THE SNOWBIRDS

A NOVEL

ANNIE JONES

Multnomah® Publishers *Sisters, Oregon*

THE SNOWBIRDS
published by Multnomah Publishers, Inc.
© 2001 by Annie Jones

International Standard Book Number: 1-59052-523-X
Previously 1-57673-623-7

Published in association with the literary agency of Writer's House.

Cover image by Index Stock Imagery

Scripture quotations are from
The Holy Bible, New International Version © 1973, 1984 by International Bible Society, used by permission of Zondervan Publishing House

Multnomah is a trademark of Multnomah Publishers, Inc., and is registered in the U.S. Patent and Trademark Office.
The colophon is a trademark of Multnomah Publishers, Inc.

Printed in the United States of America

For information:
MULTNOMAH PUBLISHERS, INC.•POST OFFICE BOX 1720•SISTERS, OREGON 97759

Library of Congress Cataloging-in-Publication Data:
Jones, Annie, 1957-
    The snowbirds / by Annie Jones.
        ISBN 1-59052-523-X
    p. cm.   ISBN 1-57673-623-7 (pbk.)
1. Alabama–Fiction. 2. Sisters–Fiction. 3. Clergy–Fiction. I. Title.
PS3560.O45744 S58 2001   813'.54–dc21   2001001058

05 06 07 08 09 10—10 9 8 7 6 5 4 3 2

For Natalie—

*my wonderful daughter who can be anything she wants
but will always be my baby.*

Acknowledgments

I would like to express my gratitude to so many people who have helped me with everything from input to encouragement on this and other books.

Without the work of editors like Karen Ball and Julee Schwarzburg and their insight, guidance, and faith (and patience in working through my tos no' tyops—I mean tons o' typos!), the words and meanings would not be as focused, the plots more holey than heavenly.

Without dear friends like the PQUALs (The Princesses of Quite A Lot, as inspired by Mary Englebreit's art), whose prayers and humor have sustained me, I would have thrown entire manuscripts—and perhaps even a finicky computer—out the window and vowed never to write again!

As always, thanks to my wonderful agent, Karen Solem, and to the community of readers and writers who make me laugh, think, try harder, and always keep the faith.

Among them: the Southern Writers' Group (look, Susan P., here you are!), the Southern Porch (Y'all keep a rocker warm, the tea cold, and shoo away that sand crane, you hear?), the Woodford County Wordsmiths, my long-standing (or should that be long-suffering?) critique group—Deanna, Janella, Fran, and Holly, my on-line buds like Gerrie, Mirtika, Denise C., Merry—and anyone else whose name escapes me at this moment but whose kindness and commitment to wonderful, uplifting stories means so much.

One

Persuasion, Alabama, ain't even a town anymore, Sam Moss." The old black man drew his antler-handled knife along a thick stick. Bark curled and fell onto the cracked leather of his spit-shined wingtips. "It's just scraps and bones."

"It's not the same place I saw in my rearview mirror twenty years ago, Mr. Freeman. I'll give you that." Sam leaned one shoulder against the Dewi's Market daily special sign. The porch's gap-toothed floorboards groaned under his feet. "Still and all, I'm not sorry I came back."

"Just scraps and bones." Big Hyde Freeman's blade scraped across the soft cedar in his hand. "And the occasional predator looking for what he can finagle for himself out of the rubble."

Sam felt that time-sharpened gaze slide over him. He did not rise to the bait. "I reckon that gets old pretty fast."

Big Hyde snorted. "Live to be my age, you learn everything gets old pretty fast. Dang sight faster than you ever figured on it happening, that's for sure."

"I hear that." Sam rubbed his stiff neck. He'd driven straight through from Albuquerque and paid the price in aches and pains a younger man would not have suffered. Even so, his words remained true. He was not sorry to have come here.

He'd come for a reason. A good reason. The sooner he made

Annie Jones

it known he was not running away again, the sooner he could get to it.

He crossed his arms. A staunch, late October gust swept down Persuasion Road, the main street through town. Rust-colored leaves plastered themselves against empty buildings and settled among the old newspapers and cobwebs that collected in the recessed doorways.

"What all is left here besides the—what's the last count? A couple hundred or so families?"

"Thereabouts, if you figure in the farms and count the cottages."

No one in town counted the people who lived in "the cottages." Sam had grown up there. He stretched out far enough to look down the dirt road that wound out and away from the all-purpose market, bait shop, and social center of the tiny community. He could just see the first of the row of ten squatty, boxlike bungalows built during the Depression. The hair on the back of his neck stood up.

"Around two hundred families, give or take, that's right." Big Hyde said it like he was talking to himself.

"And obviously that's enough to keep the market in business here. What else? Cafés?"

"Just them booths in the side room of Dewi's."

"Barber shops? Beauty salons?"

"King Cuts. End of the road there."

"They do men's and women's hair?"

"Men's, women's, children. Think they'd even clip your dog, you brought it in on a slow Tuesday afternoon."

Sam shook his head. "Guess I need to start thinking of this place in more singular terms, huh?"

"How's that?"

"You know, the market, the hair cutting place, the gas station."

"The gun shop."

"The elementary school."

"The sheriff."

Sam narrowed his eyes on Big Hyde. "The bus driver."

"That no-account, never-amount-to-nothing Moss boy."

He raised his chin. "The church."

"What church?" Big Hyde tapped his foot to shake off the pungent cedar shavings. He did not look at Sam. "Ain't no church what ain't got no preacher. Had laymen and evangelizers comin' in for nigh onto a year now, but that ain't the same."

Sam straightened and tucked his hands in his jeans pockets. His leather jacket bunched up around his shoulders and chest. If he squinted, he could just make out the cross on the steeple thrusting up into the cool, gray sky. He let out a long breath. "The church in the lurch."

"For a fact."

"The sanctuary floor still slant down toward the altar?"

"Maybe you should go in and find out for yourself."

"Last time I went in I do recall being asked never to darken its doors again."

Wind rattled the tarnished gray screens on the market's front windows and set a loose shingle flapping on the overhang.

Big Hyde held up the bare stick and studied it with one eye closed. "How many marbles did you set rolling to the pulpit from the back pew that day?"

"Only as many as my pockets would hold."

Teeth white as his long-sleeved cotton shirt flashed in Big Hyde's dark face.

Sam stepped off the porch onto the wide, low stairs.

"Ain't gonna be easy for you back here, you know."

"It never was."

A humph and a mutter answered him.

Sam glanced over his shoulder. Light glowing from the market's windows gave off a sense of warmth and welcome. The aroma of long-brewing coffee and snippets of conversation punctuated by laughter completed the idyllic picture of the place.

He wanted to go inside but knew this wasn't the time for it. Still, he could not leave. Not until he knew…

"Tell me something, Big Hyde."

"If I can." He rested his forearms atop his brown polyester pants, his stony gaze trained on Sam.

He'd just been driving through today, getting a feel for the area again, when he'd spotted Big Hyde Freeman hunkering his bantamweight body into the least broken down of the chairs on Dewi's porch. Sam pulled his truck up and cut the engine then and there. If anyone had the answers to the questions that had plagued Sam since the day he'd committed himself to return, it was the man sitting before him now.

Big Hyde had driven the single bus that connected Persuasion to the Bode County school district for forty years. Every person who lived in the county knew the man—and he knew them. Knew more about them, maybe, than most people liked to think about. Kids talk. He heard the secret truths of many a family spilled in innocence from small mouths. He saw, in too many children's eyes and attitudes, the silent reality that no amount of brave words could conceal.

Big Hyde could help Sam like no one else, if he wanted to help.

"You gonna ask something, or you want me to just figure out

all on my own what to tell you?"

"I'm sure whatever you decided to talk about would prove pretty fascinating, but yeah, I did have something particular in mind."

"Then spit it out. Ain't got all day."

Someone inside the market bellowed out the punch line to an ancient joke. A round of laughter swelled then ebbed.

"Well?"

Sam put one foot on the porch proper and leaned in over his raised thigh. "Whatever happened to the Dorsey sisters?"

Big Hyde chuckled. "Now there's a name that takes me back! The Dorsey sisters."

"Do you know what happened to them?"

"I do for a fact."

Sam waited.

The old man scratched his nose.

"What happened to them?"

"Gone."

"Gone?"

"Moved away. Up North."

"All three of them?"

"That's right. Youngest left ten or so years back, right after their daddy passed. Moved to New York City."

"Little Collier's in New York City?"

"That's what they tell me."

"And Petie?"

"That Patricia?"

Sam had forgotten that Big Hyde tended to think of people the way their names appeared on his bus roster. "Yeah, Patricia, the oldest one."

"Chicago. Her and her husband—"

"Parker," Sam filled in.

"The Sipes boy." Big Hyde rubbed his thumb over a wormhole on his whittling stick. "Moved up that way when the factory closed."

"That long ago?"

"Uh-huh."

Sam slowly shook his head. "Seems to me like only a handful of years ago that Parker Sipes played quarterback for the Bode County Pirates with Petie on the sidelines leading the cheers."

"Don't tell me. I remember all of ya'll the day each one of you come to the bus stop bawling like babies on your first day of school."

"Not me."

"No, I'll give you that, Sam Moss. Never did see you turn loose of so much as a sniffle. Not even when your mama run off, nor when your daddy throwed you out."

Sam clenched his jaw.

"From that first day you come tromping up to my bus, shoes two sizes too big, torn jeans, and hair the color of dirty straw stuck out every which way, you looked a hard case."

"Looks can be deceiving."

"Never believed you was as hard as you let on."

"Maybe I was, maybe I wasn't. Does it really matter now?"

"Heard you done jail time."

"Don't believe everything you hear, do you?" Sam met the old man's gaze.

He sucked his teeth then went back to his work. "That all you got to say about it?"

"Pretty much." He hadn't come round today to talk about himself. He'd come to see what he could find out about the town, the people, and one person in particular. He exhaled to help force out some of the tension welling up inside him, then dipped his gaze to the red dirt parking lot. When he raised his head again, he cleared his throat. "So the youngest Dorsey girl is in New York, the oldest in Chicago, you say."

"I did." Big Hyde leaned back in his seat. "Their widowed mama went up there visiting one summer, too, and that was it for her."

"Oh, really?" It surprised Sam how badly the news made him feel, considering… "Then Dodie Dorsey is no longer with us?"

"Nope."

"That's a shame." And he meant it.

"Yes sir." Big Hyde turned the stick around and began peeling away the bark from the other end. "Fool woman went up to that big city for a vacation and stayed on and married a Yankee."

"A…?" Sam winced. He'd walked right into that one. "I guess for some folks that's worse than being dead."

"City fellow and a Yankee? For a fact."

"Like I said before, it's a shame." He'd have tried harder to hide his grin if Big Hyde had been looking.

"Some round here took it as a regular slap in the face to the memory of Collier Jack Dorsey. Maybe that's why the fool woman stays as far away from these parts as she can."

"Did they sell off the house?"

"Girls wouldn't hear of it. They bought it from their mama a while back, and they've managed to hang on to it all this time."

Sam turned in the direction of Fifth and Persuasion. Trees obscured the view of the two-story frame house, but he didn't have to see the place for it to stir something inside him. "That so?"

"For a fact. All their people are still here, you know. All them cousins and The Duets."

"The Duets! Talk about a blast from the past." Sam tried to picture the two sets of twins—women he had last seen in their forties who would now be past retirement age.

"What the Dorsey sisters was to your generation, The Duets was to mine and then some." Big Hyde shook his head and let out a low whistle.

"So, the Dorsey girls ever come back to visit their aunts? Their cousins?"

"Oh, sure. Sure."

"They do?"

"They're good girls. Brought up right. They didn't just take off and forget about everyone they left behind." He rolled his hand over so that the tip of the knife pointed straight at Sam.

He sighed. Sam wondered if he'd ever do anything right in this town's eyes. If he were smart, he'd climb in that truck and hightail it back to Albuquerque.

"Yes, them girls come down here every year for a spell, without fail."

"Can you tell me when?"

"Why you want to know?"

"I just…a…"

Freeman held up his hand to cut off the justification. Probably wouldn't have believed whatever excuse he gave anyway, Sam thought. "Can't say for certain when they'll show up."

"I see."

"Just know that sometime between Thanksgiving and Christmas a person'll look up, and there they come, one, two, three. Cars flying down the road. They slide around that corner just like they did when they was teenagers."

Sam could practically hear the thumpa-whomp of tires as they left the paved main road, then crunched across the rutted red dirt of Fifth.

"Them girls descend on that old place like a flock of snowbirds settling in for the winter."

"Even Nic—uh—Nicolette?"

"Even her. They all come, kids and husband in tow."

"Kids and husbands. Of course." He nodded and hunched his shoulders up. "Of course."

"Sure do liven up the place when they do, too."

"I don't doubt it."

"Just like the old days. This old town never did have too much to brag on, but one thing we did have, we had the Dorsey sisters."

"For a fact," Sam murmured.

The Dorsey sisters. Just the name charged the air with anticipation. People sitting in a room with backs to the door would find themselves drawn away from conversations, compelled to turn and look when one of those dark-haired, brown-eyed beauties appeared.

"They were something," Sam whispered.

"Were and still are."

Sam nodded. "I can well imagine."

"Don't have to imagine. You'll see for yourself. If you're still around when they show up."

"Oh, I'll still be here, Big Hyde." Sam folded his arms. The autumn wind stung his face, and a long forgotten emotion began to twist in his gut. He looked from the cottages to the church to the corner lot of the Dorseys' old house. "You can count on it."

Two

Nic, get your head out of that toilet this instant! You are a guest in my home for Thanksgiving, not at work."

"I do not scrub lavatories for a living. I own my own house-cleaning service, thank you very much." Nic shook the can of powdered cleanser twice, hard. The fine cloud that rose from the bowl burned high up into her sinuses. "And if I did scrub them, I'd hardly do it with my head!"

"What'd you say?"

"I said...I said..." She sneezed.

"What?"

She sneezed again. Her eyes watered.

Petie rapped at the door with all the restraint of a woodpecker on a sugar high. "If you expect to hold any kind of conversation with me, li'l sister, you gotta get yourself out of that rest room and join the festivities."

Nic let the whorl of flushing water answer that.

Petie knocked again.

The ungainly rubber gloves turned inside out as Nic peeled them off. She tossed them under the sink where she'd found them.

"Are you coming out of there, or do I have to come in and drag you out?"

"Drag me out? Ha! And risk breaking a nail?" Hot water gushed into the basin. "I'll be out when I'm good and ready."

"You're just doing this to hide out for a few extra minutes. Don't think I don't know it."

A few extra minutes of peace before the chaos of a huge meal with her family, with her youngest sister in charge of the food, no less. The notion did tempt Nic sorely.

She lathered up her hands. "Naw. Not me. I just love spending my day of thanks with Wally telling stupid Southerner jokes and asking us how long it takes to get used to wearing shoes again after we get back from Alabama."

"Hey, don't begrudge the man. It's his day after all."

"His day?"

"Turkey day."

Turkey. Now there was an apt description of Wally Weggler. What Mama saw in that ruddy-faced clown after a life with Daddy, she'd never know. But then, Nic was hardly the expert on men and what made a good one. Her track record made ol' Wally boy look like the catch of the century.

"I'm serious, sugar. If you're not coming out, at least let me come in and hide with you."

"After that crack about my work, I don't want you in my hideout, big sister."

"I didn't mean anything by it. I know you run a very successful cleaning service. How you've worked your way up from two houses to a list as long as your arm. And how now you even have more than one person interested in buying your business lock, stock, and ammonia barrel." Petie trilled out the facts like an overly enthusiastic announcer at a testimonial dinner. Then her voice went soft, "And you know I'm proud of you for it, too."

Nic didn't know it. In fact, she doubted very much that anyone in her family had used the term *proud* in the same sentence as her name in years. Still, she and Petie had been thick as thieves since either of them could remember. Though years apart in age, the way they favored one another and spoke about each other, people often confused them for twins, like their notorious aunts, The Duets—Lula and Bert, though, the fraternal twins, not Nan and Fran the identical ones.

"Nic? Honey? Do you forgive me? I was just trying to get you to come out of there."

"I'll be out in a minute. I have to dry off my hands." She reached for a thick guest towel with autumn leaves in gold and copper satin appliquéd on it, then froze, hands up. "Where's the real towel you want people to dry their hands on?"

"On the rack inside the cabinet."

"I knew it."

"What?"

"Nothing." She frowned into the mirror as she wiped her hands on the threadbare pink-and-white-striped terry cloth.

"You coming out now?"

From the corner of her eye, Nic caught the gleam of the brass doorknob. She toyed with the golden cross necklace dangling around her neck. Her stomach fluttered. All she had to do was press in the button at the center of that knob and…

And spend the next forty-odd years hearing about the Thanksgiving Nicolette locked herself in the bathroom? No, thank you. She'd only just now begun to live down the awful story about how she almost ran off with Sam Moss on New Year's Eve nine years ago and the trouble it put her family through. Why hand her family yet another reason to give her grief over some impetuous act or lapse in judgment? She yanked the door open.

"Collier banished me from the kitchen." Petie put her hands on her hips. Her ruby-toned nails thrummed over the pressed cotton of her full-length apron with the horn of plenty and Indian corn motif.

"Ah, so now I understand why the high anxiety to get me out of here. You want an ally."

"I just wanted someone on my side; is that so wrong?"

"Suck in the lower lip, sister. The pouting Southern belle thang does not work on me."

Nic gathered up the tissue paper mum her daughter had made for her from beside the marble sink. She fished in her jeans pocket for a safety pin to stick the big orange corsage back on.

"I'm not pouting." Petie pressed her lips tightly together. "I just feel like a fish out of water."

"That makes sense."

"I knew you'd see it my way."

"Yeah, because remember when we had those goldfish and the bowl dumped over?"

"Huh?"

"They were fish out of water, see? And if I recall, Daddy took those fish and gave them a fitting funeral at sea." She pointed to the toilet, grinning. "Is that why you wanted to get in here so badly? To drown your sorrows?"

"No, but I can't swear I won't try to drown my sister."

Nic struggled with the bulky paper corsage and pin.

"Actually I came here because Willa told me there'd been a little accident and that you were scouring the commode. Heavens, sugar, you didn't really do that, did you?"

"Why don't you just step in here and see for yourself?" She

swept one hand out obligingly. "Or better yet, you can still smell the cleanser; come on in and take a whiff—your nose is already in the air."

"Better in the air than out of joint." She pinched at Nic's baggy brown sweater and made an exaggerated face as she stepped over the threshold.

Nic clenched her jaw.

"What I don't understand is why you thought you had to do that anyway?" Without so much as a downward glance, Petie shut the cabinet door with her knee. "Why didn't you just come get me? Or Park?"

"Park? Are you sure he's still breathing? I haven't seen him so much as blink since we got here this morning."

"Football fever. You know how he is." Petie stuck her tongue out the side of her mouth and let her eyes glaze over.

Nic laughed.

"But you still should have gotten one of my family to do this." She tucked the bowl brush back in its peach porcelain kitty cat container. "Jessica or Scott would have been happy to have helped out. We ought to get some use out of them while they're home from college for the long weekend."

"I know Scott and Jessica would have helped." Her niece and nephew—two finer, smarter, more easygoing young adults you couldn't hope to find. They couldn't help it that they looked like they'd been ordered straight out of a JC Penney catalog.

"That goes for Parker, too." Petie patted her hair down. It sprang back to the natural carefree wave she invested so much time and money to maintain. "Rolling out of the recliner for dinner is the only exercise he'll get today if I don't come up with something to tear him away from the games."

"I wouldn't do that. I know what football means to him."

Parker, like any Alabama Adonis worth his salt, had moved effortlessly through all the expected stages of a well-born but not well-to-do Southern man's life. High school letterman and president of his college fraternity, he'd then bounded his way up the ladder to a comfy rung in higher middle management. But the dreams of his day in the limelight of the Bode County Pirates never completely faded from his mind.

"Well, he was the star quarterback the year they almost took state." Petie beamed. "And I was captain of the cheerleading squad, and you were second in line."

"Rah. Rah."

Petie frowned.

"Why do I have the sneaking suspicion, big sister, that somewhere in a pile in the back of your closet there's a skirt with box pleats? And a sweater bearing the face of Pirate Pete? And a couple of shaken-till-they-shriveled maroon and gold pom-poms?"

"Don't be silly."

Nic raised an eyebrow.

"The skirt and sweater are hanging in a garment bag, and I keep the pom-poms in a hatbox at our old house in Alabama. It's only fitting they stay in Persuasion, you know."

They met gazes in the mirror, then shared a laugh.

"I'm serious as a heart attack, though." Petie nudged Nic. "You should have gotten one of us to do whatever it is you did in here. You're a guest in our house. You should not be tending to our plumbing mishaps."

A person couldn't ask for kinder, gentler, more generous souls than Park and Petie and their two children. How was Nic going to survive another holiday around them without grabbing Mama's best turkey carving knife and slicing every last toggle button off their matching navy blue cardigan sweaters?

Nic closed the safety pin and the heavy corsage slouched forward, pulling her sweater collar out of shape. Not that it had much of a shape to begin with. "I didn't call you because it was *my* child that decided to flush down the leftover gobs of tissue from her flowers. That made taking care of things my responsibility."

"Well, you can see Willa's reasoning in that; we called the craft paper "tissue" paper the whole time we taught her how to make the mums."

"The pipes stopped up and orange dye went everywhere."

"Now I wish you had called me in here. I've seen blue toilet water, even green, but never orange."

"Stop it, Petie, would you just stop it?"

"Stop what?"

"Stop trying to make everything all right. To make it seem like it was a perfectly logical thing for an eight-year-old girl to do."

"I just…"

"You just wanted to smooth things over, I know. But we can't forever go through life smoothing things out for her and covering up for her when she pulls something like this—or worse."

Petie folded her arms and tipped her chin down. With the play of light and shadow on her face and the no-nonsense tilt of her head, she looked just like their own mother half a lifetime ago. "Sometimes I think you are too hard on that child."

"And do you think the world is going to be any easier on her?"

Petie said nothing.

What could she say, really? She was, after all, talking directly to the queen of how tough the world can be on people who make a mess of their lives.

"Don't you think I wish I could bundle her up in cotton and keep all the bad stuff at bay for the rest of her life?"

"Maybe as her family we *should* be her refuge from the harshness of the world."

"That's okay for you and your kids and Collier and Mama, but I can't afford that luxury." Nic's footsteps fell on thick carpet, hard and quick as her own pulse in her ears.

Petie stepped aside just in time to avoid a shoulder-to-shoulder collision.

"It's my job to prepare Willa for what's waiting beyond the safe harbor of the people who love her." *And you have no idea how far I am ready to go to do just that,* she almost added but caught herself just in time.

Thanksgiving dinner was hardly the place for her to announce that she did not plan to go to Alabama this winter. Or that she wanted to sell her share of the house there to get enough money to put her daughter in a special program. *Please, Lord, just give me the strength to get through this day with my mind and spirit open…and my mouth shut.*

She rounded the corner from the guest bath with her sister dogging at her heels.

"Mommy, am I in big trouble?"

Tiny as she was, Willa, with her tender heart in her eyes, filled up the entire hallway. Paper mums adorned her headband, the orange made bolder in contrast to her shiny, deep brown hair. More crudely made flowers circled her wrists. She held one in her hand, the fat green pipe cleaner stem twisted between her fingers. She stood so still the crackling-thin paper did not even rustle.

Nothing on earth had prepared Nic for this child. The child she thought she had given birth to, *that* was the baby she'd been ready for. Nic had read the books. She'd had long talks with her mother and sister. She had no doubt that she could be the best mom in the world to a happy, healthy child. But it seemed God had other plans for them.

Who could be adequately prepared for standing in the cold starkness of a hospital and hearing a doctor say that your baby has sustained an injury to her brain? What book or normal life experience prepares a mother for that? No, with her precious Willa, Nic had to get by on a wing and a prayer…and then more prayer.

Willa's brown eyes, made huge behind her oval glasses, grew wider still, waiting.

And then a whole lot more prayers. Nic sighed. She reached out and touched her daughter's cheek.

Willa twitched her nose, a sign of her struggle to keep in that smile that always came so easily to her.

No one had ever told Nic how deeply she would love this warm, fragile, headstrong girl. Love her so much she would let the child hate her if that's what it took to give Willa a fighting chance at life.

"You have to learn to stop and think about the consequences of your actions, young lady." She dropped a hand to the girl's thin shoulder. "Remember how we talked about that? That there are accidents and then there are consequences? Accidents could not be helped. This little incident most certainly could have been avoided if you'd just asked for some help or advice."

"Yes, ma'am."

"Now, I cleaned up the mess you made, but that doesn't mean you get off free as the breeze. Do you understand that?"

Willa nodded.

Nic nodded, trying to appear firm in her resolve not to coddle the child.

"I made this for you." Willa held out the paper flower in her hand.

The crumpled orange mum went blurry in Nic's gaze.

"For your pretty hair."

Eyes downcast, she sniffled and tucked the flower behind one ear, mindful of staying steadfast. "Thank you, honey."

"It's my Thanksgiving present because I'm so thankful to God to have a mommy like you to love me and watch out for me and fix things when I mess them up."

"And I'm thankful to have you, sweetheart." Nic wrapped her arms around her daughter and nearly hugged the stuffing out of her.

"Maybe we can find some other chore for our Willa to help out with." Petie patted Nic on the back, then let her hand rest there.

It felt good, holding her baby in her arms, having her big sister so near. It made her feel like maybe she wasn't as alone in caring for Willa. Some days, single motherhood got the better of her. It made her weary to her bones and sometimes even tested her faith. Moments like these, though, Nic knew she'd made the right choice.

But she could never have made it this far without the help of her family. Guilt settled low in her stomach over the decision she had made regarding the house in Alabama and keeping her plans a secret from the people who had helped her so much.

Willa wriggled free from her mother's grasp. "What kind of chore do you want me to do, Aunt Petie?"

"Well, let's see…" Petie draped her arm over Willa's shoulder. "Surely we can come up with something."

"A real chore, now." Nic followed close behind them down the hallway that led to the spacious kitchen. The scents of cinnamon, allspice, and nutmeg laced the air. "Not something like pumpkin pie taster."

"I hate pumpkin pie." Willa flailed her hands in short, awkward movements, her body stiff.

"Then maybe we should make you pecan pie taster, instead." Petie took the child's hands in hers and slowly lowered them. "Of course, you understand that since Auntie Collier is making the whole meal, you may not be able to tell the difference between the two."

Willa laughed. Her hands jerked upward again.

"Nope," Petie said soft as the voice of a human conscience. She pressed down on Willa's forearms.

The behaviors. Those inexplicable, often sudden actions that screamed to anxious onlookers "Hey, look at me, I'm different!" Nic worked constantly with her daughter on toning them down. Now they usually only surfaced when the girl was overly tired or excited. Petie had handled them just right and seeing her do it touched Nic in ways she had not expected.

"Here. One of your flowers is drooping. Can't have droopy flowers on Thanksgiving Day, can we?" Petie so deftly diverted Willa from the spontaneous behavior that none but a trained eye would have ever known what she was up to.

Her family deserved to know her plans. She felt a perfect heel for keeping her decision from them. They loved Willa, too, and would want the best for her.

"This way to the kitchen." Petie steered the girl to the left. "If you go straight ahead you end up in the den with the menfolks. You'll have to listen to Uncle Park spout football scores and statistics. You aren't interested in football scores and statistics, are you, sugar?"

"I like Aggravation." Willa let her aunt turn her body in the right direction.

Petie gave Nic a curious look.

"It's a board game," Nic whispered.

Petie nodded. "Well, let me tell you, darling. If you like aggravation, you have come to the right place."

The clack and clatter of utensils grew louder as they neared the kitchen. Mama laughed. Collier muttered something then gasped. Then Collier laughed, too.

"Welcome to the aggravation headquarters for the Dorsey family holiday extravaganza."

Pots and pans and casserole dishes, oven mitts, aprons, and an open cookbook littered the counters, the table, even the chairs of the usually spotless room. Potatoes boiled on the stove. Water ran in the sink. Smoke rose from an iron skillet smoldering on a trivet on the butcher-block center island.

"Wow." Willa's mouth hung open.

"I don't know why you're so shocked." Nic put one hand on her daughter's back. "Your bedroom back home isn't much neater."

"Well, at least my room isn't on fire!" She pointed to the frying pan.

"Yes, sadly, this is what it's come to at our house." Nic laced her arms over her chest. "Our expectation of neatness has now reached the if-it's-not-on-fire-then-it's-fine level."

"Why don't you get yourself in that kitchen and ask Aunt Collier if there is something you can do to help out?" Petie sent Willa scooting off with a playful swat to the behind.

The aroma of coffee, roasting turkey, and yams slowly bubbling in brown sugar with marshmallows browning on top tickled Nic's nose. She sensed her emotions mingling, moving through her consciousness in much the same way. Her desire to stay strong and independent, her need to do right by her child, and her longing to please her family all churned together just below the surface of her tenuous composure.

"Look who's here," Jessica chimed out as Willa cautiously picked her way around the room.

Nic started to go on in herself, but in one step, Petie blocked the doorway.

"Promise me you won't be too hard on her. It is Thanksgiving, the start of our special time of year."

Nic tensed.

Mama welcomed Willa's arrival on the scene with a big fuss over the mums, comparing her to a holiday parade float.

Willa twirled around, showing off for her doting aunt and grandmother.

Nic searched her sister's eyes for any sign that she'd understand the need to forgo the yearly visit south.

"This was such a small thing. Let's not ruin the day over it."

Especially when there are so many bigger things to ruin the day with.

"She was only being a kid." Petie gathered the dark waves of hair falling over Nic's shoulder in one hand. "She didn't do it on purpose."

"I know, but I—" Nic felt practically yanked out of her shoes when her sister tightened her grip.

A cheer rose from the den followed by the slapping of hands. Park and Scott hooted. Wally coughed.

Nic tried to pull away from her sister.

"Kids do dumb things." In one fluid gesture, Petie whipped the paper flower from behind Nic's ear and wound it around to secure a ponytail nice and neat. She stood back and gave a smile of uninvited approval. "You of all people know that."

"What's that supposed to mean?"

Petie ignored her, just went on fluffing the flower and talking. "No harm, no foul."

"Petie…"

"You're doing the best you can, and no one blames you for a little mishap now and again."

From love to guilt to shame, her big sister had pushed all the right buttons. Nic gritted her teeth.

Halftime music blared from the den.

Scott's big feet thundered down the hallway headed straight for the kitchen. Park's play-by-play to a grumbling Wally followed right behind.

Beyond the doorway, Mama tied an apron around her granddaughter's slender waist.

Jessica stuck a paper cutout of a pilgrim boy and an Indian girl into the flowers on Willa's headband, creating a crown effect.

Collier handed the child a wooden spoon to wield like a scepter.

Instead of being held responsible for her actions, they'd turned Willa into the princess of the party. Well meaning or not, it entirely undermined everything Nic was trying so hard to accomplish with her child. This was exactly the reason she had to do what she had to do.

"When we all get down to the house in a couple weeks, I'll make a special point to work with Willa on what goes down the—"

Nic couldn't take it. Not another minute of it. "Petie, I'm not going to the house this year."

The room fell silent. Even Scott thudded to a halt a few feet behind her. She felt every eye focused on her in utter amazement, horror, and disbelief.

Well, in for a penny, in for a pound.

Nic threw back her shoulders. She pulled the mum from the ponytail, letting her hair fall in whatever mess it may, and raised her chin. "And I guess you might as well know—I also want to sell my share of the house for as much as I can get for it."

Three

hat are you saying, Nic?" Collier dropped the lid back onto the pot of potatoes with a decisive clank. She waved away the cloud of steam swirling up into her face. "Sell your share? Not go down for winter vacation?"

"Look, I know it's an awkward time to bring it up."

"Don't you dare shrug your shoulders and play all coy about this, li'l sister." Petie looked ready to snatch her bald. "This is not like you've just announced you're on a diet and not eating pie today. You're talking about the end of a tradition—of selling our home."

"It hasn't been our home for years. We just hang on to it for holidays and the occasional summer retreat. You had to hear about my plans sometime. And like they say, there's no time like—"

"The present? Oh, I don't think so, little sister." Petie seized Nic's upper arm in the death grip that made Collier wince, probably from having felt its like many times growing up. "Not at my house, not on Thanksgiving."

"Did I hear right? Sell the house?" Mother took to fanning herself with a pot holder.

"You sold it yourself, Mother, to the three of us to do with as we saw fit." Nic flipped her hair back. "You don't even go down there anymore. What's it matter to you?"

"Don't you take that tone with me, young lady." Mother's stiffly sprayed silver hair all but bristled.

"Heavenly mercy, Nic, why do you always drop this kind of stuff on us during the holidays?" Petie cut in quick. "You just have to command center stage with some pronouncement sure to startle this family out of their senses, don't you?"

"Oh, like driving this crew out of their senses is some kind of challenge," Nic muttered, more defensive about the accuracy of her sister's claim than haughty over being scolded in front of everyone.

Nine years ago she had ruined one of the few serene New Year's Eves her family had ever known with her failed attempt to run off with Sam Moss. Not to mention the near tragic results of her response to his leaving without her. She'd spoiled that next Easter with the news that she was pregnant, caused more fireworks than the Fourth of July display with the threat of losing the baby, and aptly chose Labor Day to give birth. The only holiday gatherings she had not made a mess of yet were Decoration Day and Christmas. And Christmas was coming.

No wonder they all looked like she'd scared the daylights out of them.

"Oh, Nicolette!" Mother tossed her head back in a display of high drama that few women, short of her sisters-in-law, could have surpassed. "Oh, my…my… Just listen to the way you talk to your family! I'm having a dizzy spell, I swear I am."

"Scott, if Grandma faints, do catch her." Petie propelled Nic straight through the melee of the kitchen toward the sliding glass door that led out back. "Everyone else go on about your business."

Nic dragged her feet.

Petie gave her an extra little shove.

"What about me?" Collier slapped her oven mitt down on the butcher-block.

"*You* might want to turn down the heat on that turkey. Nicolette and I are stepping out onto the back deck for...a chat."

"Turn the heat down?" Collier cranked the knob on the oven even as she protested. "Do you have any idea how hard I've worked to time everything out to perfection?"

The glass door slid open with a whoosh! Crisp fall air flooded into the warm, damp kitchen.

Collier stepped forward. "Can't this wait until after dinner when we can sit down and discuss it calmly and rationally?"

Petie escorted Nic right on by without batting an eye.

"I mean it, ya'll. Come back here."

They did not even slow their pace.

Their youngest sister hurried to catch up to them. "Don't think you're going to leave me out of this, then."

"Me, too! I want to come, too." Willa leaped in the air.

"Stay and help Jessica watch the dinner," Nic ordered over her shoulder as Petie gestured for her to go through the door first.

"Mom, it's November in Chicago." Sweet, practical Jessica already had Willa by the hand. "You don't really plan to go outside now, do you?"

"This is between me and my sisters, sugar." Petie did not look back at her daughter.

Everyone, even the closest kin, knew that no one but the three of them had any say in what went on between the Dorsey sisters.

Wally blurted out an ugly belly laugh. "Is this what you Southern folk call getting taken to the woodshed?"

Petie and Nic stopped in their tracks.

Collier whipped her head around so fast she risked a sprained neck. She pulled up short. Save for a last minute side step, she would have collided with her sisters.

They stood in the open doorway for no more than a few seconds, giving old Wally boy the deadeye.

The room went silent again, except for the crackle of Willa's paper flowers as she bounced up and down beside Jessica.

Then, without so much as a huff to acknowledge the absolute and utter out-and-out rudeness of Wally's intrusive remark, the three sisters made their exit onto the cold porch.

"What about the call?" Park dared to stick his head out.

Nic couldn't help but liken the sight to a man voluntarily putting his head in the guillotine.

"What about it?" Petie let go of Nic, folded her arms, and narrowed her eyes.

He looked at his watch. "Well, it's nearly time."

Ever since they'd begun the tradition of sharing Thanksgiving at Petie's a decade ago, The Duets had called at twelve-thirty on the dot. Collier had gone so far as to plan to serve the meal at one o'clock to give everyone a chance to say their hellos before they ate. Nic's announcement had shot that plan straight out of the water.

A bracing wind blasted against their backs.

"What should I tell your aunts?" Park frowned.

"Just hand the phone to Mother." Petie rolled her eyes. "Might as well let them get all their fussing at one another out of the way right off the bat."

"Okay, but—"

"And do let us know when they call, won't you, sweetheart? Tap on the door or something." Petie waved her husband back into the house. "We won't be long out here."

"We'd better not be." Nic wrapped her arms around herself. "It's cold."

"Just like my debut at making Thanksgiving dinner will be if we—if you two—go on and on about this." Collier brushed her hand back through the short layers of her new haircut, the one she had made sure everyone knew some New York hairstylist assured her gave off the aura of power and confidence. Then she looked toward her cooling culinary efforts with a pout on her face worthy of a spoiled three-year-old.

The glass door rumbled along its track then clunked shut.

Petie folded her arms, like Mother warming up to a full-fledged hissy fit, and turned on Nic. "Have you completely taken leave of your ever-lovin' mind?"

"Before you get all in a lather over this, at least do me the *courtesy* of hearing me out."

"Courtesy? You have the nerve to stand there and throw the word courtesy in my face? After you've ruined my Thanksgiving dinner?"

"It's *my* dinner." Collier glanced back at the activity inside the house. "We're just having it at your house because no one in this family would ever bring themselves to come to New York City."

"That's not the issue now." Petie slashed her hand through the air to cut off Collier, then laced her arms tight again. "The issue is—"

"I did it for Willa."

Collier focused on Nic.

The rigid knot of Petie's arms relaxed, just a bit. "How so?"

"There's this program. I can get her into it, but it won't be cheap. I've already used the money I'd saved for the trip home as a deposit. That's why I can't go this year."

"What kind of a program?" Collier stepped forward. "You're not going to send our baby away are you?"

"It's a residential program, yes." Nic lowered her gaze.

"But…" Collier strangled on the next word, then held up her hands in a sign of resignation.

Collier had only been fifteen when Nic brought the little cherub of a child, Willa, to live with Mother and Daddy and her in the house in Persuasion. Nic's youngest sister had loved that little girl from the moment she laid eyes on her.

And when the trouble came a couple years later, when they knew things were not as they should be with the baby, Collier had loved her even more. Because she had instinctively seemed to know even then that sweet Willa would need more love than an ordinary child.

Petie gave a tight shiver. "I know you're trying to do what's best for Willa—"

"I *am* doing what's best for her." Nic moved her gaze from one sister to the other then back, her eyes clear and unblinking. "Public school is not working for her. They are overburdened and under-staffed for kids with special needs. I have to think about her future. I have to think about how she will survive in this world should anything happen to me—"

"It won't," Collier insisted.

"And if, heaven forbid, it should, there are plenty of people who love her and would be ready to step in and—"

"And what?" Nic raised her head. Even when the wind tossed the long coils of her brown hair, laced now with threads of palest silver, she felt a stillness about her resolve that defied the November chill.

Neither Petie nor Collier said a word.

Behind them, Park appeared at the glass door, pantomiming talking on the phone.

Petie both acknowledged him and kept him at bay with her raised hand.

Nic sighed. She shuffled a few steps inward, closing the circle of intimacy between the three sisters. "Petie, Willa is a full-time commitment now. She may well be one for the rest of her life. Much as I love my family, I can't assume that y'all would be ready, willing, and able to do whatever it takes to care for her forever."

"I would," Collier said softly.

Nic put her hand on her sister's wrist, giving a gentle but firm squeeze. "I know you would, Collier. Or at least, in your heart, you think you would, but—"

"I would." She slid her hand into Nic's and returned the squeeze.

"Me, too. In fact, with my kids gone now I—" A light came over Petie's face, then just as quickly faded. She took both of her sisters' hands. "I'm here for you always, Nic, you know that."

"Thanks. But I have to think about what's best for Willa, too."

"I can't talk about this residential program, but I can say that, in my opinion—" Collier combed back her hair.

Park tapped on the door, making everyone jump or tense up. No one made a move to go inside.

"For Willa's sake, I have to say this," Collier whispered. "Can it really be best for Willa to be away from her family this Christmas, the last holiday before you send her off to—?"

"Don't make it sound like I'm packing her off to an institution."

"I wasn't! I wouldn't!" Apology rang in her tone. "I only meant, well, isn't there some way you two can still come down for

Christmas and New Year's at least?"

"Can't afford it, sugar. Not now."

Park's rapping on the glass turned to a resounding thump-thump-thump.

"Well, if it's just money you need…" Collier held her hands up.

Just money? Nic smiled at the simplicity of the younger woman's perception. "Just money? Like you have gobs to throw away on a sentimental whim?"

Petie gave Nic a hard look. "You could always—"

"Spare me Mother's speech about tracking down Willa's no-account biological father and wringing child support out of him. You two know what it would cost me financially, emotionally, mentally, and even spiritually to drag myself and my precious daughter through a situation with no good outcome. Even if I could find the man, what are the chances he would help? What kind of mess might I be inviting into my child's life?"

"Then Park and I will pay for the trip."

Collier let her breath out in a long whoosh that formed a moist cloud in the air.

"I can't let you do that. Willa and I will just have a quiet holiday at home."

"Alabama is your home." Collier sounded wistful. "You love that house, Nic, as much or more than any of us."

If Nic had an answer to that, she never got the chance to share it.

The back door came screeching open, and Park thrust his head, shoulder, and even ventured a foot outside. "Y'all better get in here. I can only gather so much from this cockeyed, one-sided conversation, but from this end of things, seems your aunts have got your mother all worked up over something to do with the house. And the big picture is not a pretty one."

"Where is she?" Petie led the charge into the house.

"Upstairs on the extension in our room." His profile to his wife, he kept one ear toward the TV droning in the den. "This won't take long will it?"   .

"I'll try to keep your inconvenience to a minimum."

Now there were some words Petie ought to paint on a board and tack up over her doorway, Nic thought, as the motto of her life, or what her life had become these last few years.

Petie stepped around her husband and started for the stairs.

Her sisters fell in line behind her.

"Collier, why don't you go on and tend to your dinner?"

"But I—"

Petie gave her baby sister a pat on the cheek that ended any argument, then faced Nic. "And you know what you could do that would really help about now?"

"Call ahead and see if there is a group discount at the nut house in case we all need to check in by day's end?"

"Tempting an idea as that is…" Petie pressed her hand to Nic's back and gave her a gentle shove. "Why don't you get the girls around and make sure the table is set proper. Silver in the right place, ice in the tea glasses, that kind of thing."

"What about—"

"And tell the men to wash up. That'll keep them busy while I'm going to try to salvage what's left of…this lovely family gathering."

"I still think—"

"You want to handle The Duets *and* Mother at the same time?"

"Ice in the tea glasses, you said? Anything else?"

"You know any prayers for making this family behave like God's beloved children and not like the refugees in the last lifeboat from the ship of big fools?"

"I'll improvise." Nic winked then laughed.

Petie trudged up the carpeted stairs, her voice trailing behind her. "To think, I had looked forward to this day like a child waiting for Christmas morning. What a fool I was to hope this celebration would unfold as beautifully as I'd imagined."

That was it for Nic. As long as she could remember the Dorsey sisters were there for one another. She was not going to let her sister deal with her disappointment or the family difficulty alone now. "Hold up. I've changed my mind, I'm coming up there with you."

Petie paused before her wedding portrait hung between paintings of the kids when they were children. She made a striking image standing before her own image looking as tired and unsure in real life as she had looked vibrant and ready to take on the world in her portrait. "Nic, you don't have to…"

"I know, but what kind of sister would I be if I sent you into the fray alone? We're family, sugar. We're stuck with each other through thick and thin."

"Thick and thin, sickness and health, Mother and her sisters-in-law." Petie held out her hand as Nic jogged up the stairs to meet her. She gave Nic's hand a squeeze, then nailed her with a knowing look. "And money management and misguided ideas, we are in it for the long haul for *all* of it, you hear?"

"Let's deal with Mother and The Duets first." Nic pushed on ahead. "And leave the rest to the Lord—and the people directly involved—to sort out. *You* hear?"

Petie didn't answer, and the way she didn't answer told Nic that she heard but had no intention of paying the veiled demand any heed.

Nic would've stopped on the spot to make sure her sister

understood that she had made up her mind about this issue. She would not go to Alabama this Christmas. Neither those proverbial wild horses nor her big sister's mule-headed stubbornness could drag her there. But before she could say so, their mother's voice intruded.

"No, no, no, no, no! Now I mean that, Nan and Fran. You, too, Bert and Lula. No!"

"Mother, put that phone down. I'm coming to take care of everything." Petie marched into her bedroom, her hand outstretched from the get-go to take the receiver.

"Just a minute, honey."

"Mother, I love you and I love Daddy's sisters. But the mix of you all together is about as volatile as a firecracker in a fresh cow pie. And there ain't nobody in this family can run fast enough to get out of the way of that…fallout. So let me handle this."

It did Nic good to see Petie's old fire resurface. She held in her grin, though, out of deference to their mother.

"Fine. If you're going to start talking manure, I'll gladly let you handle it." Mother thrust the phone toward her oldest daughter.

"Thank you." Petie took the receiver and affected a voice so syrupy Nic figured she'd have to wipe down the mouthpiece afterward to keep bees from swarming to it. "Hello, darlings, this is Petie now. Ya'll hang on for just a sec while I tell Mother something, then I'll be right back to listen to every little thing you've got to say."

Not one hair on Mother's bob so much as fluttered when she spun on her heel, but that did not mean she was retreating unruffled.

Petie cut her off at the door, the phone pressed to her chest to keep the aunts from hearing. "Oh no, you don't."

"Don't what?"

"Don't go down there to stir up sympathy toward your side in this, whatever it may be. We've had enough drama for this Thanksgiving already, thank you very much."

"What are you driving at, sugar?"

"If I were driving anywhere, Mama, it would be away, far, far away." She managed a smile and to kiss her mother on the forehead.

Nic knew exactly how her sister felt.

"But seeing as we are all stuck here, my goal is to get through the rest of this day without any further life-altering declarations." Petie and Mother both shot Nic an accusing glare.

Nic feigned intense interest in the knickknacks on her sister's nightstand.

"You promise, Mother, not one word?"

She pursed her lips and acted out locking them tight.

"Good. Maybe we can get through the holiday then with some measure of civility, gentility, and whatever other *ility* is called for."

"How about *sen*ility?" Mother's eyes glittered with self-satisfaction.

"What?"

She pointed to the phone. "They have really lost it this time."

"You've been saying that ever since I can remember. After all these years, what could they possibly have left to lose?"

"How about the house, for starters?"

"They've *lost* the house?" Nic blinked.

"Apparently you do not fully grasp the concept of no more life-altering announcements, Mother," Petie spoke through clenched teeth.

"We own the house." Nic cleared her throat to chase away the hint of panic in her tight voice. She had staked far too much of her daughter's future on that house and what would happen with it. She did not find her mother's joking about it one bit amusing. "They just look after it while we're away. How could they have lost it?"

"It's not lost as in gone, but just ask them what they've done. They might as well have lost it, and it's not something you're going to straighten out on the phone, either. Whether you want to or not, Nicolette, you and your sisters are going to have to go down there and sort this out in person."

Four

Nobody listened to Sam. No one listened—or talked to him, for that matter. The regulars at Dewi's nodded and muttered greetings whenever he came in, but they never offered an invitation for him to join them over coffee, or shared any of the twice-told gossip that passed for news around the place. The church ladies had brought by some ham and a couple congealed salads in recycled whipped cream and margarine tubs, not their usual good plastic dishes with their names on the lids in permanent ink. Their gestures, Sam understood, only skirted the most basic level of good manners. It served to remind him that no one had asked him to come and no one expected him to stay long.

In the town where he had been born and raised, he remained an outsider. He'd thought that would change when he got settled into a place, started letting everyone know why he had come back and what he hoped to accomplish.

A blue-and-silver truck pulled in next to his battered pickup where he waited outside Dewi's. The door slammed so hard, Sam felt it through his worn seat springs.

"You just gonna sit there on your brains or you coming inside?" Lee Radwell, a fellow cottage kid who now owned the gas station stood on Dewi's porch, glaring through the windshield at Sam.

"Hello, Lee." Sam rolled down his window. "You inviting me in to join the boys for coffee?" Sam knew better. Of all the people who held his past against him, Lee was the worst.

He grunted his contempt at Sam's suggestion. "Just saying them parking spaces are for paying customers."

Sam chose not to point out how those paying customers often sat in Dewi's all day spending all of the price of a bottomless cup of coffee. "Not to worry, Lee. I'll gladly give up my spot if somebody comes along who needs it."

"Too bad it ain't that easy to fling you out of the pulpit you got no business hiding behind."

Proverbs taught that a soft word turned away wrath. Sam understood a man like this would not respect softness, that Lee would mistake a gentle response for weakness and try to use it against him at every turn. "I don't hide behind my faith or my calling, Lee. In fact, I am more than aware of how it often makes me a target to people with other agendas."

From the day Sam had arrived in town, Lee watched for missteps and waited for misunderstandings he could use to his advantage. He felt, like many in town, that a kid with Sam's background, one who had thumbed his nose at the town and at the things it held dear, had no place here. He went to great strides to make Sam feel unwanted and unwelcome—in the place everyone should have been received without malice or judgment.

"But I wasn't called to take the easy path. I wasn't called only to walk through friendly doors. I came here to help make things better for everyone, even those who don't want me, and I will be staying for a while."

Lee snorted and stuffed his hands in his pockets. "We'll see about that." As he walked inside, his heavy boots scuffed over the old boards like a schoolyard bully kicking up dirt on the playground.

Sam sat back in the worn seat of his pickup and fixed his gaze on the steeple of the Persuasion All Souls Community Church. Come next Sunday, would the place be as empty as it was last week? Given the resistance of people like Lee and the church's state of decline, was that really possible?

Big Hyde had tried to warn him. But that hadn't prepared Sam for the reality of the forsaken church or the coldness of the town's people. What had he expected? The seed of the idea got planted in his brain so long ago that he hardly remembered anymore where his realistic plans left off and his idealism took over.

The screen door of Dewi's opened and slammed shut again, but Sam had not noticed who had gone inside. Whoever he was, he had certainly not taken the time to offer a wave or invite Sam to come inside and warm up. No, warmth was one thing no one here extended to him. What had he been thinking coming back?

Maybe the real question was, *who* had he been thinking about? He told himself he'd come back to serve his hometown, to try to build a future for children growing up here now, and to make amends with people he'd hurt when he was nothing but a troubled kid himself.

He ought to know by this stage in his life that the lie you tell yourself is the most dangerous lie of all. He shut his eyes and rested his head on the back of the seat.

Nicolette.

He could see her in his mind's eye just as clear this moment as she had been on the night he left her standing on Reggie LaRue's lawn on New Year's Eve. Nic had told her mother she was with a girlfriend, then sneaked over to Reggie's, the scene of wild goings-on the likes of which a girl like Nic would never have even imagined if she hadn't gotten hooked up with Sam. She would not have gone for that kind of party even at Sam's bidding, but she did go to Reggie's that night. Not for the party but for Sam. He had promised to marry her and take her away from Persuasion forever. That night, Nic learned once and for all how easily a man who made a promise in passion to a woman could break that promise—even if he knew it would also break her heart.

It was the lie he told himself that allowed him to do it. The means he found to justify his selfish behavior, to take the easy path instead of doing the right thing. Looking back now, he understood it had been a pivotal point in his life, the thing that had set him on the *right* path. But he dared not let himself start thinking there was anything noble or forward thinking in his actions that night. He just got scared, and being a young man, became arrogant in his fear. So he ran off, telling himself he was doing it for her own good, and left the girl he loved standing in Reggie's yard sobbing.

Might have worked out that way, but it was a lie that made hurting her so badly palatable to his ego. He had not done it for her.

But he had moved back for her. At least partly. He moved back for all the fine reasons he'd recited again and again to the people he left behind. But in his heart, he always made himself add, and for Nic. *I'm moving back for Nic.*

And she didn't live here anymore.

Sam opened his eyes and sighed.

He tugged the collar of his black leather jacket up around his neck and stared at the stark outline of the cross against the white, winter sky.

He'd stay until Easter. If he hadn't made any headway by then, he'd just have to admit it wasn't meant to be and move on. In the meantime, he had work to do. He'd wasted too much time already.

He wasn't going to think about Nicolette Dorsey anymore. Wouldn't give her another thought.

He had his mission, his goals, his hopes. They deserved his undivided attention if he truly planned to accomplish anything here. He cranked the key in the ignition, and the engine grumbled, sputtered, then hummed to life.

He'd come back to find Nic, but he had a greater purpose for his homecoming, for his life as well, and he would focus on that alone. He stretched his arm over the back of the seat and turned to check behind him as he slowly backed the truck out of the space in front on Dewi's.

Beep. Beep. Beeeep! He heard the friendly warning blasts of a compact car before he caught the gleam of the front bumper followed by a flash of silver. Without thinking he lifted his hand to acknowledge and thank the driver but the car was gone. Almost immediately in its place, framed by the back window of his truck, another car appeared, one of those monstrosities of a vehicle that looked more suited for patrolling the wilds of Africa than tooling around the quiet streets of Persuasion. Following in short order, a dark blue station wagon whizzed by so fast Sam could not tell how many people were in it or who was driving.

But then he didn't have to get a good look to know, did he? The cars took the corner of Fifth and Persuasion with the skill and showmanship of NASCAR drivers roaring around a banked curve. They made the transition from paved to dirt road like they'd done it all their lives.

Because they had.

"Sometime between Thanksgiving and Christmas a person'll look up and there they come, one, two, three. Cars flying down the road. Them girls descend on that old place like a flock of snowbirds settling

in for the winter." Big Hyde's prediction rang in Sam's ears even as his own resolve faded to a sweet, aching memory.

Put Nicolette out of his mind? That was the last thing that could happen now, and he wasn't exactly sure what to think about it.

"You had no right. You had no right at all to rent out our house without our consent." Nic never spoke a cross word to her aunts in her entire life, but this…this was just too much to let slide with a smile and a soft response.

"Honey, it isn't a matter of rights. It's a matter of right versus wrong." As Fran spoke, Nan nodded her head, her expression the mirror image of her twin.

Fran and Nan had never married. Despite the fact that their mother had given them the nonidentical names of Francine and Nannette hoping to encourage individualism, to this day they shared a home, a matching wardrobe, the same sweet but stubborn disposition, and a penchant for doing as they durn well pleased.

"Why have you got yourself all riled up, child?" Aunt Lula rubbed Nic's back in a slow, soothing circle. "We didn't rent out the whole house, just the master bedroom and bath."

"With kitchen privileges. No good having a place to sleep and—" Aunt Bert normally would have said something blunt enough to curl a mule's tail.

"Little pitchers have big ears," Nic warned and made a quick eye movement toward Willa, who had plunked herself on a chair on her knees. The child stretched her upper body out over the table to play with the objects there.

She had not wanted to take this trip at all, but her aunts' actions had forced it. She refused to take Willa back to begin her new school experience sounding like grumbling old Roberta Dorsey Bolden.

"Mama, these aren't pitchers, these are salt and pepper shakers." Willa held up a pair of plump pink ceramic pigs in overalls and straw hats.

"So they are." Nic smiled and patted her sweet child's back. She saw no need for lengthy explanations about old sayings and their meanings. It would mean little to Willa. Besides, in a world where it did not happen often enough, she liked letting her daughter be right about something.

"As I was saying, we had to include kitchen privileges. What good's a place to sleep and to *do your business,*" Aunt Bert lowered her voice to a whisper to make sure her far gentler euphemism did not lose all its impact.

Nic tried not to grin at the woman's tenacity.

Bert folded her soft, flabby arms over her round tummy and resumed her normal gruff tone. "If you haven't got a place to make a cup of coffee and eat a biscuit?"

Nic looked around the very kitchen her aunts had recently granted some stranger the right to use. Big and airy, with tall windows that looked out onto the overgrown backyard, this room had been the heartbeat of the home in her childhood. No matter what the occasion, friends and family always seemed to collect here, filling the six chairs around the oak pedestal table, curling up on the window seat, even leaning against the counters when no other space presented itself. Just being here was the thing they all craved.

And the noise that created! Chatter and laughter, the clunk of the broken-hinged oven door plopping open then slamming shut again, the whoosh of gas burners coming on suddenly at full flame as Mother or one of the girls took a turn keeping everyone well fed and welcome.

But there was one person Nic did not feel like making welcome here. "Look, I know you mean well, but this renter, this border you've taken in, has got to go."

Fran and Nan, Aunt Bert and Aunt Lula exchanged bemused looks.

Nic wished she could moan and groan and pitch a pure-de bona fide hissy fit but she just didn't have the heart for it. Ever since the birth of her daughter, Nic no longer let herself get bogged down in the petty nonsense of finessing around others to get her way. Straightforward was now her style. But where her aunts were concerned it might as well be straight forward into a brick wall.

Petie should have handled this. Of course, not ten seconds after they hit the front door, her older sister had dashed upstairs, claiming she had a bad feeling about something and had to call home *immediately.* Collier offered no help either. Still breathless from the life-threatening hugs of the Duets, the baby of the family had breezed into the kitchen, checked the refrigerator, put on a pale, woebegone look, and proclaimed she had to go to Dewi's to pick up a few things or they'd all starve before sundown. Sometimes Nic hated the dramatic streak the other women in her family so enthusiastically embraced. Other times she was just plain agitated that she hadn't thought of employing it before they got the chance.

"The thing is, we…that is, I…" Nic fidgeted with the edge of the quilted place mat in front of her on the table. "We had other plans for the house that did not entail renting out any part of it."

"Well, you never told us." Nan poured stout black coffee into almost translucent china cups.

"This is the first we've heard of any plans." Fran handed a filled cup to Lula, who placed it just so on a delicate saucer.

"You did leave us in charge of things here, to do what we saw fit." Lula passed the steaming drink to Bert.

"To do what you saw fit about taking care of the place, upkeep, maintenance. I thought for sure y'all understood that." Thought it? Nic *knew* they understood it. She did not buy this innocent act for one moment. Her dear, darling elderly aunts were up to something. Well, they could just *understand* this—it wasn't going to work. Nic had too much at stake to let their kindly mischief-making get in her way. "None of this matters, of course."

"We didn't think so, sugar, not now." Lula moved to set a cup and saucer in front of Nic.

"Because you're going to have to tell that boarder to leave."

Lula gulped. The cup clattered against the saucer. Coffee sloshed over the rim. Her eyes grew wide and she sank into the chair as if that were her only hope against fainting dead away onto the cold, pocked linoleum. "Leave?"

Nic took the cup and saucer from her aunt's hands without so much as batting an eye or spilling a drop. Drama had its place, she supposed, but it had nothing on the calm determination of a mother doing what she must for her child's well-being. "Yes, that's right. Leave. Hit the road. Don't let the door smack ya from behind on the way out. So long. Good riddance. Buh-bye."

"But…" Nan's mouth hung open.

"But…" Fran's did, too.

"We never could…." Lula wrung her hands.

Bert puffed up her already sizable chest and huffed. "No."

"Excuse me?" Nic sat the coffee down with a thunk.

"We're not going to do that, Nicolette." Bert scowled. "Now, I'm sorry if that interferes with some plan of yours, but we've made a promise, and if it's one thing The Duets do not do, it's go back on a promise."

"If it's one thang tha dyuettes do nawt do, it's go bayck on a promise." Willa held the ceramic pigs up belly to belly, smiling snout to smiling snout as she parroted Aunt Bert's drawl.

Nic wanted to wring her sisters' necks for leaving her to deal with this alone. Like she didn't have enough already on her plate with worries over Willa and money and… She shut her eyes and put her head in her hands.

"You know something, Willa, honey?" Aunt Lula's grandma-sweet but gravel-throated voice flowed over Nic's frazzled nerves like the warmth of a fire-lit hearth on a rainy winter night. "Here it is just three weeks from Christmas and we haven't even got the decorations out of the back bedroom closet. What say you and me and Nan and Fran go see if we can't dig them out and see what's what?"

"Dig 'em ouyt and see whut's whut!" Willa echoed, clapping her hands and all but bouncing off her chair.

Nic mouthed a thank-you to the three women creating a lovely distraction for her child. And for her, too, truth be told.

Just the mention of the deep, dark, cedar-scented closet that kept hidden away the wonderful treasures of her childhood like the photo albums, beach umbrella, and Christmas decorations flooded Nic with emotions and memories. The thrill of birthday parties, the tranquility of sitting on the porch swing on a summer night, the joy of catching fireflies in a jar, and the marvels of many, many Christmases spent in this very home with everyone she loved close at hand warmed her thoughts.

By selling the house she would be taking all that away from her child. She was no fool. She knew that.

But what would Willa reap in return? That's what Nic had to focus on. Yes, she would have to sacrifice something of the past, of Willa's roots and her own, but she would give her child a better future. Or so she hoped.

Nic shut her eyes. *When, Lord, when am I going to have a clear direction? When will I see the right path laid out before me, open and waiting for me to go forward? When will I stop feeling as if the only choice left open to me is not the clear and perfect way but simply the lesser of two evils? Why can't You just shine a light on the right way to go so I can't make another mistake?*

"I see how this troubles you, child." Aunt Bert heaved a weary sigh. "But you have to understand, we've given our word. We can't toss someone out on the street because you got a bee in your bonnet."

A sudden surge of frustration, anger, and apprehension pushed Nic to her feet, her voice louder than she intended. "I don't have a bee in my bonnet, Aunt Bert! I have a child! A wonderful, precious child who has got all these needs…"

The words strangled in the back of her throat. They always did as if saying it aloud somehow made her a bad mother and a woman too small in her faith. As if admitting the truth of Willa's problems sounded too close to giving up on her baby girl, and on the mercy of God to make that child whole. Nic blinked back the tears and swallowed before going on, softly. "She has these needs…these special needs, and I have got to find some way to provide for her."

"Then I reckon you'd welcome the extra rent money."

"It won't be enough, Aunt Bert." She pictured the file in her suitcase with the bill for the first year's tuition. "Not nearly enough."

"Then perhaps you need to think about other resources—"

"Don't you think I've used every resource available already?"

"I can think of one—"

"Don't start in on relying on God, Aunt Bert. I already do that."

"Yes, I know you do."

"I have prayed and I have prayed. I have prayed until my throat was almost as raw as the ache in my heart for that fragile, innocent angel I brought into this hard, hard world."

"I know you have, honey. We all have and do. But I was thinking more of an earthly solution to your problem."

"I have an earthly solution. But for it to work, you first have to get rid of this boarder."

"Maybe it would be better if you would get rid of the idea that you have to shoulder all the responsibility for that child all by yourself. She has to have a father somewhere who—"

"No."

"That's pride talking."

"It's reality talking. Trying to locate Willa's father is not an option, and even if it were, I cannot imagine it would be worth the time, money, and sacrifice it would require." Nic folded her arms around herself and pulled her shoulders up tight. "No, we are going to do this my way."

Tires crunched on the gravel drive outside. A purring engine cut off.

Nic sighed. Collier was back. Collier would be on her side. Any minute now, her little sister would walk through that door to back Nic up and all would be resolved. Just that easy.

"You don't understand, Nicolette." Bert set her jaw and her eyes went positively beady behind her small oval glasses. "This renter is—"

"History."

"The new minister."

"Oh." Even Nic felt a twinge of guilt over tossing out the first new minister the town had snagged in over a year. "Maybe he could stay until the place sells. Or better yet, maybe he'd be interested in buying it from us! What do you think? Do you think the new minister might want to buy this place from us?"

"Don't know. Why not ask him yourself?"

Nic followed the line of Aunt Bert's gaze, turning in her seat just in time to see her worst fear step up through the battered back door.

Five

inister? *Minister?*" She slammed her hand flat-palmed on the table, knocking over a plastic napkin holder and setting the salt and pepper shakers wobbling. "I don't know what kind of con game you are running, but I'm not falling for it. Not for one minute!"

"It's good to see you, too, Nic." He said it like he meant it—because he did. She was *here.* He'd expected as much, of course, but the reality of seeing her standing in this kitchen, so close he could reach out and touch her, overwhelmed him in ways no man could fully prepare for.

She folded her arms and shook back her hair like she knew he could not take his eyes from her and wanted to provide a little flash and strut for his benefit. She stole a quick glance at the doorway that led to the rest of the house. So quick he would have missed it if he hadn't been totally transfixed by her every movement.

She licked her lips, a sure sign of nervous energy. She seemed to weigh her options in a split second and then leaned toward him, her right hand still flat on the table, her expression a shade away from fury. "How dare you come back to this town, pretending to be a preacher, no less. And worse still, worm your way in as a boarder in my home. *My home,* Sam Moss. What kind of bald-faced lies have you been feeding my aunts to accomplish that?"

Miss Bert's cheeks went positively florid. "Nicolette, you apologize to Reverend Moss this very instant!"

Sam held his hand up. He had as much coming from Nic, that much and a whole lot more. "I'm not pretending to be anything that I'm not. And while it is now my job to feed my flock, bald-faced lies are no longer the daily bread of choice on my menu."

"And you expect me to *swallow* that?"

He grinned at her quick follow-through. "Like the whale devoured Jonah."

She narrowed those heart-wrenching brown eyes on him. "So, you admit there's something fishy about all this, huh?"

"I admit…" He bowed his head. The leather that had protected him from the cutting winter wind now laid heavy on his back and shoulders. A film of sweat beaded up on the back of his neck. With a sidelong glance to size up the prospects of Miss Bert's cooperating, he shrugged out of the jacket then held it out to her. "Would you hang this up for me, Miss Bert? It's hot as the devil's frying pan in here. You ladies sure do like to fiddle with that thermostat when you come in for a visit, don't you?"

"Well, if you didn't keep it like an iceberg in here." Bert played along with believable gruffness. Might have worked, too, if she'd have gotten the phrase right.

"Iceberg?" Nic sighed. "Don't you mean ice*box?* Not to mention the fact that barring some kind of bizarre weather event or turning on the air-conditioning, the coldest anyone could keep a house in Persuasion in December is a cheap plastic ice chest."

Sam conceded with a wince that the older lady invoking an iceberg in Alabama did give a false ring to Bert's complaint.

"You never could think on your feet, Aunt Bert. If you had to throw in with this…this…this imposter of a pastor, you could have at least made your bit *sound* credible."

"Maybe I don't think on my feet, young lady, but I sure as fire can walk on them, and that's just what I'm going to do." She lumbered up from her chair and started for the door. "If you need me I'll be calming my nerves with my sisters."

Calming their nerves was Duet code for venting their frustration by chattering a mile a minute about whatever or whoever had gotten on their bad side. Sometimes all four of the ladies calmed their nerves at the same time, often each on her own subject without seeming to notice they had no common topic. Miss Bert moved off at her uneven gait, the grumbling already begun just under her breath. "Come in here and start picking on the only preacher we've had in over a year, I swear. Gonna scare the man off; then where'll we be?"

"Better off, that's where you'll be," Nic called after her aunt, who waved the answer away without looking back.

"You have every right to believe that." Sam started to fold his arms but decided that looked too defensive. He pulled out a chair to sit beside her.

Her scorching glare warned him not to try it.

He grabbed the back of the chair instead and braced his arms straight, leaning in enough to keep his voice down and his eyes fixed on Nic. "You have every reason to think that your aunts, my church, and this town would be better off if I hightailed it back to New Mexico and left things here to go on like they have until they all but faded away."

She pressed her lips together.

"But I can't do that."

"Why not? You didn't have any problem nine years ago leaving this place and…and everyone in it."

"I had a lot of problems nine years ago, Nic. You of all people know that."

She looked toward the window. The yellow-checkered curtains softened and warmed the pale sunlight streaming into the silent room, but Nic's expression stayed hard and cold. "And now you've come back with this cockamamy story about being a minister."

"I don't blame you for not believing it, but it's true nonetheless."

She tucked her hair behind her ear, then stole an anxious peek over her shoulder.

"Maybe we should take this discussion someplace more private."

"What discussion? There is no discussion here, Sam. You are out."

"Out?" He managed not to grin too big over that bold pronouncement. "Out where? Out of luck? Out of my league? Out of—"

"Out of my house." She curled her hand into a fist. "Out of my aunts' lives. That's all I have any say over."

"Actually, you don't—"

She nailed him with a glare that would have sent old Scratch running for cover. But Sam had looked the devil in the eye more than once and had no fear of him—or of one stubborn, impossible woman who mistakenly thought she had right on her side.

"I've signed a lease here. It's legal. Your aunts are all adults who can associate with whomever they see fit. You won't be running me out of this house or this town anytime soon, no matter how many daggers you shoot at me with those big brown eyes of yours."

"You are wrong about that." She stood slowly. "Just like you were wrong to come back here."

"This town and its one tiny church are in a lot of trouble, Nic."

"Then they don't need any more."

Sam chuckled. "If I didn't know better, I'd swear you'd been talking to Big Hyde."

"I don't need outside input to help me form an opinion about you." The quiet clatter of her cup and saucer as she settled them in the sink underscored the crisp tension in her words.

"No, I suppose you don't." He looked at his white-knuckled hands gripping the back of the painted kitchen chair, then forced himself to ease up and let go. "I don't expect you to understand this now, but I want you to know that I came back seeking peace, Nic. To offer peace and to live every day in the power of forgiveness and redemption, that's my goal here. There is no other place on earth God could have called me where I could more ably do that than my old hometown."

"Then there is no place on earth God could have called you where you would be more apt to fail," she said it, not in anger or spite but more like a gentle correction. A tender warning from one wounded soul to another.

Sam blinked. What could he say to that? In his heart, deep where he pushed down all his fears and misgivings, he had a nagging apprehension that she spoke the unflinching truth. Still, he came to this town to accomplish something. He wanted to do the work God led him to do, willing to risk comfort, pride, and crippling failure in this simple act of obedience. "Nic, I—"

"Whatever you are up to, it won't work, Sam."

O ye of little faith, he wanted to tease. Knowing it would only fan the flames of her doubt about his sincerity, he cocked his head and put his hands on his hips and asked instead, "Why won't it work?"

"Because if it's not real, if you are not telling the truth, these people who, mind you, already expect the worst of you, will eventually see through you." She leaned her hip against the old blue-tiled kitchen counter. "And they will not take kindly to being made fools of, especially not by a Moss."

"Fair enough." He nodded, bowed his head for a split second, then fixed his gaze on her, his voice low. "And if I am for real, if I am telling the truth?"

She straightened, her gaze never wavering from his. "Then you may find that this town has little tolerance for those who embrace true forgiveness. That they have their own brand of redemption around here. And that they have no interest in practicing what you intend to preach."

"You say that like the voice of experience."

She pinched the neck of her Christmas red sweater between her thumb and forefinger and sank her top teeth into her lower lip. From the far end of the house, The Duets' voices rose in excitement. A discovery of some kind, it sounded like as their indistinct words ebbed and flowed like waves from a not-too-distant shore.

Nic focused on the yet empty room beyond the kitchen. "Maybe we *should* try to find someplace more…"

He stepped between her and the large, arched doorway that opened to the rest of the house. "We could go to my office in the church."

"I don't—"

"You'll be perfectly safe with me. I promise." He'd meant it as a joke, but even with the jest still hanging in the air between them, he saw that Nic did not find it funny. Well, maybe neither did he. He'd made promises about taking care of her before, and how well had he done honoring those?

"No, Sam." She put her hand up, almost touching his chest.

Whether she started it as an overture of comfort and kindness or if she wanted to keep some barrier between them, he could not tell. Maybe she had only pulled up short from physically pushing him away.

The old Sam would have pressed on for the answer—the answer he wanted to hear, of course. He conceded to her wishes with a nod. He would have plenty of time to make inroads with her, to reach out to her, to make some kind of peace between them. She had come home for Christmas, and her home was now his. Sam saw no reason to rush anything or push for answers neither of them might be ready to hear.

"Mommy! Mommy! Look what I got here!"

"Mommy?" The endearment buzzed softly over Sam's lips. He whipped around just in time to see a tiny slip of a child parading into the kitchen with her cupped hands before her, bearing some unseen treasure. "And who might this be?" Sam asked, his eyes on Nic's daughter and his mind unable to fix on any one thought or emotion.

"It's baby Jesus." The child held the tiny carved wooden figure aloft, still cradled in the hollow of her small hands like a fragile baby bird.

Not a far-off description for the girl herself. She darted past him and headed for Nic, who had dropped back into a chair and welcomed the child with open arms.

"So it is." Sam bent at the knees to put himself eye level with the girl. She looked to be all of five or six if Sam judged correctly based on the kids who gathered around him Sundays for the children's sermons at his old church. He peered between the child's parted fingers. "It is for a fact, baby Jesus."

Nicolette's daughter. Funny, he'd never thought of Nic as having children. He did not have children. He had not gotten married. He had made no home or family although his church had been those to him. For some reason he had always pictured Nic the same way. Never in all these years had he thought of her as somebody's wife, as somebody's mother.

He smiled at the sweet thing laying her head on Nic's shoulder. He had never imagined her existence, but suddenly, seeing this delicate girl, her eyes wide as saucers behind doll-like, pale blue glasses, Sam could not fathom a world without this precious life in it. The power of that realization hit him hard and at the same time made his heart light. "And what's your name, sweetie?"

The child tipped her head. "Willa, what's yours?"

"Sam."

"Mister…that is, *Reverend* Moss." Nic ground his title out through clenched teeth.

"Pleased to meet you, Willa." He held out his hand to the child.

She eyed it, then slid just her fingers into his for a fleeting handshake.

Sam had to smile. He might have personally dealt Nic an unfair hand, but God had fulfilled His promises and given her this incredible gift. Given to Nic and her husband, Sam reminded himself, this darling child.

Willa turned to her mother. "The Duets told me to bring the baby Jesus to you so you could see about hiding him for us to find on Christmas Eve, Mommy."

"It's a family tradition." Nic smiled, weak and wary, but a real smile all the same.

"I recall. Christmas Eve day, Dodie and Collier Jack hid the baby Jesus figure from the nativity for you and your sisters to look for on Christmas Eve."

"Not just for the kids, right, Mommy?" Little Willa craned her neck to look up into Nic's face. An awkward rhythm halted the child's words, not quite slurring but something he could not quite put his finger on.

"That's right, sugar, not just for the kids." Nic smoothed the girl's hair down.

Willa waved her hands and did a sudden jerky jumping movement like a startled baby unable to control its limbs.

Sam cleared his throat not sure how to respond.

Just that fast, Nic had quieted the girl's excited flailing with strong, sure hands.

"No one should be left out from finding Jesus. Not grown-ups…or kids…or…or…" Willa blinked slowly, her huge brown eyes magnified by the thick lenses.

He did not know if the girl had a sudden attack of shyness or just paused to size him up.

In the silence of waiting for Willa to go on, tension radiated from Nic like heat from glowing coal. She kept her child close and her eyes trained on Sam's face.

Protective. That's all he could think. A mama protecting her little one. But from what? Sam posed no danger to anyone here, least of all this extraordinary wisp of a child.

"Or even someone who isn't like everyone else. Looking for Jesus is something anyone can do, even me," Willa finally said, a soft kind of sadness weighing down on her words.

"Even you," Sam whispered, understanding at last. Something *was* different about cherub-faced Willa. No wonder Nic felt compelled to protect her so fiercely, even from a man who, under better circumstances, could have been the girl's father.

"Jesus is for everyone." Willa held open her hand with the painted figure of the holy baby in it.

Sam smiled at her, then lifted his gaze to Nic. "That's right, honey. Jesus is for everybody. No matter how badly someone messes up, Jesus can still make something wonderful out of his life."

Overhead the hurried pounding of footsteps in the upstairs hallway did a fair impression of Sam's pulse as he waited for some acknowledgment of his assessment from Nic.

She narrowed her eyes at him, her jaw clenched.

The footsteps came to the back stairway, a cramped passageway with tight turns and steep steps that no one liked to use unless she needed to get straight to the kitchen unseen or in a big hurry.

The noise broke the spell of the hushed anticipation between him and Nic.

In a flash, Nic took the figure from Willa's open palm and plunked it on the table by the salt and pepper pigs. "I'll tend to hiding the baby, Willa. You better scoot now and see about helping The Duets set up the nativity. Otherwise they may get in an argument like last year, and someone's bound to end up with a camel in her coffee cup."

Willa pressed both hands over her mouth, hunched up her thin shoulders, and giggled.

Sam held his hand out to the child. "Maybe I should take you back in there then. This sounds like a job for a wise man."

"A wise man, yes. Some wise guy? No thanks." Nic gave Willa the gentlest of pushes in the right direction. "You run along, sugar. I'll be there in a jif."

"I could have—"

"No." Nic shook her head and her hair shimmied over her stiff shoulders. "I won't have you trying to get to me through my daughter."

"Nic, I—"

"No. No." She stood and walked the length of the kitchen, then turned and leaned against the back door.

He half expected her to fling it open and order him from the premises.

"Now, you and I are going to have to talk."

"Okay."

The clomping from the back stairway grew louder.

"Someplace private."

"Sure."

"But not intimate."

"Of course not. In fact, you should probably include your husband in our meeting to avoid even the hint of impropriety."

"I don't…that won't be possible." Her expression darkened but did not give away any deeper meaning behind her response.

"I see."

"Besides, this is between you and me. I want to keep it that way."

"In other words, you don't want any witnesses." He grinned.

"I don't want any funny business."

"Regardless of whether you believe it or not, I am a minister now, a changed man. The last thing I want is to give so much as the appearance of inappropriate behavior."

"Good. Good. Because I won't stand for any of that kind of nonsense."

"The Dorsey name means something in this town. I understand that. I won't allow it to become tainted by innuendo or speculation."

She shut her eyes and turned her head, her mouth open to add something to his take on things, or to discount it, he wasn't sure which. She didn't get the chance to do either.

"Heavenly mercies, Nic, I am so glad it's you down here." Petie came out of the stairwell like she'd been shot out of a cannon. She *landed* with her arms looped over Nic's neck, short of breath, but somehow able to go on raving. "I have a problem and I have got to tell someone. Now promise you won't fly into a panic about this?"

"We're not alone, Petie, sugar. Sam Moss is here." Nic extricated herself from her sister's grip and waved a hand in Sam's direction. "The Reverend Sam Moss, that is."

"Sam? A reverend?" She put both hands to her forehead like she had to shade her eyes just to gaze at him.

"Good to see you, Petie. If you want me to make myself scarce I can—"

"Oh no, no! By all means stay. Stay. Before this is all said and done, I may need the services of a man of God."

"Has something bad happened, Petie?" he asked even as Nic demanded to know, "What is it this time?"

Petie straightened up and gave her sister a look that would frost a firecracker. "Bad? Well, I guess you could say something *bad* has happened. If you consider it bad that I have probably, without malice aforethought mind you, *killed* my husband."

"What?" Nic's mouth hung open.

Sam scowled.

"I've killed Park. It's his own fault, of course, the fool. If he had just listened to me. But he doesn't listen, does he?"

"Can you blame him?" Nic muttered for Sam alone to hear.

"Why don't men listen to their wives?" Petie directed the question to Sam.

"Well, I can't speak from experience, not having a wife but—"

"Isn't there something in the Bible that says 'men listen to your wives and ye shall not be killed by doing something stupid'?"

"Not that I recall, but—" Given that the woman seemed more peeved than grieved by this turn of events, Sam had no idea whether to offer advice or comfort…or the phone number of a good Christian counselor.

"Well, there should be. Don't you think there should be?"

"I'm not big on second-guessing what should or should not be in the Bible, Petie."

"Then just take my word for it. Somewhere there ought to be written down a set of guidelines for men, and the very first one should read—" she smacked the back of her hand into her open palm for emphasis as she rattled off the first rule of Petie's proclamation for men—"Husbands, pay attention to your wives when they tell you things for your own good. One day it may save you from eating spoiled tuna casserole that was left on the counter, who knows how long, and was supposed to have been sent down the disposal weeks ago."

"That's what this is about?" Nic rolled her eyes. "You think Park keeled over from eating bad casserole?"

"I can't reach him by phone. I called the neighbors, and they can't rouse him by knocking on the door."

"Oh, well, call the undertaker and book the church basement for the postfuneral dinner."

"Don't be smart with me, Nic."

"If you really believe something that awful has happened to Park, why not go back home and check?" Sam stood back and waited humbly for the acknowledgment of his brilliant and logical solution.

Both women looked at him like he had that bowl of killer casserole under one arm, a spoonful of the deadly dish in his mouth, and had just said, "Hey, this don't taste all that bad to me."

"Parker Sipes is a grown man, Sam Moss." Petie huffed and rolled her eyes.

"But you just said—"

"If he has been sent to his heavenly reward by rancid mayo, stinky tuna, and slimy noodles, what good would my going back there do?" She put her hand to her practically sculpted hairdo. "Comes a point in every marriage when a woman may love and honor her husband and feel great concern if she thinks something is amiss with him. But she'll be switched if she'll hop in a car and drive the breadth of the entire country just to see if he has survived his own stubborn stupidity."

"Gotcha." He nodded. "Then I guess the best I can offer is to put Parker on my prayer list."

"Would you?" she asked, then without waiting for his affirmation added, "I appreciate that."

"Anytime." In fact, Sam pretty much had already decided he might ought to grant ol' Park a permanent slot on the prayer list.

"That made me feel a whole lot better, Sam." She gave his arm a squeeze as she passed by on her way toward the archway and the rooms beyond.

"Then that's the most productive thing I've done all afternoon." He gave Nic a pointed glare. "But that could be about to change."

"Absolutely, it could. There's still enough daylight left for you to get quite a lot done."

He could not read her face, but her tone put him on guard. His goal, the only goal he had since he'd seen her car whiz past earlier, was to get her alone, to talk to her, to clear the air with her, and to listen to her. He could not do that in this house with most of her family around. To have this discussion, to give them the chance to begin to heal the rift between them, they had to get out of this house if only for a while.

"Here's an idea for something productive, Nic. Why don't we grab a couple of sodas at Dewi's, then walk over to the church and have that talk."

"Fine by me." She laced her arms over her red sweater and leaned back against the door again. "I'll wait."

"Wait? Wait for what?"

"For you to pack a bag. No need for anything big, an overnight case will do. You can come back and get the rest of your things tomorrow."

"Very funny."

"Not joking. You cannot stay in this house another night, Sam Moss."

Not stay? Judging from the determined look on her face, he did not dare *leave*, not even to go to the church office, for fear he'd return to find his belongings boxed up on the porch and the doors locked against him. "I can and I will stay here, Nic. Another night, another week, at least until my lease is up this spring. And you can't do a thing about it."

"Don't be so sure."

"But I am sure."

"Fine, let's go have that talk in your office."

"Actually, I've changed my mind. Think I'll stick around here this afternoon."

"Stick around? What for?"

"Put up Christmas decorations."

"Christmas decorations?"

"That's what The Duets are doing, isn't it?"

"Yes."

"So, I think I'll join them. A tinsel rope here, a lighted snow globe there."

He lowered his gaze to hers, leaned in, and touched his finger to her quivering chin. "It's the little touches really, Nic, that bring on the holiday mood, isn't it? The little things that will make *your* house *my* home?"

He did not see the salt shaker pig as it flew by what had to be just inches from his back. But when it bounced safely on the carpet a few feet ahead of him, he laughed out loud. Neither of them had gotten what they wanted today, but these were the holidays and who knew what God had in store for them?

Six

Nic laid her head on the kitchen table. She would have banged it on the table if she thought it would have cleared her mind and helped her see what to do regarding that awful man—who did not seem to be quite so awful after all.

Her chest tightened and she squeezed her eyes shut. Still, the memories flooded back of that December when she and Sam had made big plans for their future. She could see him as he was then, lean as a stray dog with the snarl to match. And a quick scowl that never really concealed the fear and longing underneath the façade of toughness. Even then there had been a presence about him, a sense that there was something more there, something good, almost golden under the hard exterior.

A boy, really, yet so fearless and bold—or was it reckless and foolhardy? Looking back through the filter of time, with the lessons learned and the supposed wisdom of growing older, Nic realized it was the second. He had been reckless, with his life, with his actions, and with her heart. She had taken a long time to forgive him for that and now…

Now this man for whom she had been ready to surrender everything—her home, her family, her better judgment—was like a stranger to her. Worse yet, a halfway decent stranger. It did not improve her disposition to think that from that one pivotal point in their past, Sam had gone on to build a good and meaningful life while she had taken one miserable misstep and detour after another.

She thought of her sweet Willa and made an instant correction, a few missteps and detours that had redefined her life but had not robbed it of its meaning. She was Willa's mama and that counted for something. She was God's own and washed in the blood of Jesus, and that was nothing to dismiss. His grace was bigger than even her sins. She'd sorted her life out now evidently in the same way Sam had gotten his back on track, with the love of God and a lot of hard work.

She tried to reconcile the tall, lean man who had come through her family's door with the scraggly youth who had pitched pebbles at her window to get her to talk to him. Even now in his early thirties there remained a boyishness about Sam that made it hard for her to hang on to her anger toward him. His dark blond hair might not have that devil-may-care look of his teens, but it still had more of a wayward streak than most small-town Southerners were inclined to want in a minister's hairstyle. His eyes held a mix of compassion and humor that somehow got beneath her well-hewn defenses. He'd always had that way about him, at least where she was concerned.

And now they were back where they'd begun. Only things had changed dramatically. Instead of wanting to go off with him, she wanted him to just plain go. How could she accomplish that while stirring up the least amount of trouble for everyone?

Her original plan, to sell the house without coming back, had suited her needs to a tee. Uncomplicated, tidy, quick, and guilt free. That's how she had planned the transaction. The Duets and Sam had seen to it that that was now impossible.

A banging on the back door startled Nic out of her musings. She leaped up and, seeing her younger sister's face in the window, yanked the door inward.

Collier balanced a brown paper bag on one knee and clutched another under her arm. "Whose truck is that in the driveway?"

Nic took one bag, turning her back before she answered in her best matter-of-fact tone, "Sam Moss."

"Ha, ha, very funny. Who is it really?" Collier clunked the second bag on the table. "One of The Duets have a boyfriend?"

"No, it's—"

"Oh, I'll bet it's the new boarder. Right?"

"Bingo."

"Bingo?" The door slammed shut with a wham that rattled the glass in the windows. "Bingo who? Any relation to Mango Potter?"

"Bingo you got it right, not Bingo as a name." Why did talking with her family too often resemble living in an Abbott and Costello routine?

"Oh, Bingo as in I got it right. Got it." She dove into the bag and began fishing out canned goods which she simply stacked on the table. "So, who is it? What is his name?"

"I told you." Nic grabbed up the cans as fast as Collier could set them down and shoved them into the cupboard where they belonged. "It's Sam Moss."

Collier froze with a can of pork and beans in one hand and a container of dried onion rings in the other. "You're kidding."

Nic frowned.

"You're *not* kidding?"

"Some things even I won't kid about, baby sister."

"Sam Moss." She said it like someone who had to get the name out there, had to hear it aloud to make herself believe it.

Nic understood exactly how she felt. "Sam Moss," she repeated for her own benefit as well as Collier's.

"B-but Aunt Bert said they'd rented out rooms to the new minister. Surely that can't be—"

"Sam."

"Oh, Nic."

"Tell me about it."

"What are you going to do?"

"I've already asked him to leave and he said no."

"Have you told him why you need him out of the house?"

"Not yet."

"Why not?"

"Collier, it's…" How did she explain this to someone her family had taken great measures to shelter from the events that now shaped her reasoning? Nic sank her fingers into her hair and temples and massaged the aching muscles there. "Let's just say it's complicated and leave it at that, okay?"

Clearly, Collier did not want to leave it at that, but she did not cross Nic. She did clench her jaw and made far too much fanfare out of folding up the paper bag she'd finished emptying.

Nic pretended to ignore her and set the last of the cans on the proper shelves. Then she turned her attention to the second bag, sitting at an odd tilt on the counter. She pulled a stalk of celery and a carton of milk out and started for the fridge.

"Where is he now?" Collier's tone rivaled the open icebox for chilliness.

"Putting up Christmas decorations with The Duets, Petie, and Willa." She put the milk up and turned toward the table.

"Willa?" Collier stepped in Nic's path. "Do you think that's wise?"

"Sure. Why not? He met her a minute ago and was very sweet to her."

"Well, he would be, wouldn't he?"

"You mean because he's a minister?"

"You know I don't."

"Because she's such a darling little girl?"

"She is—just a darling little girl. But don't play it coy with me, Nic. You know what I'm driving at. Everyone thinks they kept me out of the loop because I was so young back then, but you know better than anyone there is no such thing as keeping secrets in this town."

Nic clenched her teeth. Without looking at her sister, she grabbed up the empty paper sack and began folding it down into a neat, flat square.

"I heard the gossip back then, and time and again people have seen fit to question me about Sam and you and the New Year's he stood you up and you spent all night out at that party—"

"Stop it right there, Collier."

"My not talking about it won't make it go away, Nic. With Sam back in town and you here and the holidays upon us—people will speculate."

Her lips pulled tight against her teeth. The bag in her hand crinkled as her fingers curled into fists in the brown paper. "That's nothing new."

"Yes, but this…this situation is new. It's bound to draw attention, especially if you make a show of throwing Sam out of the house he rented from The Duets. Some folks have probably taken that as a sign that, well, that he had no connection to our family that would make our aunts harbor any ill will toward him, if you know what I mean."

"You know I do."

"Of course if he stayed, some would take *that* as a sign that there was a reason for him to be with our family, with you and your child, over the holidays...."

"Condemned if I do, condemned if I don't." Nic put her hand over her eyes. She wished she were the kind of person who could sit right there and weep and wail and get it all out. But self-pity over her plight was a luxury she had not allowed herself since she first found out she was carrying Willa. Her daughter's disabilities only strengthened her resolve never to give in to that vulnerability. "Well, I have to do something."

"You can start by telling Sam."

"No."

"Nic, c'mon, you have to tell him that he's—"

"No." She held her hand up to stop Collier midsentence. She could feel the fierceness of her beating pulse all the way up into her throat. Still, she swallowed hard and raised her chin. "I am not going to sit here and allow you to repeat that unfounded snippet of mean-spirited gossip."

"Nothing mean-spirited about it. Honest." Collier slid the crumpled paper back from Nic's shaking hands. "I just think a man has a right to know—"

"Don't finish that sentence."

"Nic, you're being unreasonable. It's me, your sister. You think I don't know?"

"I know you *don't* know."

Nic stood up. All her life she had despised, or at least disdained, the dramatic flair that seemed to come so naturally to the women in her family. Now she found she had no other choice but to employ it—or let this pointless and hurtful debate with Collier rage on. Head high, she flipped her hair over her shoulder and moved to the door. "You don't know because I don't know myself. But I will tell you what I believe with my whole heart. What I have had to believe in order to go on with my life every day of these last nearly nine years—Sam Moss is not Willa's father."

Collier gasped.

Nic glared at her, daring her to say anything more about the subject.

Her face pale, her sister clutched the grocery bag to her chest.

Nic started to turn away.

"What are you going to do?" Collier whispered.

What was she going to do? She picked up the figure of baby Jesus from the table and turned it over in her hand. She'd do what she always did, trust in God, act in faith, and fly in the face of anyone who wanted to force her to live in pain and shame the rest of her life over a scarlet stain that had been washed white as snow a long time ago. "I am going to go in there and tell Sam Moss that I've changed my mind."

"You are? You have?"

"Yes. It may not be the perfect solution, but it does seem only fair and right. I'm going to tell Sam he can continue to rent his room here until we sell the house."

"You're not!"

"Oh, I'm not, am I?" She gave her sister a sly smile over her shoulder, then squared her shoulders and headed toward the room where the others had gone to sort through the decorations, calling back, "Just watch me."

"Sam? Willa? Don't ya'll want to come into the living room and help The Duets set up the crèche on top of the coffee table?" Petie held on to the door frame and leaned into the room where a wooden crate and countless smaller containers of all kinds littered the floor, the lowboy, and the high antique bed.

Willa looked up at her aunt for only a moment then took a slow, methodic turn and stared at the bounty filling the room around them. "You can set the crash up, Aunt Petie. I'm not done looking."

"Can't hardly argue with that. There is a powerful lot to see here." Sam paused from his job of pulling smaller boxes out of big ones to make his own survey of the room.

Strands of tinsel glittered on the chenille bedspread, beaded ropes in gold, silver, and braided red and green lay in pools or spilled over the top of storage boxes. Old Christmas cards dribbled glitter on the floral carpet. Handmade ornaments of pinecones and paper peeked over the top of silk holly, plastic candy apples, and packages of ribbons. A snowman of painted macaroni and colorful buttons glued to a cardboard cutout and several small, delicate angels of crocheted yarn dipped in sugar to make them stand stiff cluttered the top of the dresser.

"You sure, Willa, honey? We could use your vote in deciding where to put the animals, you know. You always do a good job with that."

The odd edge in Petie's voice finally broke through Sam's dense hide. She didn't care all that much about the child participating in the setting up of the manger scene. She wanted the child with her, to keep watch over her. Though he could not explain exactly why, Sam understood that feeling. It was the same feeling a good-hearted person had when he found a wounded bird, the need to help, to be God's hands on earth. This fragile little girl had that effect on most people, he suspected, but most profoundly on the family that loved her so dearly.

"She'll be all right with me, Petie."

Her eyes met his. "Sam, you might not realize this, but Willa is a...special girl."

"How could anyone take one look at that precious face and not realize what a special person she is?" He smiled then watched as the child picked up a large, tinfoil star with a cutout of Jesus taped to the center. Sam recognized that picture from the programs he'd found of last year's Christmas Eve service. "You can go on, Petie; she's in good hands."

Hesitance, then relief washed over her face. "Well, all right, you two carry on with your treasure hunt. We're just in the living room if you need us."

Sam nodded without looking back to see if Petie had gone. He took a deep breath and found the mingling of dust, old pine needles, and cinnamon-scented candles more appealing than he had ever imagined. Of course he would. They smelled like home—a place filled with traditions and laughter and holidays and love. A place that he had never really known, even after he'd moved away and gotten his life straightened out.

Funny how a man could get more sentimental over the things he never had than he could over the many real experiences that had made him who he was today. Funny how until today he had not ever really felt that. Being in this home with the Dorsey family babbling and bickering in the background, the decorations that told of a lifetime of memories—being so close to Nic again and to her sweet, extraordinary daughter—he suddenly missed the life he had forsaken so many years ago.

The creak and jounce of the mattress springs just over his left shoulder broke his introspection. He shifted his legs on the hard floor and craned his neck in time to see Willa dump a plastic tub full of bread dough ornaments onto the bed. Stretching out, she rummaged through the pile before her with both hands.

"Are you looking for something special?"

"Yes."

"What?"

"Yes, I'm looking for something special." She raised her head, then tipped it to one side and blinked as she added, "Sir?"

Sam smiled. "Okay."

She pushed the shellacked bread bears and rocking horses aside. She grabbed an old candy tin and popped off the lid. Concentration colored her face, and just the tip of her tongue stuck out the corner of the determined line of her mouth as she peered inside.

He laughed at how much she reminded him of her mother, and though he had no idea what he was searching for felt compelled to join in. He sank his arms elbow deep into the crate in front of him on the floor to see what he could come up with.

"My birdie! That's where Mommy put my birdie." Willa scrambled off the bed so fast she almost took the fluffy white bedspread with her.

"Birdie?" Sam rotated the dusty pink shoe box in his hands until he saw the illustration of ballet slippers on the tan lid mended with yellowed masking tape.

"My birdie. I remember now. I wanted to take it home with me, but Mommy said that wasn't a good idea."

"Oh?" A cold sensation crept low in Sam's gut.

Willa stood beside him now. "She put it in that box so it would be safe forever."

"I see." A vision came to mind of a dried-up parakeet in a coffin of cardboard accidentally packed away with the decorations in the rush to put things up and go home. He had no reason ever to believe Nic or any of her family would be so careless as that. Still, something about this dark-eyed child reaching for the object in his hands put him in high protective mode. "You sure this is a birdie? It looks like ballerina shoes."

Instead of the smile or gentle laugh Sam expected, a tenseness he could only describe as controlled panic came over the child's entire body. Her shoulders rose slightly, her leg jiggled at the knee, her arms drew in tight to her body, and her hands jerked upward and began to flutter as quick and light as bird's wings themselves. But it was her eyes that got to him.

Big, innocent brown eyes that in no more than a flash filled with an apprehension beyond her tender years. A caged, helpless look of someone who knew too well that she was at the world's mercy. The look of someone who had everything to lose, no power to choose, and only a heartbeat to decide where to lay her trust.

"I was only teasing you, honey." He capped the top of her head with his cupped hand. "If you say your birdie is in this box, I'm sure it is."

She relaxed a little, but her hands continued to flail.

Did she want him to hand her the box? Was that the best thing to do? Sam considered calling for Petie or someone, fearing the wrong move might worsen the child's anxiety. He'd dealt with a lot of anxiety in his life and ministry, a lot of fear and desperation and people feeling helpless. He had reached out to so many with God's love and assurance. How could one child fluster him so?

Because she was different? How different did a person have to be not to want what we all want? Love, support, a friend. Slowly, Sam lifted his open hand to Willa's then gently slid his fingers into hers as he whispered, "It's okay, sweetheart. Your birdie is safe. You're safe. It's okay."

She sighed, and with that breath the last bit of tension seemed to leave her body. She took his hand and met his gaze and held it a moment. Then she smiled.

Sam had known few rewards in life he would cherish more than that one, totally trusting, sincere smile.

"Big Hyde carved my birdie for me." She touched the lid of the box with her free hand as she made herself quite comfortable on Sam's lap.

"Big Hyde?" Sam let her settle in, wrapped one arm around her to make sure she was secure, then dared at last to give the box a shake. Something heavy rustled in a nest of tissue paper. "Carved, you say?"

"Out of wood."

"Oh, wood? Not out of soap? Or butter? Because, you see, the only things I've ever carved have been out of soap or butter. Unless you count carving my initials on trees and, um, the occasional school desk or church basement floorboard."

She gaped up at him. Her mouth hung open like she didn't know what to make of what he'd just said. Either that or like she had just noticed this vantage point gave her a decidedly unpleasant view right up his nose.

Sam cleared his throat. "Well, now, what kind of birdie did Big Hyde make you? You want to open it up and show me?"

She nodded vigorously, but even as her fingers worked to fit between the lid and the lower half of the box, she announced with unabashed pride and dignity, "It's a snowbird."

"A…?"

"A snowbird." Nic's voice sank straight into his bones, warm but husky, like silk rasping over a rough patch.

He looked up, unsure of how she would react to seeing the man who had hurt her so badly, the man she wanted out of her home, befriending her only child.

Nic smiled. Not a sudden burst of a smile. A slow one that seemed to have traveled from someplace deep within her, arriving in fragments until they finally added to one precarious, halting smile.

"A snowbird," she said again. "I suppose you don't have those in Albuquerque."

"Actually we do. They come in by the droves to escape the northern winters."

"They do?" Nic stepped into the room.

Willa tore through one of the pieces of tape holding the box closed.

"You can tell them by their distinct plumage," Sam went on, delighted in how his words and her own curiosity seemed to draw Nic closer. "You can spot the males by their bold Bermuda shorts and black socks with sandals. The females sport lavish headgear and have been known to carry purses that require their own luggage rack on the back of a luxury RV."

"Oh, you." Nic snatched up a handful of tinsel and tossed it at his head.

It made a graceful arc in the air, then plummeted only inches away from her, drifting down to decorate the toe of his shoe.

"We're talking about the real snowbirds." She tapped the sole of his boot with the toe of her shoe. "Surely you remember those. Little birds with heads and backs the color of slate and a snow-white underside?"

"Like this." Willa tugged an intricately carved wooden bird

from a nest of wrinkled tissue paper in the box. It dangled from her slender fingers by a gleaming golden cord.

"Very pretty, Willa." Sam stroked one finger along the plump underbelly as carefully as he would had it been a live creature suspended there before his eyes. Truth to tell, he half expected to feel the downiness of feathers, the warmth of a living body, and the rapid beat of a bird's heart beneath his touch. The work was that real. "Did you paint this?" he asked Nic as he nudged the snowbird to twirl it a quarter turn so he could examine the dark black eyes, reddish beak, and the painstaking layering in shades of gray and charcoal that defined the wings and tail.

"Yes, it took me a while to get it right."

"You did. It looks real enough to eat seed out of my hand. I remember you always had an artistic flare. Good to see you didn't let that go to waste."

Her back went straight. Her gaze dipped. She wet her lips and twisted her hair around one finger. When she raised her eyes, she focused first on Willa then on him. "So, you remember these birds now?"

"I think so. You'd see them in flocks around old ladies' houses?"

"Old ladies' houses?" Nic smiled.

"Probably had the best bird feeders, and they know how to rig up tinfoil pie pans to keep the squirrels away,"

"Snowbirds are ground feeders," Nic said, a wistfulness in her tone that seemed ill matched to the subject.

"Big Hyde says they blow in on the first storm of autumn." Willa lifted the ornament away from Sam's touch and began picking her way through the disarray on the floor.

Nic watched her child navigate the chaos with the unusual treasure swaying above one open palm. "He said when he'd look out the window and see the snowbirds huddled under a bush in the yard, it was the Lord's way of telling him to take in the porch swing and get out the lost-and-found box for all the stray hats and gloves that kids would leave on the bus."

"I've been around town a while now, and I don't think I've seen a single one of them, though." It was small talk and he knew it. He did not care. Small talk, big talk, no talk at all, he was in favor of anything that kept Nic close to him, that gave him a chance to make a connection that he could someday build on.

"Big Hyde has a theory on that as well." Nic tucked her hair behind her ear. "He says even the snowbirds have given up on Persuasion."

"My first day in town he called you and your sisters snow-birds."

"Did he?"

Sam nodded. "So that begs the question, doesn't it? Have the Dorsey sisters given up on Persuasion as well?"

"Willa, careful with your birdie now." She never gave him so much as a sidelong glance in reply to his question. "Carry it on in to show The Duets and your aunts, then bring it back to the box, you hear?"

"Nic? You didn't answer me."

"Maybe I should go with her."

"Will you not run away if I promise to mind my own business?"

"I'm not running away from you, Sam. I never have and I never will."

He deserved that and had the decency to wince at the reference to the selfish cruelty of his past. But he did not let it make him turn loose of the conversation or of Nic's presence. "Good. If you're not running away, then you can sit down and tell me how you came to know so much about the snowbirds."

"I suspect you could care less about birds, snow or otherwise." She smiled.

"'Foxes have holes and birds of the air have nests, but the Son of Man has no place to lay his head.'"

"What?"

"The Bible makes a lot of references to birds: how God cares for them, how they carry messages." He scowled and rubbed his knuckle over his jaw. "For some reason that verse was impressed on my heart just now. It's from Luke, when Jesus was trying to get some peace from the crowds who wanted so much from Him."

She nodded as if the verse made perfect sense to her.

God was often like that, of course, His living Word speaking to people in ways others did not always understand. Sam nodded too, only once, as if sealing some kind of agreement with Nic.

She sat on the edge of the bed. "Dark-eyed juncos."

"Beg your pardon?"

"The snowbirds. At least what we called snowbirds. They're dark-eyed juncos."

"Ah. And why the fascination with them?"

"Why not?" She tipped her head to peer out of the open doorway in the direction that Willa had disappeared moments earlier.

"Isn't there more to it than that? Don't feel you can't tell it to me because it's a long story. I'm not going anywhere."

She whipped her head around so fast that Sam wondered that he didn't hear a swish and a crack.

He did not back down. He held her gaze.

She narrowed those almost painfully earnest brown eyes at him. "Why do you care if my daughter likes snowbirds?"

"I'm not the self-involved, scared, wounded young man you knew nine years ago, Nic. Give me some credit." He wanted to reach out to take her hand but settled for picking up the empty box that Willa's ornament had been in and offered it to her.

She accepted the undersized shoebox in one hand. The room grew intensely quiet as she stared at the crisp white paper with the small hollow in it where the bird had nestled all summer.

For a minute he thought she would break down and pour her heart out to him. He braced himself for whatever would come.

She dropped the infant Jesus from the nativity inside, where it fell deep into the crumpled paper, sighed, shook her head, and pulled her shoulders back. "Maybe we can talk about snowbirds and…and Willa another time."

"Time? I thought I'd run out of time where you're concerned."

She put the lid on the shoebox. "You were very sweet with Willa."

"How could anyone be otherwise?"

"Oh, trust me, they can."

He clenched his jaw and gave that short, sympathetic nod again. He pushed himself up from his seat on the floor, and this time he did offer his hand to Nic.

She took it without meeting his eyes and stood. They started to walk from the room without touching or speaking. But just before they got to the door, Sam put his hand on her shoulder to hold her back only long enough to say, "Nic, if my being here causes you any pain or creates even the slightest problem, just say so and I'll be out so fast—"

"No." She pressed her lips closed, then shut her eyes. "No."

"No? No what? What do you want me to do, Nic? Just say it and I'll do everything in my power to comply."

"I want…" She raised her eyes to meet his gaze. Doubt and anger and a weariness that weighed down on Sam's heart like lead filled her expression only to slowly be pushed aside by resolve. "I want you to stay."

"Stay? Are you sure?"

"I'm not sure of anything right now, but I am willing to give it a try on a temporary basis."

"Even a bird needs a place to nest, huh?"

"And a fox has his hole."

"So, I'm still the fox in the henhouse here, is that what you're saying?"

"I'm saying that I'll give it a try. That despite what some people around this town might think, this is the kind of home where the Lord abides and there will be peace. Unless of course—"

"Yes?"

"You cross the line, Sam Moss. Then don't think for one minute I won't snatch you by your collar and toss you to the curb like a dried-up, old Christmas tree in January."

"Yes, ma'am."

Some other time he'd ask what made her change her mind. For now he could only thank the Lord for her change of heart and pray that this was the first step toward a real sense of forgiveness from her and a chance to rebuild from the ground up.

Seven

ic's heart raced. She moved stiffly through the living room, her skin prickling with the awareness of Sam at her side.

Willa was just there across the room, spinning awkwardly on tiptoe while holding a plastic angel over her head. Reaching higher and higher still, oblivious to the chattering of the women around her, the child made long—and surprisingly graceful—loops and arcs with the oversized figure. The angel's slightly bent wings didn't move, but the crocheted dress one of the sisters had dressed it in years ago swished over its bell-shaped lower body. The thing had not been a part of the original nativity set but had kept watch over the family nativity for as long as Nic could recall. It seemed as oddly out of place and yet as natural as Willa herself, twirling lazily in the midst of the quiet, old home and the discord of the vibrant women of their family.

While Willa whooshed and whirled, Collier stood nearby with her hands on her hips and a smart-aleck look on her face. "If we had some tape we *could* stick the angel to the long pull cord on the ceiling fan, and she'd look just like she was flying over the manger."

"Collier, that is not funny." Petie shot the giggling Duets a warning glare.

"Why not?" Collier trained her gaze on Nic's daughter. "Willa thinks it's a great idea, don't you, honey?"

She might as well have spoken in Latin. The question seemed to have so little effect on the child.

Nic did not have to check over her shoulder to feel Sam studying the little girl lost in her own world. Her stomach knotted. All of Willa's life she'd felt this protectiveness, this need to stand between her often helpless child and a world too quick to judge those who did not fit the easy expectations. While her defenses twitched just below the surface even now, she did not feel that urge to turn on Sam, outrage at the ready.

The image of Willa in Sam's lap, of the two of them admiring the snowbird Big Hyde had given her overwhelmed Nic's thoughts. That was why, she assured herself, she trusted him not to make some hurtful remark about her daughter. She refused to entertain any other possible explanation for her ease around him and about Willa.

"We're not going to tape an angel to the pull cord and that's that, Collier. It just smacks of disrespect or…or something." Petie looked mad enough to pinch their baby sister, but she didn't do anything more threatening than shake her finger.

Collier laughed.

The Duets laughed and said things that sounded cute coming from the over sixty set. "You go, girl."

"No, *you* go, girls." Petie clucked her tongue at her aunts. "Y'all go find a nice tall vase or something we can set that angel on top of to keep things tasteful around here. I know the four of you came over here and rearranged everything to your liking as soon as we left last year."

Aunt Bert grunted.

Lula hopped right up and helped her twin get up off the couch. "We know what you are up to, Miss Patricia."

"And far be it from us…" Fran gathered Nan's coffee cup up with her own. "To stay…"

"Where we're not wanted," Nan finished for her identical twin.

"Uh-huh." Petie shooed them off with both hands, her face a mix of tenderness and exasperation. "Then why don't you just stand off to the edge of where you're not wanted, like say in the kitchen. That way you can talk about us while still keeping an eye on what we're up to."

Their aunts said not one word to that. Though Bert did chuckle under her breath and Nan did a little thing with her head that conveyed a "what do I care about keeping an eye on *you*" attitude as she passed by. In short order the parade of elderly aunts had passed by.

Sam cleared his throat, which hardly covered his amusement over it all.

Collier did an imitation of the dispatched biddy brigade, got caught, and winced apologetically at Aunt Bert who just shook her head and tipped up her nose.

Nic captured the blond-haired, pink-lipped angel as Willa whisked past, scooping it up in both hands the way she'd seen magicians hold doves before releasing them into an awed crowd.

Willa hardly even seemed to notice. She simply spread her tiny fingers and adapted, swooping around like an angel or a bird set free all on her own.

"Well, it's about time the two of you came out of that room." Petie dropped onto Grandmother's love seat and kicked her feet up onto the footstool Nic had made in summer camp by covering a circle of juice cans with padding and fabric.

Nic thought of kicking those cans right out from under her sister, or worse. She clutched the angel in her hands so tight that the silver thread in the yarn dress scratched her palms.

Sam stepped up behind her, and as if he knew how badly Nic wanted to throw that innocent little angel right at her smart-mouthed sister's big head, he took the thing from Nic's hands. "So, Petie, what do you plan to do about this potential murder-by-tuna situation back home?"

Nic thanked him with a sidelong glance for turning the spotlight onto her sister, the troublemaker.

"I'll thank you not to make light of my likely impending widowhood, Reverend Moss." She looked like anything but an impending widow. In fact, she went positively petulant and pouty like she was still seventeen and captain of the cheerleading squad. "It's unbecoming of a man of the cloth."

"Do you got a cloth, too?" Willa came out of a spin perfectly positioned to tilt her head back and look straight up at Sam.

"Too?" Sam bent at the knees and cocked his head. "Do you have a cloth, Miss Willa?"

"My mommy does. She has a garage full of them, and every week a big smelly truck takes the dirty ones away and brings clean ones all wrapped up like presents."

"Is that right?" he said like he found it fascinating, not like he doubted her for one second.

"Willa, darling, a man of the cloth means he's a preacher." Collier nudged Petie's feet from the footstool and sat down on it. "That means he's God's servant."

Willa reached up for Nic's hand, which still held the angel. The child wound her fingers in the hem of her mother's shirt instead. "Mommy's God's servant, too."

"I'm sure she is." Sam smiled up at Nic.

The sight warmed her more than she wished it would.

"With a hefty emphasis on *servant.*" Petie's teasing doused the subtle mood like water on coals. "See, Sam, Nicolette cleans other people's houses for a living."

"I own my own business." She spoke to Sam as if her sister were not even in the room.

"A *housecleaning* business," Petie interjected like it just galled her to let Nic have the last word on it.

"What's so bad about a housecleaning business? If a certain someone I could mention would have done a more thorough job cleaning her own house, maybe she wouldn't be worried her husband had done himself in eating something she should have thrown out a week ago."

"This is where I came in." Sam stood.

"I'm going to go try to call Park again." Petie shot out of her chair and rushed off.

"I'll come, too, in case you need someone to catch the receiver when he answers and you fall into a dead faint." Collier took off on her sister's heels.

Nic mouthed a thank-you to Sam. Heaven help her, she was still too proud and too mad at him to say it aloud.

He offered his open hand to Willa. "As I recall your mom said we should put your snowbird away until we can hang it on the Christmas tree. Want me to help you do that?"

"Oh, she won't—"

Sam put his hand on Nic's shoulder. She instantly knew he'd done it to keep her from saying anything that might make her daughter shy away.

Willa slipped one hand into his, then grabbed Nic by the fingers with her other hand, looked up, and smiled.

For one moment, no longer than that really, they formed a tight circle—mother, child, and…old friend. There was no reason for this sweet passing interlude. Nothing had precipitated it. Nothing had prepared her for it. It just happened. It seemed so right and yet so entirely apart from her reality.

Nic tried to make sense of it all, but her mind and senses reeled.

Willa's soft voice finally broke the almost reverent hush between them. "Can we wrap my snowbird up in your cloth to keep it warm until we get a Christmas tree?"

"I don't actually have a—"

"That's what happened with a snowbird we found when I was little. It got cold and sick and went to sing for Jesus on His birthday."

"I see." Sam curled his fingers around Willa's hand.

"I want Jesus to have a happy birthday, but do you think He'd mind if we kept Big Hyde's snowbird here, wrapped in your God cloth so I can have this one for always?"

"I think…" Sam took in a deep breath and lowered his head. "I can't think of anything more wonderful than wrapping up the ones we care about in God's love."

"God's glove?" Willa blinked. "It's not a cloth?"

Nic opened her mouth to try to explain, but Sam spoke first.

"Love. God's love. It's not a cloth like this." He reached into his back pocket and tugged free a white handkerchief. "But we can wrap ourselves up in it every time we remember the promise of His grace, and we can wrap the people we love in it every time we pray for them and ask the Lord to keep them in His care."

Willa pulled the hankie from Sam's hand. "Birds, too?"

"Birds and beasts, all God's creatures."

"Then I'm going to put my snowbird in God's cloth." Willa stared down at the stark white square covering her open palm, never taking her eyes from it as she walked toward the table where her snowbird lay among a flock of ceramic sheep. "So God will always look after him."

"Sam..." Nic looked up, but he didn't take his eyes from the small, determined girl tackling her task.

He asked no questions, made no assumptions, and most importantly offered not a single recrimination about her fragile, broken child. He just watched and waited. Like a kind man. Like an old family friend. Like a faithful minister. Like...

Nic's throat closed. Her eyes burned with unshed tears. She clenched her jaw and tightened her fists, but she could not close her heart and mind to that final frightening, unimaginable insight. Sam watched and waited for Willa. With that one look he wrapped her more securely in God's love than most members of her old church had done in a lifetime of promised prayers. He watched the extraordinary and sometimes heartbreaking child in a way no one had ever looked at her before—like a father.

And that fact nearly scared Nic half to death.

Eight

What are we planning to do about a Christmas tree?" Petie stood at the picture window in the living room, the morning sun warming the spot always reserved for the tree in a lifetime of Christmases past.

"We did not come here to put on some kind of Dorsey family holiday extravaganza." Nic tidied the pillow on the love seat. "We came down here to sort out the situation with our new boarder and to put this house on the market."

"Sam wants to go with us."

"Why should he go with us? What place does he have horning in on our family celebration?"

"Some *family* celebration." Collier crinkled her nose and ruffled her fingers through her short hair. "Mom and Wally-boy are spending the holidays with his kids. Your kids aren't coming in until a few days before Christmas, Petie. And poor old Park has probably wolfed down one too many spoonfuls of your rotten casserole, stumbled into the bathroom to be sick, pitched forward, and clunked his head on the sink."

"Collier!" Nic punched a throw pillow to fluff it up.

"Most likely he's lying in some hospital bed right now suffering from amnesia and can't remember who he is much less where he's supposed to spend Christmas." Collier laid the back of her hand over her forehead and leaned back in the wooden rocker at the side of the window, her face the picture of dire drama.

"That's enough." Nic dropped the pillow into its proper place.

"What? My version's a whole lot better than Petie's. She had poor ol' Parker sprawled out dead on the kitchen floor, a spoon in one hand and greasy potato chip crumbs from the casserole on his cold, cold lips."

"Sure, make a joke of my misery."

"What misery?" Nic rolled her eyes. Petie would not know true misery if it bit her on her perfectly pedicured big toe. "You've only tried twice in the last twenty-four hours to get him with no luck. That hardly qualifies you to play the lead in some movie-of-the-week tragedy."

Petie ignored her sister. "I should have set the alarm and tried calling him in the middle of the night."

"Yes, you should have—if you really wanted to get ahold of him."

"You're implying I don't?"

She hadn't intended that, but now that she thought about it, maybe she was. Petie had a way of milking her imaginary woes long past the point when anyone, even her family, cared about them. The oldest of the sisters had always loved attention, and when the spotlight strayed, she found a way to draw it back to her.

Sam's appearance in Persuasion, his very presence in this house, had become the new focal point. With him living in the master bedroom downstairs, and Nic and Willa occupying her old room on the second floor, everyone in town was bound to hone in on that and forget all about Petie. If she made a point of calling Park at a time she knew she would reach him, her drama would come to a quick and ridiculously dull end.

"Get a grip, Petie, I was just—"

"Get a grip?" Petie's eyes flashed. "Get a grip? That's the way you talk to someone who has done so much for you? Who would do anything for you and your sweet baby girl?"

Nic hated like the dickens to be shamed, but shamed she was. She had crossed a line that, as sisters, they had often found only the blurred suggestion of a boundary. But with her snotty tone, her rigid body language, and her very words, she chose to belittle Petie's feelings from the get-go. She had gone too far.

"Maybe I don't, deep down, think that Park has died of food poisoning brought on by my indifference and his total inattentiveness."

Bingo. They had a winner. Finally she understood something of what prompted her older sister's moods of late. Nic chewed on her lower lip.

Petie fidgeted with the small rhinestone buttons on her pink quilted robe. "My concern over not reaching Park is very real."

She believed her sister. Indifference, inattentiveness, concern, and not reaching her husband, *those* posed the real problem behind Petie's drummed-up drama over the lethal leftovers. Nic saw it now plain as the daylight streaming in through the picture window onto the faded living room rug. Too bad Petie didn't see it or wouldn't admit to it.

"Obviously your concern about Park is real, but let's not play games about what's really going on here, okay?" Nic folded her arms.

"C'mon, you two, let's not do this now." A glint of pleading filled Collier's eyes. The baby of the family never could stand much dissention between them. "There are so many things we need to take care of."

Collier had a point, and Nic had enough to worry about without alienating both her sisters by shooting off her mouth.

"Tell it to Nicolette. She's the one who started it."

"Well, of course she is. She's always the one who starts it." Collier grinned like she meant it as a joke, but underneath the jab, they all recognized the kernel of truth in her accusation.

Always the one who starts it, and always the one who finishes it. That was her, Nic thought. While it went against her nature to rein in her opinions and she certainly would not want to lie, Nic cleared her throat and shook her head. "I was just saying, that's all, Petie. If you're really concerned about reaching Park, make a point of calling when he just has to be home to answer."

"Which is what I said I needed to do, thank you."

She did not look Nic's way. But then she didn't have to for Nic to look right into her heart. Petie needed support. She needed comfort. She needed someone on her side. No matter how ridiculous the story she spun to ask for those things, Nic should have responded. They were sisters. If you couldn't count on your sisters to understand you, who on earth could you turn to?

How she wished Willa had that kind of support system. If she did, maybe the whole residential program would not be the only option. If there were a team of family members to help, maybe they could keep her home and help build the kind of future Nic longed to secure for her child.

"Come on, you two, no sulking." Collier leaped up from the rocker. "It's Christmas, after all! Don't forget that's why we're down here."

"It is not!" Nic clenched her jaw, her mind freshly fixed on what she must do for Willa. "We are down here to get this house ready to sell so I can take care of my daughter."

"Maybe if you weren't so tense, you'd figure out there could be another way to take care of your daughter without selling our family home." Petie's tone never even hinted at harshness.

"She's only tense because of Sam." Collier grinned.

"Won't even let the poor man come with us to pick out a Christmas tree." Petie gleefully joined the teasing.

"I never said he couldn't come with us."

"There's a word for that kind of reaction, isn't there, Collier?" Petie put one finger to her cheek.

"Denial." Collier pronounced it with slow emphasis.

"Okay, maybe I did, but it's because we can't let ourselves get sidetracked. We are not here for Christmas; we are here for business."

"Right. And the whole family is supposed to just ignore the wonder and joy of the season of Christ's birth because it doesn't fit into your plans this year?" Petie folded her arms.

"No." That hardly sounded convincing, even to her. Nic wet her lips. "No, of course not. Let's just not go overboard."

"*This* family?" Collier put her hand to her chest. "The last bastion of good taste and subtlety in the greater Bode County area and all parts north to Chicago and east to New York City? Go overboard?"

"Nevah!" Petie cried in an accent straight off a movie set.

This was a battle she could not win. Nic knew it. Why waste her time and energy squabbling over trees and decorations and things when she had so many demands on her already? She sighed. "Okay. All right. One last big, sparkly, over-the-top, too-many-gifts and way, way-too-much-food blowout of a Christmas in this house."

"The voice of reason at last." Collier laughed.

"But on December 26—" Nic put her hands on her hips— "this house goes on the market."

Saturdays were the worst for Sam. That hadn't always been so. He used to like them. Used to relish them. Used to consider them the calm before the storm, the quiet before the hectic, fulfilling demands of the large, energetic church he'd left behind.

Of course, in his wayward youth he'd slept away most Saturdays, only crawling out of bed or off the couch in time to launch himself headlong into another round of self-indulgent misbehavior. The prospect of having to get up the next day for church or anything remotely connected with God and godly conduct had never intruded on wild times then.

Now the realities of his small church and doing the right thing preyed on his mind almost constantly. Saturdays most of all. For the first time in his life in the ministry, he had begun to worry over things he'd taken for granted before. Attendance. The offering. Plumbing.

He spent far too much time, time when he should have been contemplating the needs of his flock, wondering instead if the groaning pipes would last the hour or if they would burst and re-create the great flood in the Noah's ark-themed nursery. If anyone had ever told him in seminary that he would expend so much energy tending to things like worn-out washers and clogged fixtures, he would have...

He wouldn't have changed a thing. Handling hardware had proved a far easier and more rewarding task than winning over the hard hearts he too often encountered since his return. The coldness that greeted him day in and day out grew worse on Sunday when the church sat nearly empty. That's what made him question his choices most. Not the decision to enter the ministry; he would never regret answering that calling. But he often marveled at his innocent belief in the wild idea that he could come back to a town filled with self-satisfied sinners in the guise of righteous Christians and challenge them to do and be more. What had made him think he could make a difference here? Why did he even care if he did or not? No one else seemed to care.

Keeping his tiny, struggling church afloat, literally and figuratively, had become his main preoccupation, and no one seemed to share his concern. How much of an impact could he have in Persuasion under the present circumstances? He asked himself that each Saturday morning as he looked toward the next day and the next set of problems it would bring. And why did it matter so much?

This town didn't mean anything to him. He'd had to go far, far away from this place to find real success and the greater truth of God's love. What was so important about trying to bring what he'd learned elsewhere home?

Home? Is that what this anemic excuse for a town was to him? His home? Hardly. He snorted and cinched the belt of his thick terry cloth robe more tightly around his middle. He had on a T-shirt and sweatpants. He slept in those out of a sense of decency at having so many women in the house, even though none of them had any reason to come near his rented rooms. Still, he felt compelled to throw his robe on over his sleeping clothes. Having to take that kind of precaution in his own home, first thing Saturday morning before he'd even had a cup of coffee, only darkened his already grumpy mood.

Sam bypassed the living room where he heard the distinct buzz of intense feminine conversation. Barefoot, he padded silently through his private bathroom and out into the hallway that led to the kitchen. He only had to step lively once as he dashed past the doorway into the living room. From the fleeting looks he got from the sisters' faces, he doubted they would have noticed if he had paraded past with a drum strapped to his chest and cymbals clanging on his knees. Still he sighed in relief as he slipped by the door and his feet hit the cold kitchen floor.

Coffee. That would do the trick. A couple of cups of good, stiff brew. Then he could face the day without dwelling overmuch on the difficulty of dealing with a church that did not embrace him in a town that gave him no reason to call it home. Coffee and quiet. Time alone to think and draw on his inner strength. That's all he asked for a few minutes this morning.

"Hi."

The small, sober voice startled the living daylights out of Sam.

"Don't do that," he said, shutting his eyes and pressing his hand over his thundering heart.

"Sorry." The apology came out before he'd even finished speaking. The child was that ready to accept the blame for his overreaction though she hadn't been even remotely at fault.

Instantly, Sam felt like a total heel. "No, I'm sorry, sweetie. Your sitting there took me by surprise. My mind was somewhere else."

"That's okay. Sometimes my mommy says my mind is wandering. I don't think it's such a bad thing, but it scares her sometimes on account of it's a scary world."

Sam had no idea what to say to that. He rubbed his fingertips back through his hair. "Yes, it can be at that. 'Course if you're walking with God, it's not so scary then."

"Mommy prays for God to watch over me every day."

"I'm sure she does." Only knowing this child less than twenty-four hours, Sam had already added that very prayer to his own list.

"And angels."

He smiled. "Angels?"

"Angels to watch over me, to go before me and to guide me, to lift me up and to shelter me, and to help me find grace and gratitude in all that God has given me." Willa must have heard those words many times before. So many times she carried them in her heart and in her mind that sometimes might wander but already knew how to focus on what was true and right.

"And angels, for all those things," Sam murmured.

She pushed her glasses up on the bridge of her nose and gazed expectantly at him.

He had no idea what she wanted. Aside from children's sermons and visits to vacation Bible school, he really didn't have a lot of interaction with children. And almost none with children who were as special as Willa.

He cocked his head to study her. She looked positively lost in the stark sun-brightened kitchen with its floor to ceiling white cupboards and bare countertops. The big table came up to just under her heart-shaped chin. Her red-and-green-checkered robe bunched where the buttons had been fit into the wrong slot. Her feet, swinging back and forth as they dangled a foot above the floor, sported one purple crocheted house shoe and one pink ballet slipper at least two sizes too big.

Her straight dark hair lay matted against one side of her head with her bangs falling forward like a tangled mop over the top of her blue glasses. He thought of how his own hair had always been in disarray as a child, and how kind people like his teachers and even occasionally Big Hyde had helped him comb it out because his father could not be bothered to get up and help him with it.

She yawned, and it finally dawned on Sam that she had probably just gotten out of bed and come down here without a soul in the house even knowing she was up.

"Does your mother know you're awake?"

Willa shook her head.

He reached up into the cupboard to pull down the coffee filters and the can of special roast blend he indulged in on weekends only. "Should I go get her for you?"

Again, a soft shake of her head was the child's only answer.

With the smell of fresh grounds still in the air and the gurgle of the coffeemaker at work in the background, Sam leaned back against the counter. "I make oatmeal for breakfast during the week, but on Saturdays it's nothing but sugar-coated junk cereal. Does your mom or dad let you have that?"

"I got no daddy."

"You mean your dad's not here?"

She shrugged and took the salt and pepper shakers in both hands and without a sound began making the pig figures dance around the table. "My mommy and I never had a daddy in our family."

So many thoughts whizzed through his mind. No wonder Nic had avoided his questions about a husband. She never had one. But what was Willa's story? Was she born that way, or had some accident or illness made her as she was? And just what was she? Impaired? Retarded? Neither seemed quite to fit.

He wanted to understand her for Nic's sake and for his own. He wanted to know how to help them both and how to minister to them. Though they had not asked it of him, he felt compelled to be ready if they should need him. This was Nic's little girl, after all, and despite the fact that he had forfeited all right to care about what happened to Nicolette or any children she might have, he did care.

Admitting that conjured up new questions about why it still mattered so much, where he expected his feelings to lead, and how he thought he was even entertaining those feelings.

Sam turned and flung open the door to the shelf where the brightly colored boxes of cereal stood. The clutter of choices did not distract him from the one question that nagged him most. Where was the man who fathered Willa, and why didn't he play a role in her life—and in Nic's?

Glancing over his shoulder, he smiled at the child, who appeared totally absorbed in the imaginary life of the salt and pepper pigs. "Willa?"

She tapped the pigs together, seemingly unaware of his presence.

"Willa, honey? What do you want?"

She paused in her play and lifted her head but didn't turn toward him.

He cocked his head to one side, prepared to read off the names of the cereals for her.

Before he could rattle off a single brand name, she sighed like a lonely heart who had wanted all her life for someone to ask that simple question. "I want…"

Sam waited.

"I want to stay here."

"You want to stay in the kitchen?"

She shifted around in her chair and peered at him between the spokes of its back. "I want to stay in this house." Her voice was subdued but strong. "I want to live here and be here for more than just Christmas."

"Oh?"

"I want to string up the hammock in the summer like Mommy

and Aunt Petie and Collier said they did and get orange sodas from Dewi's to cool off when it's hot 'nuff to fry an egg on the side-walk."

Sam nodded. He more than anyone understood that longing for the things he had never had but knew existed beyond his narrow, difficult life.

"I want to see the snowbirds come in on the storm."

The power of her wistful tone made Sam ache to see those birds, too. The quiet conviction of her simple description of his hometown made him see it in a new light. Yes, it had its share of snobs and gossips and hypocrites, but where could he go outside of heaven that would not? His job, his very calling as a believer was to stand against those things wherever he found them. By Christ's example he had to try to make wherever he found himself a better place, not go looking for the place where things came ready-made to his liking.

"Don't you like where you live now, Willa?"

"I like it here."

Sam glanced around at the simple surroundings and exhaled slowly. "So do I, honey. So do I."

Finally she let go of a tentative but absolutely heart-melting smile.

Sam grinned. "You know you're pretty smart for a little kid."

"I'm not so little. I'm just small for my age."

"Oh? How old are—"

"How long have you been up, young lady?" Nic breezed into the room and swept her child up in a hug that ended any hope of Sam continuing the discussion.

He knew she had not planned it, but he felt a twinge of frustration aimed her way just the same. His conversation with Willa had only deepened the mystery about her, not given him any answers.

"I hope she hasn't bothered you too much." Her cheek against her daughter's, Nic fixed her wonderful brown eyes on him.

"Not at all." He picked the pot up off the burner and filled his cup with dark, steaming liquid. "We were just going to have a chat over coffee."

"You didn't give her coffee!"

Willa giggled.

Sam laughed. "Give me some credit, Nic. I may not have any children of my own, but I have spent some time around them. I was even a child myself once, you know."

"You were never a child, Sam." All the kindness Sam would ever need in this cold old town he saw at that moment in Nic's warm eyes.

"Well, I can't argue with that." He pulled out a chair and settled in at the table. "But even if I didn't have much firsthand experience with a real childhood, I do know a thing or two about kids, what they need and what they want."

"Such as?"

Willa snapped her head up. Her fingers wound tightly around the ceramic pigs in each hand. With only her eyes, she begged him not to divulge what they had talked about, what she had said she wanted.

Sam brushed his hand over her head, then smiled at Nic. "Let's see, it's a Saturday morning in December."

Nic scooted Willa over to share the kitchen chair with her child. "And that matters because—"

Sam stroked his chin. "And we've already unpacked the decorations."

"And left them strewn all over the back bedroom." She gave

them each a warning glare.

"It's way too early for wrapping presents."

"Unless you want to wrap empty boxes."

"Too soon to start baking cookies."

"Oh, goodie, a man who bakes."

"Given those circumstances, I don't have to be *too* bright to figure out what a kid wants."

"Lucky for Reverend Moss, huh?" Nic winked at Willa. "So, tell us, given those circumstances, what is it that a kid wants, oh, not *too* bright one?"

"To go shopping for a Christmas tree."

"Oh no," Nic whispered.

"Hooray!" Willa threw up her arms.

"Yes!" Sam pumped his fist in the air.

Nic opened her mouth, shut her mouth, then shut her eyes and groaned. "Okay, okay. I did agree that since we are here, we could have one last family Christmas celebration in the house. I guess a Christmas tree fits in with that just fine."

Willa climbed to her feet on the edge of the chair and shouted. "Hooray!"

Sam shot his hand out to steady the child at the exact same moment Nic grabbed the girl by the waist. Their fingers brushed over each other. She lifted her gaze to his.

He grinned and bellowed, "Hooray!"

"A small tree," she said, tight lipped.

"Hooray." He adapted his cheer accordingly to barely a whisper, but in his heart it felt as loud as a triumphant shout. With his new insight, courtesy of Miss Willa, and the pure delight of a day filled with holiday fun ahead, his usually gloomy Saturday had just taken a turn for the better.

Nine

"A small tree. A *small* one," Nic warned Sam and Willa as they disappeared into a forest of trees of various shapes and sizes. Nic wound her arms around her body and hunched her shoulders against the chill of the brisk morning air. She drew in the scent of pine.

A row over and three trees down, Sam plucked up a perfectly acceptable ponderosa pine from where it lay on the barren ground. He held it upright and stepped back. It stood just tall enough for Willa to put the angel on top without climbing on a chair.

"That one will do nicely," she called out.

He ran his hand upward over it. The branches rustled almost indignantly. Needles rained down on the toe of his tennis shoes.

Before Nic could make a comparison to the sad tree that only needed love in the Charlie Brown Christmas special, the pine toppled to the ground. Sam and Willa moved on.

How had she gotten roped into this? She had only made a small concession, allowing for one small tree. To go with a small celebration and the small delay in her plans to sell the house and get out of Persuasion forever. It went perfectly well with her small bit of backpedaling and the small amount of room she intended to open in her heart for any sentimentality over this—with no room at all left over for Sam Moss.

Two rows over a six-foot blue spruce wobbled and swayed. Nic closed her eyes and clenched her teeth.

Willa giggled.

Sam muttered something.

The spruce went still.

Nic sighed but her relief was short lived. When the tip-top of an absolutely enormous fir trembled, then twirled, then toppled from its place towering above every other tree in the lot, she had to bite her tongue to keep from letting out a far from small yelp.

"Oh, no you don't!" She reached them in a few long, hurried strides.

"Why not? It's perfect. Just what I had in mind." Sam stood back to admire the full, lush tree.

"It won't even fit through the door."

"Then we'll just have to set it up outside."

"Outside?"

"Outside! Outside!" Willa twirled and danced in the aisle made by the low swaying branches of the other trees.

"You can't have our family's Christmas tree outside; it's just—"

"This tree is for the church."

"The church?"

"Yes. I thought it might be a community-building activity to come together to decorate it."

She hated to admit it, but it was a good idea. A very good idea. This town and that struggling church did need something to unite it—something other than speculating over her personal business for a change. A tree might just do the trick.

"What about a tree for the house?"

"We've found the perfect one." He pointed to the end of the lot to a cluster of long-needled trees, each resting in black plastic tubs. "It's a living tree. We can replant it after the holidays to enjoy all year round."

"Enjoy all year round?" Talk of memories and even the hint of permanence had no place in her plans. "But we're selling the house. It won't be a memory for the new owners, and we'll be gone."

"I'll still be here. I like the idea that whenever I drive by the old house, even though the Dorsey sisters won't be coming back anymore, something of them is there for me to see and cherish. My very own first Christmas tree."

"You mean your first Christmas tree since moving back."

"No, my first tree ever."

"You never had a Christmas tree?"

"My father didn't…let's just say he wasn't one for the Christmas spirit." He put his hand in his pocket. "Later, well, it wasn't a priority."

"You had a hard life."

"I made a hard life for myself—and for most everyone I loved."

Loved. The word hurt and frightened her. Had he truly loved her once? She had believed he did just as she had believed she loved him. Then he left her. But that had been so long ago and so much had happened since then.

"You really never had a Christmas tree, Rev'end Moss?" Willa blinked up at him.

"Well, the church secretary always set one up, but I never had one in my home." He brushed back Willa's hair with one hand, then raised his gaze to Nic. "The holiday season was always so busy for me. I never thought I'd get much pleasure from one. Besides, with no one to share it with—"

"This year you have lots of us to share it with." Willa reached up to take hold of his jacket sleeve.

"Yes, I will. That's the kind of thing I'd like to remember."

"All right, get the live tree. But on the twenty-sixth when I am putting up the For Sale sign in the yard, *you'll* be digging the hole to plant it, got that?"

"Got it." He winked at Willa.

She attempted a wink back. Once, twice, on the third time, she did it!

Nic laughed. It wasn't a deep, robust laugh, but it was far more sincere than she would have guessed she could manage. And somewhere, deep inside, she did feel a little lighter. She dismissed it as the fleeting flicker of the joyous holiday mood. Because if she let herself suspect it might be anything else, she would have hightailed it out of there faster than eight fabled flying reindeer could carry her.

Sam hoped a hole for the live tree wasn't the only hole he found himself digging in this situation. But somehow, as he watched Nic hug Willa from behind, quietly enveloping the child's fluttering hands in her own, he knew he was getting in deep.

"Two trees? Mercy, y'all have jumped into the season's spirit with both feet now, haven't you?" Bert slid a stubby pencil—which Sam suspected she'd appropriated from the back of one of the church pews—from behind her ear and began marking on a fat receipt pad.

"Aunt Bert, what do you think you're doing working at Hyde Junior's Christmas tree lot?" Nic all but had to drag Willa away from the tree they'd singled out, but the effort did not lessen the volume of her voice or the sting of her reprimand.

"I'm helping a friend." Bert didn't even look up at her niece. "Hyde Junior had to run his momma over to the doctor's. That's an all-day trip, time you factor in a hot meal and a trip to the druggist."

"I hope everything's all right." Sam put his hand on Bert's shoulder to draw her attention. Big Hyde Freeman and his family, along with The Duets and a couple families from the cottages, had been the backbone of his church so far. If anything were wrong with Theda Freeman, he would want to know so he could offer prayers and support.

"Aw, no, Theda's not feeling poorly; she's just not young any-more. Once you reach a certain age, can't hardly go to a doctor but he writes up a sack full of pills for you to take." She bore down hard on the thin paper with the blunt pencil, then glanced up, her tongue poked out between her oddly perfect false teeth. "So you're taking a ten footer *and* a live tree? Whooeee, where in the house are we going to put them both?"

"The big one is for the church," Nic volunteered the information before Sam could think up a way to throw Bert off the question entirely.

"The church?" She sounded as surprised as if he'd announced he bought a beer keg for the fellowship hall.

"I..." He scratched the back of his neck and kicked at the ground with the toe of his shoe. "It's probably a crazy idea, but I thought it might help if we could gather people together to decorate it."

"Pardon my saying so, Reverend, but a congregation our size could gather together around a twig."

"I know." That old Saturday dread jabbed at him low in his gut again. "But I thought we might draw in more people if we had something that they could enjoy as a community. I plan to ask everyone at the service tomorrow to invite their friends and neighbors to a townwide tree decorating party. What do you think?"

Bert nodded, the corners of her mouth turned down. "Used to be just about everyone turned out for the children's Christmas pageant."

"We don't even have enough children in our Sunday school for a...well, for a Sunday school, much less a pageant. And no time to organize one if we did."

"That's true. Well, then a tree it is."

"You think it will work?"

"We'll make it work."

"I like your attitude."

"It's called faith, Reverend." Bert slapped him on the back.

He laughed, though somewhere deep inside he did not find the humor. "Faith. *That* I have in abundance when it comes to the Lord, but when it concerns the people of Persuasion?"

"Can't separate the two. It's a package deal. You trust in the Lord and let Him work on the folks around here."

"It's a deal." He spoke with a confidence that was, indeed, more faith than certainty. "Now let's see how we can get these trees over to the church and the house."

"If your sisters had come with you this morning, it would have been light work for Sam to tie the cut tree to one of their cars and carry the balled tree over to the house in his truck."

They both waved as Sam and Willa drove off the lot to deliver the tree for the church. Nic had wanted to go with them, but the tree was so big they'd had to open the back window in the truck and poke the trunk into the cab, only leaving room for two to travel safely. Willa had wanted to go with Sam, and he had insisted she would be such a big help. What else could Nic do?

She had no doubt that Willa would fill her in—in minute detail—what went on when Sam returned to retrieve Nic and the live tree to take them all home again. "I know it would have been easier if Petie and Collier had come along, but when they found out I agreed to let Sam come with us and pick out a tree, they suddenly claimed a million things to do around the place."

Bert's old eyes twinkled. "Pretty flimsy job of playing at matchmakers I'd say."

"What?" Nic wadded her collar closed in one fist. "Me and Sam? That's…that's…"

"That's only natural, given the situation."

"There is no *situation!*"

Bert could have called her on that. Could have dragged out who knew how many stories about how Nic had mooned over Sam Moss as a teenager. And, of course, the tale about the party and its repercussions. She settled for giving her a stern look.

"I'm doing this for Willa." Nic's protest strayed to the weak side.

"Of course."

"And for the rest of the family."

"Then why ain't the rest of the family here today?"

"They are not matchmaking. They know better than that. It's just that, well, if you must know the truth, we are not getting along at all these days."

"Y'all aren't getting along, or they aren't *going along?*"

"I don't know what you mean."

"Like fire you don't, girl." Bert clucked her tongue. "Think I don't know how things go between sisters?"

"It's different with us. We're not twins, and we did not grow up then live our lives all within a three-mile radius of one another."

"You're blood. You're Dorseys. You love one another with a bond no other humans could possibly share. That's all that matters."

"Aunt Bert, you don't under—"

"In the end that's all that matters. You are sisters, and you cannot run roughshod over them to get your way."

"Running roughshod? That's a bit harsh, isn't it?"

"Is it?"

Nic tightened her jaw.

"Oh, don't feel ashamed that you're the stronger personality, Nicolette. It might surprise you to know that I can sometimes be the tiniest shade more assertive than my sisters, myself."

Laughter burst from Nic's lips at the understatement of the century. A cold glare from Aunt Bert shut her up quickly, though Nic almost strangled trying to accomplish it.

"My point is, girl, that they are your sisters. They will be there for you today and ten years from now and ten years after that. As long as one of you draws a breath they will be a part of you every day of your life in some way."

"What are you trying to do, scare me?"

"I'm trying to wake you up to the blessings you have in your hands right now. Girl, I *see* you. I know who you are. From the very first day you learned to stamp your foot and holler and set your sisters running, you have wielded that power like a benevolent despot."

Nic blinked. She wasn't sure which surprised her more: the

accuracy of Bert's earnest evaluation or the fact that her simple old aunt knew a term like *benevolent despot*.

"Exactly what are you driving at, Aunt Bert?" She folded her arms and stood toe-to-toe with the much older, more stout version of herself. "This isn't about Petie and Collier not tagging along to get the Christmas tree."

"No, this is about what Petie and Collier *are* tagging along for, and against their wishes I suspect." She folded her own arms, her nose inches from Nic's. "Selling that house we all love so much."

"Fifteen thousand dollars." Nic's pulse ticked hard along the side of her neck. "That's one year's tuition at the school where I need to send Willa. And that's not counting books and fees."

"Lands! I had no idea."

"So you see, Aunt Bert, even selling the house is only a temporary solution. Even if we get top dollar, it will only help for a couple years. But maybe that will buy me the time to find something better. And it will get Willa off to a better start. She's floundering in that great big system now."

"We have pretty fine schools here."

"Not for a child with as many needs as Willa."

"I thought the law provides for children with special needs."

"The Bode County school system is just too small to—"

"This one's too small, that one's too big. The one you want is too fool expensive."

"Tell me something I don't know."

"All right. Sometimes it don't take a fancy degree to know what's best for children, to do what's right for them, and to teach them how to make good lives for themselves."

"I know that."

"You don't act like it."

"What are you saying?"

"I'm saying, well, just look at Willa and Sam."

"Don't go there." Nic held up her hand to cut that nonsense right off. Did her whole family have that flimsy matchmaking gene or what? Or worse, did they all just naturally assume that Sam was Willa's father and that Nic should be doing something to reunite their bedraggled family unit? Either way, Nic had no intention of encouraging their conduct. "I do not want to hear another word about Sam Moss, most especially in regard to my daughter."

"Fine, then let's look at the way Willa is with the family. That child just blossoms when she spends time in the company of people who love her and show her discipline, patience, and understanding."

"People who spoil her." Nic covered her mouth almost as quickly as she had blurted out the groundless and defensive remark about her family. Guilt drove her to say it. Love, understanding, and discipline—Nic had those in abundance for her child but not patience. In that way she knew she failed her little girl. She did not have the aptitude to work with her in the same way that Petie, Collier, and now even Sam had shown. Guilt knotted in her stomach and burned high in her throat. "I'm sorry, Aunt Bert. I spoke without thinking. I know the family wants what's best for Willa. And I agree that she does respond best to people who have the right touch in dealing with her."

"People who love her but don't bear the world's heavy weight of preparing her for the future, of setting her on the right path to make a meaningful life for herself despite her difficulties." Bert slipped her ample arm around Nic's waist. "In other words, someone who is not her mama."

"That's why I want to enroll her in this special school. Why I must hand over her care to professionals."

"And pay dearly for it."

"It costs a lot to provide that level of care."

"I wasn't referring to the monetary costs you'd pay, honey. But if it gets down to that, no amount of money in the world can buy the level of care she gets from her family."

Nic's lower lip trembled. "She's eight years old, and she cannot read her own name. I'm so afraid—"

"Don't make decisions out of a position of fear, honey. Especially something as important as this."

"What other position can I make them from regarding a help-less child like Willa in a scary world like ours?"

"How about on your knees?"

"I keep my child in prayer constantly," she whispered with her defenses dropped and tears filling her eyes.

Aunt Bert gave Nic a squeeze. "I know you do, as do we all. I'm talking about praying for yourself."

"Myself? How could I be that selfish when my daughter is the one who has so many needs?"

"How can you know what's best for your child if you don't ask the Lord to show you the way?"

Nic shook her head.

"Maybe it's something you should have a talk with Sam about."

"Sam, Sam, Sam! Why does this family insist on pushing me toward Sam Moss every chance and for every cooked-up excuse they can find?"

"Because he's a minister, honey. And a right fine one, by my account."

"Oh. Yes. That's right." She put her hand to her temple. "It's still hard for me to remember that."

"I can imagine."

She shot her aunt a warning frown.

"Talk to him."

"Don't see how he could help, really. He doesn't have children, so how could he know?"

"You don't have to have a child by blood to love a child." Bert stood back, not having to remind Nic aloud that Bert's own two children came to her through adoption. "You obviously already trust him with the world, with your Willa. Why not trust him with your troubles, too?"

"It's not that simple. I came here with a plan—a well-thought-out plan—and I can't just up and—"

"Sure you can."

Nic pressed her lips together.

"Nothing is set in stone yet, honey. I'm just suggesting you talk it over with someone a little more objective, someone who has a godly perspective and the compassion of an old family friend."

"When did Sam become an old family friend?"

"All right then, a new family friend." Bert placed a kiss on her cheek and gave her an affectionate shake. "I worry about this choice of yours, Nicolette. If you sell your home, where will your heart come when it needs a rest?"

Nic's heart did need a rest. Aunt Bert was surely right about that. As a girl misguided, a woman trying to head both a business and a single parent family, and the mother of a child who might always need an advocate to stand in prayer and act in faith on her behalf, Nic's heart did need a home.

"But a home is not a house, Aunt Bert. It's not a place."

"No, a home is where the people love you most and where the Lord abides."

Her throat closed with emotion, Nic could only nod.

"Do you really think you will find those things for Willa at that fifteen-thousand-dollar-a-year school?"

Sam's truck pulled into the lot and stopped. For an instant he looked up and caught Nic's eye. He smiled.

"Do you think you can find those things for yourself with Willa gone off somewhere else?"

Nic swallowed hard.

Willa bounced on the seat next to Sam. He leaned over to help her out of her safety belt, then opened the door for her with the tenderness and care of someone releasing a mended bird back into the wild.

The December air stung deep into Nic's lungs as she held her breath. "Aren't you going to tell me I can't find those things without a husband, Aunt Bert? Without a father for Willa?"

"Me? Meddle like that?" Bert snorted and tucked the pencil behind her ear again. "Can't imagine where you'd get an idea I'd ever do a thing like that."

"Yeah, go figure."

"Get yourself on over here, Reverend. Nic can't manage things all on her own, you know."

Before she could chide her aunt, Sam was at her side and Willa had her by the hand. She was outflanked and outnumbered and out and out unsure of what she should do next.

Ten

hey had reached the eleventh day of Christmas in the old carol when the wheels of Sam's truck bumped over the dirt road and into the gravel drive of the old Dorsey homestead as Nic's father, Collier Jack, liked to call it.

"Eleven la-la, hmm-hmm," Willa bellowed. She did not let the fact that they'd all forgotten what gifts arrived on what days after five golden rings get in the way of her carrying on with the song.

The old Dorsey homestead. Driving up to it, even after the short trip from the Christmas tree lot, gave Nic a feeling no other place on earth could rival. If she had never come back for this last visit, if she'd never agreed to spend one last Christmas here, if she hadn't listened to Aunt Bert, maybe she could have sold the house without so much as a backward glance. But she had done all that and more, and now she knew she could not just let this house go without the input of her sisters. That was a conversation long overdue and it could not wait another minute.

They had hardly slid out of the truck and their feet had not hit the ground before Nic started barking out orders. "Sam, will you go out and check in the garden shed around back for a wash-tub or the like to set that tree in once we get it inside? We need something big enough to hold the root ball but not so big that the tree tips over."

"Can do." He gave a little salute.

"And, Willa, honey, you go with him and see if, between the two of you, you can find the dark green, long-necked watering can." Nic added descriptive hand motions to her request, hoping that would help her child focus on the simple but important task.

"Dark-necked, long green water can." Though she didn't get the words verbatim, Willa's hand copied her mother's gestures to a tee.

"We'll need that inside, too, so we can reach under the branches to water the tree without knocking decorations off." Nic looked to Sam as a backup, to make sure he understood what she wanted.

"Not to worry, we won't let you down."

Of the half dozen or so things she might have replied, all Nic could murmur was a hoarse, "I know."

Sam extended his hand in her direction.

She braced herself for his touch on her shoulder.

At the last instant he withdrew and tucked both hands in his jeans pockets. "And while we're unearthing the necessities from the darkest recesses of the garden shed, what will you be doing on the Christmas tree prep front?"

"Nothing."

"Aha!" Sam gave Willa a conspiratorial look. "She gives the orders, but she doesn't carry out the orders, just like a—"

"A benevolent despot?"

"I was going to say like a Dorsey woman but six of one, half a dozen of another." He grinned.

"Go!" She feigned an authoritative scowl. "And take your time, please. I need to have a talk with my sisters."

"Big confab on what to do in the house with a live tree?"

"Big confab on what to do with the house, period."

"Oh?"

"Don't look smug. I haven't changed my mind about selling it. I just realized I never talked it over properly with Petie and Collier."

"Then you're right, you should." He nodded his head. "Personally I value the opportunity to talk things over with people I trust, to get feedback and an honest exchange. It often works wonders to help me see where they are coming from and for them to appreciate my point of view."

"Point taken, Mr. Obvious." She held her hands out and stepped back.

"Maybe this evening you and I can finally have that private talk in my office?"

"Maybe." She retreated backward another step. "But first, I really need to spend time with my sisters. I need their special insight, to seek their guidance."

Sam raised his gaze skyward and pointed. "You do realize that you should take this—"

"Yes, yes, of course I realize I should take this all to the Lord. Don't think I haven't. But I also need to see eye to eye and come heart-to-heart with the people who will always love me and put up with me no matter what."

"Always a smart move."

"You know my sisters are my lifeline. They are both so well grounded and levelheaded. They really care what happens to me and Willa, and they are—"

"On the roof."

"I beg your pardon."

Sam pointed upward again. "Your levelheaded, well-grounded

sisters are both, at this very moment, climbing out the attic window onto the roof."

She turned in time to see Collier regain her footing just seconds before she would have gone sliding on her backside down the steep pitch of the gabled roof.

"Those blockheads!"

"So much for wise and caring advisors to the headstrong, dominant Dorsey daughter."

Petie flicked a string of Christmas lights trailing out of the window high in the air to hook over the weather vane on the very top of the single attic dormer.

"I'd cook up a scathing rejoinder to that, Sam, but I haven't got the time right now. This benevolent despot has got to go knock some sense into her beloved subjects."

"What are you thinking crawling out onto the roof when both Sam and I are gone?" Nic climbed out the window without a moment's hesitation to confront her foolhardy sisters. "What if you had fallen off and broken your silly necks? Who would you have come running to for help then?"

"If we broke our silly necks, we wouldn't come running to anyone, least of all *you*." Petie jabbed Nic in the shoulder with one perfectly manicured fingernail, then plunked a bundle of tiny lights into her hands. "Now either make yourself useful or go back inside."

"I am making myself useful. I'm trying to keep you two from…" She inched along behind her older sister as Petie draped lights down the side of the dormer in no particular pattern. Nic stood back, frowned, then reached up to slip the green wire into the tiny hooks their father had put up two decades ago to hold the lights in place. "I am trying to keep you two from hurtling your-selves off the roof and crashing into Mama's rosebushes. Do you know how long it took her to get those filled in like that? One careless misstep by you two and *splat,* years of good gardening squashed."

"We're not going to fall anywhere." Collier guided the heavy strand of larger ceramic lights into place outlining the front eaves of the house. "And if we do that's our problem, not yours."

"Oh, sure, like I wouldn't be the one stuck with the messy cleanup detail." She pointed to a spot her younger sister had missed, causing the string of lights to droop.

"Your concern is too touching." Petie took the last of the small lights from Nic's hands and squeezed past her. "But if the only rea-son you came out on this roof was to nag us…"

"Will you listen to what you're saying? What are you two doing out here anyway?"

"Irish step dancing." Petie didn't even look her way. "What does it look like we're doing?"

"Petie and I decided that if this was our last ever Christmas in this house, we wanted to do it up right. We haven't hung the lights on the roof since Daddy died. It just seemed the right thing to do this final time."

A tumble from the rooftop probably would have had less impact on Nic than Collier's words and the sad, longing look in her eyes. She had come back to talk to her sisters about their home and ended up yelling at them instead. Aunt Bert was right; she was bossy and tyrannical to the people who loved her most, and not so benevolent when things did not go her way.

"We ought to put the star up, too," she said softly.

Petie and Collier exchanged glances.

"I'll go get it." Collier started back inside the window.

Nic stopped her with one hand on her arm. "No, wait. Sit with me a minute."

"On the roof?" Petie shifted her feet on the grayed shingles and crinkled her nose as if she had just realized where they were.

"Yeah, on the roof." Nic settled herself down and patted the spot next to her. "It's a nice view up here. Really gives you a sense of the big picture, and that's what I want to talk to you two about."

"The view?" Collier sat cross-legged at Nic's side.

"Uh-huh, the view. Your view and Petie's." Nic looked up at her older sister. "It's coming a little late, but I want to hear what you think about my plans, about these decisions I took upon myself to make for everyone."

"Oh, *this* I have to sit for." Petie lowered herself slowly, then situated herself with her elbows braced on the windowsill behind her. "You want to start first or shall I?"

"You've heard my side." Nic held her hands up. "Cut loose on me."

Petie put one hand on her head, flattening what little poof her hairstyle still held. "I don't even know where to begin."

"I do." Collier straightened her back. "I don't want you to make us sell our home. And I don't want you to send Willa away to some school where— I don't want you to send her away. Period."

"Okay." Nic tried to keep any reaction she had to her little sister's directness under control.

"I don't think it's good for her and I don't think it's good for our family. Plain as that, Nic."

Nicolette bent her head until the rough weave of her blue

sweater scratched her chin. She looked to her left and a little behind her to catch Petie's eye. "Is that how you feel, too?"

For the first time in forever her sister would not meet her gaze.

Nic sighed. "I never even asked, did I? Just told you I needed the money for Willa and you both were willing to make the sacrifice."

"We love you and our sweet Willa more than any old house." Petie's lips trembled but finally formed a faint smile. "It's just wood and glass, some furniture and mementos, and a whole lot of stuff that's just a yard sale waiting to happen."

Nic mustered a faint smile at the description.

"We can sell this place if you need us to," Petie said. "It won't touch our memories. We'll always have what this home has meant to us, what we mean to each other."

"We're sisters." Collier's voice rasped. "If you say it's got to be this way for Willa's sake, we won't fight you on it. But it's not what I want, not what I would ever choose for you, for us, or for her."

The sweater's sleeve chafed Nic's cheek as she dipped her head to wipe away the silent tears filling her eyes. She sniffled. "Petie?"

"If I had the chance to have my children home with me again, even for a little while, even knowing they would grow up and leave me all over again, I don't know what army could take them away from me."

"But your children are strong and healthy," Nic whispered.

"So is Willa."

"But what if…" Nic could not finish. The questions were too big and too many.

"What if we say that no matter what you decide, we'll support you." Collier scooted nearer. "If you promise to spend the next few days thinking and praying about all the options?"

All Nic could do was nod.

In a heartbeat, Petie was at her side.

Collier wound her arm into Nic's and laid her head on her big sister's upper arm.

Petie snuggled close and laid her arm over both of them, pulling them into a tight knot, sisters bound by love and hope. Nic did not know what she would do. But as she looked out across the town where she had grown up, with her faith in the Lord and her sisters there to lend support, she knew she would make the right choice.

By Christmas day, she told herself, she would have chosen a course and she would not look back.

Eleven

ot so much on this side. People passing by the house
will want to see the decorations through the window, too, y'all." Nic gave Collier a little shove to get
her started toward the side of the tree that didn't face the living
room. After that she pointed to the spot where Willa and Petie
were weighing down the branches with various hand-done
baubles. "Don't put all the homemade ornaments together like
that; break that grouping up with the store-bought ones."

Even something as simple as decking out the tree saw Nic in
charge with a style and flare that no one, except for a few mumbled
unrepeatables from Petie, questioned. When she couldn't stand it
anymore and got in there herself to replace a cotton ball and a
thread spool lamb with a plastic snowman drinking a soda pop,
Sam chuckled.

"What are you laughing at? Your job did not end with hauling
the tree in and getting it to set straight, you know."

"Hey, I'm no good at this kind of thing." He held his hands
up. "Remember, I never had a Christmas tree before."

"No excuses. It doesn't take a rocket scientist to figure out how
to fling tinsel."

"Fling tinsel?"

"That's our job." She pointed to herself and then him. "Soon
as the others get the ornaments done, we'll switch on the lights so

we can see where to put the tinsel. This being a live tree we don't want to get carried away, I figure. But if we layer the tinsel in just so, then it'll catch the light and look perfect."

"Perfect," he whispered, making not even the slightest reference to the appearance of the tree. Nic still had it. She was still strong and vibrant and sure of herself in ways he never could be. How he could use her won't-take-no-for-an-answer attitude around the church, too. Imagine the things she could accomplish, even with his small congregation, if she set her mind to it. She'd make a wonderful partner in that respect.

She bent down to scoop up a handful of glittering silver tinsel. As she stood upright again, the lights on the tree flicked on and she turned toward him and smiled.

Who was he kidding? She would make a wonderful partner in any respect.

"Well, what are you waiting for?" She extended the hand filled with tinsel toward him.

"Everything in God's time." He grinned, then groaned as he pushed up off the couch to flavor his response with just the right touch of humor. Still, when he moved close to Nic, close enough to see the tiny twinkling lights reflected in the depths of her brown eyes, he found it no laughing matter.

What was he waiting for? If they had been alone in the room, he would have brushed the thick waves of her soft hair away from her face, laid his hand along her neck, and looked long and deep into her eyes. If he saw mirrored back just a glimmer of the hope and heartache he felt whenever he stood near her, he would have kissed her.

But they were not alone. And big lumbering fool that he was, even he knew she was not ready for him to pour out his soul and admit he'd come back to Persuasion in part to find her.

She held the tinsel out to him.

"What should I do now?" he asked, edging in until he felt her warmth radiating into his chest.

"Now?" It came out more like a sigh than an audible question. She glanced down, paused, then plucked a few thin strands between her thumb and forefinger. "Now we proceed with care; don't want to go ruining a good thing by getting heavy handed."

She turned away and tossed the tinsel into the air.

Sam watched it float and drift, then drape over the bristling needles of the plush green tree.

"See?" She faced him again.

He let his gaze sink into hers. "I think I can handle that."

"Good." She pushed half the tinsel into his hand. "Then start over there. Remember, be gentle."

"I will."

"Don't rush this."

"I promise."

"And whatever you do—"

"Yes?"

"Don't clump."

"Nice job, huh?" Sam sipped the dregs of the hot chocolate they'd mixed up in the spirit of the day's activities, his large hand easily encompassing the whole delicate cup. "I can't believe Petie and Collier didn't want to sit here with us for a while and enjoy the quiet mood."

Nic did not believe it either. Still, she saw no reason to point out to Sam that they had once more become the victims of a well-intentioned but probably inappropriate matchmaking scheme.

"You heard Petie, when she found out that Collier had brought her laptop along, she wanted to see if she could reach Park by e-mail."

"I hope she does. At this point *I'm* beginning to worry about the guy."

Nic laughed. Park and Sam had never had, to put it politely, any love lost between them. In everything from their upbringings to their involvement with Nic and Petie, they could not have been more different.

"Maybe you should put him on your prayer list," Nic teased.

"I did." Sam seemed genuinely surprised that she would suggest otherwise. "I told Petie I would, remember?"

"Yes, I just…lands, you really are a minister, aren't you?"

"Guess you'll find out how real tomorrow morning. Y'all are planning on attending the service, aren't you?"

"For the chance to see Sam Moss standing in the pulpit of Persuasion All Souls Community Church? Wild horses couldn't keep me away."

"Drag you away," he corrected. "Then again… Maybe I ought to check around and see if there's been a rash of wild horse sightings, 'cause something is keeping everyone else away."

"You're worried about that church, aren't you?"

"What church?" For the first time weariness and disappointment colored his voice.

"Sam?"

He shook his head like he could shake off the mantle of care weighing down on him, then smiled, but only a little. "Just repeating what Big Hyde said to me the first day I showed up back in town. He tried to warn me I wouldn't find much in the way of acceptance here."

Nic understood that feeling better than any other person on

earth. She laid her hand on Sam's arm. "What are you going to do?"

"Pray."

She curled her fingers closed over his shirtsleeve.

"Work hard and pray," he amended.

She had nothing to add to that. No advice or words of encouragement came to mind. Finally, to fill the gnawing silence, she patted his shoulder and said a bit too brightly, "Maybe your idea about the tree will help."

"I hope so."

They sat in silence, watching the lights. It had not been cold enough to build a fire in the nearby fireplace. Still, the moment had its own warmth.

"Thank you for including me in your family celebration, Nic. It means a lot."

Nic curled her legs beneath her on the sofa like a contented cat and lifted her head to bask in the glow of the tree in the darkened living room. "It wasn't anything special."

"It was to me." His voice, his posture, even the way he tipped his head to one side as he gazed across the room reminded her of the Sam she had known so long ago.

Or was it so very long ago? It was all of Willa's lifetime. Yet in the grand scheme it didn't seem like so many years stood between now and the time she had fallen for Sam. Fallen for him in the way innocent young girls too often do for cocky young boys ill-equipped to handle those emotions—fall hard and without reservation or one scrap of common sense.

But it had been easy to care for Sam back then. She had seen beneath the life-toughened exterior to glimpse the good in him that had, in fact, with God's hand, grown to fruition in the man sitting here today. Nic sighed. "I'm glad you're here to share the holidays, Sam."

"Are you?"

She nodded.

"That means a lot to me to hear you say that." He brushed his crooked finger over her cheek.

She shut her eyes and savored the comfort of Sam's closeness, the coziness created by the glowing lights in the darkness. The scents of fresh pine and lingering hot chocolate completed the sensation of utter contentment.

"Nic, I—" His weight shifting made the old sofa creak and the cushion dip toward her. His shirtsleeve swept over her upper arm as he took her shoulders in both his strong hands. She didn't have to look to know that he was planning to kiss her.

For a second she lifted her chin and thought of letting him follow through with it. Then her not-so-distant thoughts about the young man who had crushed her tender heart so long ago intruded before he drew her to him.

She opened her eyes and pushed him away with both hands on his chest. "It took a lot for me to admit I like having you here, Sam. Let's not risk spoiling the moment by pressing it any further than that."

"You're right." The sofa groaned and sagged as he sat back again. "You're right, of course."

She was right, but that did not keep her from feeling a twinge of regret that he gave in so quickly. The old Sam would have pursued his goal a little longer. The man with her now was definitely a changed person. Mentally and emotionally she welcomed that realization, but her been-too-long-alone ego would have appreciated just a bit more protest on his part.

She huffed out a long breath, then twirled her finger in her hair, trying to think of a nice safe topic that would keep him here a while longer. "My favorite part tonight was the final touch—putting the star on the top. Collier made it when she was little, and Willa stuck the picture of Jesus on it last year. That makes it extra special."

"I can well imagine."

"It's sort of a family tradition to put it on last, then stand back and ooh and ah."

"For a minute there I thought Willa would have to let one of the more experienced star sticker-on-ers take over." He watched her as he spoke. Not in the way he usually watched her, which was unnerving enough, but with an interest that reached beyond the surface of the simple remark. He was testing the waters with her regarding Willa.

Nic sat up, her gaze on the star and her back stiff. "Thank you for lifting her up like that; I could tell you wished she'd hurry it up there toward the last."

"That's okay. She's just a tiny thing, doesn't weigh very much."

"She wanted to get it just right." A sentiment Nic appreciated tenfold.

"She sure got a charge out of the lights, didn't she?"

At last, a safe topic—Christmas decorations. A logical enough leap not to stir Sam's suspicion over her shift in subject. Yet something she could milk for a few minutes more with Sam before saying good night. "Who doesn't like the lights? I think we should all go for a drive one evening this week to see how everyone has their houses done up."

"I'm game. I still can't get over Willa though."

Willa was not a topic Nic considered safe nor one she wanted to linger over. Especially not with Sam.

"Imagine wanting to eat her dinner out here by twinkle lights." He shook his head.

"I kind of liked the effect. Don't you enjoy holiday decorations?"

"Sure, I like them okay. I liked the company better." He smiled. "I guess the lights in the background did give the mac and cheese a more festive touch."

"Well, Collier's cooking can use all the help it can get."

"Ah, it was fine."

Nic relaxed her shoulders and started to lean back.

"Willa told me that was her favorite dinner."

Her spine went rigid before it ever met with the sofa cushion. She faked a smile but had no illusion that Sam bought her light expression. "Willa would live on macaroni and cheese if she could. I make sure she eats her fruits and veggies, though."

"I'm sure you do. Anyone can see you're a great mom, Nic."

"Great?" She huffed and ran her hand over her forehead. She neither felt deserving of the accolade or comfortable with the person giving it. She could not talk about Willa with Sam without being aware of the fact that some people suspected he might be her father. How did you put a thing like that out of your mind? Nic had resolved the issue of Willa's paternity years ago and had committed herself, as an act of pure faith, not to dwell on it again. It was the past, and a past for which she had been forgiven. The old sins were gone, but if she was not careful, she would let being in Persuasion and seeing Sam dredge them up again.

"And Willa's a great kid."

"Okay, *that* I'll give you. I have been blessed."

"Blessed. That's exactly the right word for it, isn't it, Nic?

Despite…well, whatever… I can see that Willa is a true blessing to you and to this entire family. To me, too."

"You?"

"Yeah, she really took my mind off worry over the church today, for one thing." He rubbed the back of his neck and kept his gaze focused somewhere across the room. "And when she showed me her snowbird ornament that first day, she gave me a glimpse of how terrific it is to love and nurture a child. A blessing if I ever saw one."

"Thank you for being so good with her," she said before she could stop herself. So much for steering the conversation into safe waters. "She really thinks you're something special, too."

Sam shrugged.

She couldn't tell if the response came out of modesty or nonchalance. That gave her very little to go on in deciding what to do next. Nic wet her lips. What harm could there be in letting Sam in on how much he had meant to Willa in the short time she'd known him? Willa would probably tell Sam herself at some point. Why hold back when there was nothing more to it than a child's response to a kind man? "She told me when I tucked her in that she thought you were the nicest, handsomest man she'd ever met, except for her Uncle Park, cousin Scott, and the man who hands out suckers at the drive-thru bank."

"Pretty highly esteemed company."

"You've struck a chord with her, connected. That's not always easy to do."

"Well, I realize she has some…difficulties, but she's still real young, Nic. And pretty articulate for her age, assuming…what is she, about six?"

If he'd asked straight out, she'd have answered in kind. But his hesitance, the roundabout way he came at the question put Nic back on full alert. "She does score high for her age group on verbal tests."

"I can see that." He folded his hands together and waited, not saying any more, just watching her. She had seen so many doctors and counselors do this very thing, hoping that in an anxious need to fill the silence she would spill her guts about feelings and expectations. Well, if he thought that was going to happen, he had the wrong girl. She had a million thoughts and emotions swirling in her head now about the house, her goals, her sisters, her precious child, and even Sam. She did not want to chance muddling those things up and blurting out who knew what because he played some ultrabasic psychological game with her.

She folded her hands and mirrored his position.

He said nothing.

She held her peace.

Upstairs they heard shuffling.

Petie and Collier's voices rose then quieted.

Nic relaxed a bit to remember she and Sam were not really alone and to know she could always use her sisters as an excuse to make a polite exit. She tried not to feel too silly after trying to prolong the conversation so she could spend just a few minutes more with Sam. She now wanted a backup getaway plan.

"So you're not going to tell me?"

She tried not to gloat that he had broken first. Besides, she needed to stay sharp so she didn't let down her guard too much for vague questions obviously intended to draw her out. "Tell you what?"

"Willa's story."

"Willa's...?" She put her hand to her throat. Beneath her palm her heart thudded in a furious, frightened cadence. Sam wanted to know Willa's story. Of all the things she had wanted to suppress since coming back to town, he had to ask the one thing that she feared most telling him—the one thing she knew that someday, no matter what happened between them, she would have to share with him.

"Okay, I worded that poorly, but I had no idea how better to put it. After getting to know that sweet, special kid, I didn't have it in me to look in your face and ask you what's wrong with her."

"Wrong?"

"I'm sorry but I don't know the proper term for what's, you know, *different* about her, Nic."

She let her breath out slowly. She tried to find her equilibrium again without an obvious show that she had almost lost it entirely. She ran her hand through her hair and tucked a strand behind one ear. She let her gaze drop and focused it on a splash of wayward glitter brightening the leg of her faded jeans. "What's different about Willa is that she is brain injured, Sam."

"Brain…?"

"Injured." She looked up. She had always spoken frankly about Willa's condition, no reason to change that now. "Brain damaged."

"Oh, Nic. When? How?"

"Probably at birth. We can't prove that; though, believe me, we did try."

"I don't understand."

She shut her eyes but that did not dispel the emotions welling up within her. "And I don't want to talk about it, not now, at least."

"Nic—"

"I'm not trying to hide anything from you."

"I never thought you were."

She bit her lip and nodded.

"This is obviously very painful to you."

"Every bit of it. The cover-ups, the outright lies, the casual disregard for a child's well-being, and a parent's right to know and best care for that child." She cut herself off. She wasn't making sense and she knew it. "It is, Sam, very painful. What happened when Willa was born and in the time shortly after that shaped my life and the decisions I made regarding caring for her in ways you cannot begin to imagine."

"I believe you."

Nothing else he could have said would have meant more to Nicolette. He believed her. The level of trust implied in that simple sentence spoke volumes to her bruised self-esteem. She put her hand on the side of his face. "Oh, Sam. Thank you."

"For what?" He stroked a tear from her cheek with the side of his thumb.

She had no words to explain it to him. She sniffled, shut her eyes, and shook her head.

When he drew near, she did not lurch away. When he kissed her temple, she took a deep breath and turned toward him. When he slid his fingers under her chin and gently coaxed her into the perfect position for a long, sweet kiss, she—

"That's it! No ifs, ands, or buts." Petie seized the living room like Sherman bearing down on Atlanta, her jaw clenched, her eyes bugged, and her hair woolly as wildfire through a hayfield. "It's official. Parker Sipes is either dead or he will soon wish he were."

Twelve

"C alm down, Petie." Sam bolted up from the sofa, trying not to look too much like a teenager just caught stealing a kiss.

"Calm down?" She plunked her hands on her hips. Her feet, in stretched out, wool hunting socks, remained planted firmly on the threshold between the living room and kitchen. "Ohhh, I hate that."

"Sam didn't mean anything by it." Collier breezed past her older sister like she hadn't a care in the world, but the dark look she shot Nic and Sam said otherwise.

"Why do men insist on telling any woman who is simply expressing an honest emotion to calm down? Why is that, huh?" Petie strode into the room, dominating the once serene setting with her bright blue bathrobe, her quiet but commanding tone, and her blazing brown eyes.

The sofa springs drowned out Nic's exasperated groan with an eerie, low creak as she edged forward but stopped short of standing at Sam's side. "Petie, no one said—"

"He did." She pointed dead center of Sam's chest. "Calm down. That's what all men say when they want to make a woman feel like she's suddenly gone careening out of control. And all because she doesn't feel the need to suppress and deny what's going awry in her life in order to appease the empathy-impaired men around her."

"Fair enough." He held both hands up, knowing when he had met his match. "I take back my 'calm down' and substitute a nice, friendly, gender neutral 'sit down' instead."

Petie glowered at him.

He motioned to the sofa.

She dropped into the overstuffed chair on the other side of the coffee table.

Sam sat down, mindful of not landing in Nic's lap, or even close enough to her to imply some kind of intimacy between them. "I don't suppose you'd like to talk about this to a potentially empathy-impaired male but otherwise good-hearted minister and old family pal?"

"What's to talk about?" Petie wrapped her chenille robe around her like armor.

"All right then." Sam slapped his hands on his thighs and made a move to get up again. Excuses about the long day past and the even longer one ahead of him began to form in the back of his brain. Even though, in truth, he would rather do anything than go to bed and lie there thinking about services tomorrow and what they would bring, he figured Petie's reticence to talk was his clue to leave the sisters alone. "I guess I'll just scoot on to—"

"My husband of twenty-two years has left me."

Nic gripped his arm, as if desperate to keep him in his place.

She shouldn't have wasted her strength. After a remark like that, he wasn't going anywhere.

"Petie, what exactly are you talking about?" Nic asked.

"Park." She crushed the belt of her robe into a ball in both hands. "He's left me."

"Now you don't know that for sure." Collier perched on the arm of her oldest sister's chair.

"I know," Petie whispered. "Either he has left me or something horrific has happened to him. Those are the only possible explanations."

"For what? Details, girl, give us some useful details." Nic managed to sound compassionate yet annoyed at the same time.

That alone gave Sam more information than anything the other Dorsey siblings had offered since flouncing into the room a minute ago. Obviously she had some concern for her sister's experiences, but underneath it all suspected yet another play for attention on Petie's part.

"You have to understand I'd never have done this kind of thing under normal circumstances."

Sam turned to Nic. "I shudder to think what qualifies as 'normal circumstances' in this family."

"But Park and I, well, the lines of communication have constricted somewhat this last year, what with both kids gone off to college."

"You know that's not all that unusual, Petie." If he had been sitting closer, he'd have given her a reassuring pat. "You've heard about the empty-nest syndrome."

"Empty nest? Of course." Nic sighed.

Though he faced away from her, Sam could feel her relief in the way the couch sagged as the tension left her body.

"Your little chicks have flown the coop, Petie. That's why you've been all on edge and unfocused these past few months."

"Me? When did this get to be about *me?*"

"When is it ever *not* about you?" Collier let out a burst of laughter, then got that deer-in-the-headlights look on her face as if she probably just realized what she'd said, who she'd said it about, and that she'd said it aloud. "I, uh, I didn't mean that as an insult, of course."

"No, of course not, why would I take it as one?" Petie went so stiff it looked like even the hint of a smile would crack her face, like one of those masks that women wore for their complexions. "You are only taking a very painful situation in my life and using it as a springboard to loose your pent-up vindictiveness against me."

"I never—"

"A springboard to loose pent-up vindictiveness?" Nic was off the couch and striding across the floor. When she pivoted she stood behind her sister's chair, but she railed on like an impassioned attorney making a closing argument. "That's exactly the kind of thing that made Collier say that about you. It's this weird need you have to blow things that so much as touch your life way out of proportion. And *you* don't even need a springboard to send you flying off on some tear about you, you, you!"

"Me? Me? *Me?*"

"Petie, listen to yourself."

"Heaven knows we've had to listen to you long enough," Collier muttered.

Petie wedged her elbow between her youngest sister's backside and the arm of the chair, then used the leverage to unseat her so quickly Sam did not have time to call out a warning.

Collier spilled with a thump to the floor.

Nic ignored her completely. "Why can't you just admit you might be making a bigger deal of this than it warrants? Why can't you, for one minute, stop playing the victim of everybody and their dog and consider that maybe your perspective is colored by the fact that your life has changed and you don't know how to cope with it yet?"

"Why don't you come over and sit on the arm of my chair and say that?" Petie patted the spot from which she had just unceremoniously dumped their baby sister.

"Oh, if I come over there, it won't be to sit on your chair, missy." Nic folded her arms.

Collier tilted her chin up from her spot on the floor. "Do it, Nic."

"Like she'd ever have the nerve." Petie smoothed her hand down the lapel of her robe.

"Oh, do not tempt me, Petie, not after the past few days I've just gone through."

"Hold it right there, ladies." Sam held both hands up, boxing referee style. "Let's keep this focused on the real issue here."

"Butt out!" The three sisters spoke in unison but with varying degrees of vehemence.

"This is between sisters, Sam." Nic raised her eyebrows at him.

If it was intended as a threat or merely a way of emphasizing her point, Sam could have cared less. It was at the very core of his being, a part of his very calling in life to help people sort through their problems and find peace. He had not had success accomplishing that in his new church. If he also failed at it in his home, how could he live with himself?

"You're letting your relationship as sisters and a whole lot of stored-up anger and frustration over nit-picking nothings intrude on the real issue. Can't you set your annoyance with Petie's dramatics aside long enough to see your sister seems genuinely hurt and worried over whatever has happened regarding Park?"

Nic bristled at him in sulking silence.

Collier hung her head.

Petie tugged her robe lapels closed just under her chin and gave him a nod of approval befitting a queen. "Thank you, Sam."

"Now come over here and sit back down on the couch—Collier, you can have my place." He stood to make room for the girls who grudgingly made their way to the old sofa. "Now are you ready to hear what Petie has to say?"

Collier smiled up at him. "Yes."

Nic heaved a sigh.

"Petie?" Sam folded his hands, hoping he looked authoritative enough to keep the others quiet while seeming sympathetic and supportive enough to allow Petie to open up. "Why do you think Park has left you or met with some horrible accident?"

"Because I…" She bowed her head.

Sam believed that if she had had a hankie, she'd have dabbed her eye with it, just like some actress in an old-time, black-and-white movie.

Nic tapped her foot in rapid tempo against the leg of the coffee table.

"Go on, Petie," he urged. "You can tell us. No matter how hard it is to talk about, we're listening."

"Like I said I'd never do this normally. I trust Park…or I did." She sniffled. "Maybe I was wrong to do that. I have to ask myself if I'd been more vigilant, would things be different today?"

"If you don't move this along, you'll have to ask yourself if things would be different tomorrow because it'll be past midnight." Nic's machine gun-paced foot tapping did not let up.

In counterbalance, Sam walked slowly across to Petie's chair. The floorboards squeaked under the faded nap of the floral carpet. Above the cold, empty fireplace, the mantel clock ticked out the passing of each second like raindrops dripping into a metal bucket. The lights of the Christmas tree blinked and twinkled and, with the glow of the overhead light from the kitchen, illuminated the faces of the three lovely Dorsey sisters.

Seeing them now, like this, they hardly seemed a day older than when he had known them so many years, so many mistakes, and so many changes ago. Sam's heart filled with joy at being here to help these people in their time of need who had been so much a part of his life.

With his eyes locked on hers, he knelt by Petie and took her hand. "It doesn't do any good to dwell on 'if only,' Petie. The thing to do is to take hold of the situation as it is and deal with it, head-on, no delaying, no fear. The Lord is with you in this, you know, and so are we."

She nodded and gave his hand a squeeze.

"Why do you think Park has left you, or that something awful must have happened to him?"

"Because—" She choked up just enough to garble the end of the word.

Nic made a sound that Sam had no trouble interpreting as a wish to finish the job of choking her sister into complete speech-lessness. But she did stop thrumming her foot on the table leg, and for that he was truly grateful.

"Petie?" He infused his hushed tone with all the ministerial solace he could muster.

She sighed.

The girls on the couch leaned forward.

Petie wet her lips, raised her chin, and with a look he'd only seen on paintings of martyred saints, blurted out, "Because he hasn't picked up his e-mail."

"His…his what?" Sam tightened his grip on her hand.

"*That's* the big crisis du jour?" Never known for her aim, Nic sent a small sofa cushion sailing and missed Petie by a mile. It skimmed the backside of Sam's head.

He glared at her and not all of his agitation had dissipated when he turned to Petie again. "And how does not picking up his e-mail translate into death or impending divorce?"

"Because people always pick up their e-mail. I check mine twice a day, and I don't use it for business or anything."

"So, you sent him an e-mail and—"

"No, no. That's why I said I wouldn't normally do this. I…well, we have different screen names with the same on-line service. So I signed on under his and found he hasn't picked up his e-mail in two days!"

"That hardly screams accident or abandonment in my book," Nic grumbled.

"You don't understand. After our chat up on the roof, I got to feeling all cozy and nostalgic and had this compulsion to try to reach Park again. So I called his work."

"Which you'd done before."

"Only to be told he was out and they didn't know where to or when he'd get back. Today was different."

"Oh?" Sam adjusted his weight to keep his knees, still in full crouch, from starting to ache.

"Today the receptionist transferred me to his boss, who seemed quite surprised that I didn't know that Parker had requested some time off in addition to time he was supposed to have off to come down here for the holidays." She swept her fingers over the motionless waves of her hair, then fixed her eye on Sam and dropped the last detail like a bomb. "Beginning two days ago."

"Okay, that's a little odd, I'll grant it, but if he was able to call in for time off, at least you can be thankful the tuna didn't do him in."

"If that's your best brand of counsel, Reverend, I suggest you shop around for something new and improved."

Nic's dark eyes sparked with amusement at his fumbled attempt to console her sister. "But Sam does make a point. He's obviously fine and just wanted some R & R."

Collier perked up. "Christmas is almost here. He's probably taken some time off to get some Christmas shopping done."

"Parker Sipes?" Petie snorted. "There hasn't been a gift box come into or gone out of our house since the day we were married that he even knew the contents of, not for y'all, not for his family, not even for the kids."

"Are you really sure you mind all that much if he has left you?" Collier laughed just enough so that everyone knew she was trying to make light of things to pacify, not bedevil, her sister. "The way you talk anymore it doesn't seem like it'd be much of a difference."

Petie sighed and cast her gaze downward.

"Oh, get real now, Petie. You cannot go reading something untoward into every unexplained action." Nic pushed her unruly hair back behind both ears. "We all know Park. He's just not the type to sneak off and leave you."

"You think you know Park. I thought I knew him but…"

"A man who gives his wife the password to his e-mail account is hardly the type who has anything to hide." Sam patted her arm.

"He didn't give me his password," Petie whispered.

"What?" Sam cocked his head. "I didn't quite get that."

"I said he didn't give me his password, okay?" She pushed up from the chair and started toward the kitchen. Halfway there she stopped and spoke without looking back. "I broke into his account."

"You read his personal e-mail?" Nic half shouted the exact thought that had gone tearing through Sam's mind.

"No, I didn't read his e-mail. I just checked when he last signed on and glanced over the list of saved mail. All of it was filled with addresses from work on subjects like 'database backup memo,' that kind of thing. Oh, and scads from his administrative assistant titled 'Meeting Reminder.' Even if I intended to snoop, there was nothing there that seemed even remotely intriguing."

Sam tried not to believe she sounded a tad disappointed at that.

"Oh, and I poked around to see what kind of places he had bookmarked on the Internet. No surprises there: sports sights, travel info, boring stuff."

"My sister, the spy," Nic muttered.

"Actually I showed her how to do it. It wasn't hard, really, since they share an account with two different addresses. We just had to keep trying until we figured out his password." Collier had the good taste not to sound boastful.

"That hardly qualifies as a challenge." Nic laughed. "Let me guess—his number from his glory days in football?"

"The year he captained the team when they almost took all-state?" Sam ventured, feeling only a tiny bit guilty at playing along.

"Yes and yes, with his college fraternity nickname in between." Petie held up both hands. "I don't know whether I feel worse that I did this, or that in doing it I confirmed my greatest fears."

Nic was off the couch and beside her sister in a flash. She put her arm around Petie's slumped shoulders. "It doesn't confirm anything. Not a thing."

"Oh yes, it does." She turned enough to face her sister in profile. "It confirms to me what I've suspected for far too long now. After all these years, I can no longer deny where my husband's priorities lie—with himself and himself alone."

In a heartbeat, Collier joined the others. They stood silhouetted against the yellow light from the kitchen, framed in the large, arching doorway.

Sam wished he knew what to say or do to help. Or maybe he just wished he knew a way to become a part of it all. He had never known this kind of family kinship and caring. He didn't pretend to understand the kind of love that moved from quarrels to conversation to commiseration as fast as the need arose. But he wanted to know it. All his life he had wanted that kind of bond with someone, to build that kind of family for himself. He had come the closest with Nic and her family but had messed that up horribly.

Now more than ever the blind selfishness and fear that had guided his choices that long-ago New Year's haunted him. If not for that, he might be a part of this family now. And he might be of more help. "Petie, if there is anything I can do—"

A sniffle answered him. The girls moved apart.

"No." Her voice was thick and hoarse. "No, but thank you, Sam. Just talking has made me feel better, and let's face it…none of this really means anything."

"It could all be very innocent," Sam assured her.

"I sure do hope so." She smiled at him.

"Everything is going to look a whole lot better in the light of day." It was a lame promise at best, Sam knew. Yet, looking at these sisters, he couldn't help but believe it. They had each other; they had family and home, faith and hope. No matter what came their way they could handle it, couldn't they?

Thirteen

his just looks awful!" Nic kept her voice low and her head down as she practically went slinking along behind Aunt Bert into the third pew from the front. She hated to leave the first two pews empty but told herself that maybe having her whole family front and center would throw Sam off. Besides, only the goody-goodies and women with new hats they wanted to make sure everybody saw sat in the front pew.

"Where is everybody?" Petie slid in behind Nic.

Collier, then Nan, Willa, and Fran rounded out the row. Willa had insisted on sitting with her doting great-aunts. Nic knew that move had as much to do with the fact that they would feed her pink peppermints from their huge pocketbooks all service long as it did that Nic would expect Willa to sit still and behave. She leaned out to send a warning glance at her already fidgeting child. Willa grinned back at her, her cheeks puffed out like a squirrel storing nuts for winter and a stomach-medicine pink on her teeth. Nic smiled at the sweet child then sighed and made a quick survey of the rest of what could hardly be called a crowd.

Across the aisle a family from the cottages sat. Nic did not know their names. She would not have known they lived in the old cottages if Aunt Bert had not specifically told them when they walked in to "sit on the side opposite that family from the cottages." She had not said it with any prejudice against the people dressed in not quite their Sunday best clothes that Nic could discern. They seemed nice, to look at them. The woman pressed a bundled baby to her shoulder while the man flipped through the hymnal, jiggling one leg up and down.

A row behind them sat the Stern family. An aptly named household of serious-faced people who had spent many years as missionaries before settling in Persuasion where Mr. and Mrs. Stern pretty much ran the high school by teaching and taking on every extracurricular activity they could manage. Despite their sometimes off-putting expressions, they were some of the nicest, most generous, most faithful Christians Nic had ever known. It did her heart good to know they supported Sam and his effort to rebuild the church that had once been the center of the community.

Behind Nic and her family, Mrs. King and her daughter scooted to the center of their pew. The pair who ran the town's lone beauty parlor sat down demurely, their posture perfect and their hairdos right out of the latest issue of *Modern Hair and Beauty*—the only reading material besides the Bible and current religious tracts they kept in their small salon.

Two generations of the Freeman family took up both back rows. A couple of older folks that Nic did not know rounded out the sparse congregation.

"Surely there are more people than this attending church?" Petie nodded to the people across the aisle.

"Maybe they are late getting out of Sunday school." Collier craned her neck looking around.

"Not this late." Nic flicked her younger sister's arm to remind her not to gawk.

"They haven't had regular services here in a long, long time. Could be they found church homes in Cordy or Fayton or Gilbertville." Petie settled in as if she'd hit the reason on the head and any further speculation was unwarranted.

"Don't kid yourself. We saw all the cars parked down at Dewi's." Nic glanced over the bulletin. "That lot's fuller this Sunday morning than it was that New Year's they brought in the live dance band."

"The Twelve Tunes," Petie murmured.

"What?"

"The name of that band. It was the Twelve Tunes. I remember because Park and I walked over there that evening after Scott and Jessica drifted off to sleep."

"Were they good? The band, not Scott and Jessica," Collier asked.

"Let's just say their name overexaggerated their repertoire. But Park and I sure had a wonderful time."

"See, you do feel better toward him this morning, don't you?" Collier wriggled in her seat, all smug and satisfied.

"What was I thinking? There has to be a logical explanation for his behavior. Park isn't the kind to do anything crazy or rash. We're talking about a man whose idea of going hog-wild is wearing jockey shorts with a pattern on them when it's not even Saturday night!"

Nic and Collier giggled at the apt description.

"Shh. You girls behave yourself during church. You are not too big to get a pew pinch."

A pew pinch was the Dorsey family's favorite form of church discipline. The adults, who always placed themselves on either side of a child, scooted in closer, then closer until said child could scarcely move a muscle. Nic looked at Aunt Bert with her ample attitude on one side and Petie with her pent-up emotions over Nic's bad behavior last night on the other and decided not to risk it. "As soon as the service starts, I'll behave and so will everyone else. We want to set a good example, and I can't wait to see Sam in action."

"In action?" Petie clucked her tongue. "Honey, he's preaching a sermon in the All Souls church, not blowing away bad guys in some blockbuster movie."

The long, low creak of the back door swinging open made every head in the place turn. Aunt Lula waddled in on her grandson's arm with her daughter following dutifully behind.

Nic gave a wave to her cousin, who pretended not to see as that small segment of the family walked right on past to the very first pew.

"What's that about?" Nic whispered to Aunt Bert. "Gone all front pew on us, have they? And Aunt Lula not even with a new hat to show off for it."

"It's your cousin's doing. She drives over from Cordy to take Lula to services once a month. I reckon she marches them right to the front of the church so everybody sees she's done her duty."

"Now who needs a pew pinch?"

Bert snorted. "I love my sister and my sister's children, but sometimes…"

"I hear you on that," Nic muttered.

"You tell it, Aunt Bert," Petie added.

"Uh-huh," Collier lent her agreement.

"You know she'll convince Lula to go off to her place for the holidays rather than bring her brood over to be with the rest of the family." Bert's large, soft body rose then slumped a little as she heaved a hard sigh. "'Course I'm not one to talk, what with my young ones trading off spending either Thanksgiving or Christmas at home every other year."

"They have to take their in-laws into account." Petie reached over Nic to pat Bert's age-spotted hand resting on the skirt of her navy blue polyester dress. "With Park's parents living here until they passed and Collier and Nic not married, we don't have that problem."

Nic stiffened. Though she never came out and said it, it remained pretty clear that Petie enjoyed her personal brand of superiority in lording her married status over her sisters. But with them in church and her marriage potentially crumbling, Nic decided now was not the time to pick a fight about it.

"When's this going to start? We've been sitting here for more than ten minutes." Collier leaned past Petie to ask Nic.

Both sisters gazed at her expectantly.

"How would I know?" Nic adjusted her shoulders and tugged at the neckline of her dark green velvet dress. She'd intended to wear this dress to Christmas Eve services. But this morning as she started getting ready, it just seemed the right thing to do to put on her very best for when she heard Sam preach for the first time.

The altar looked beautiful, decked in fresh greenery and the colors of the season. The old brass candlesticks gleamed as if newly polished. The wood of the organ, benches, altar, and pulpit glowed with a new coat of wax, obviously the result of hours of elbow grease and patience. It both did Nic's heart good to see it like this and weighed down her spirit to think how few others in town were reaping the benefits of Sam's loving work.

She inched closer to Aunt Bert to ask in the woman's ear, "Where is everybody? What's the holdup?"

"I think Big Hyde went down to Dewi's to see if anyone could be persuaded to give the church a chance."

"What's with all those cars there on Sunday morning anyway?"

"Well, you know, used to be we'd have a traveling preacher in once a month and got so a bunch of the menfolks drove their wives and families in, dropped 'em off at the church, then went to Dewi's to drink coffee and chew the fat."

"Okay, I can see that. But there aren't any wives and families dropped off here today. The men just drive into town to meet there out of habit?"

"More out of spite than habit. When Sam showed up, it made a lot of people pretty unhappy."

"Because of his reputation as a kid?"

"Yes, and because of where he came from and how his father acted. Because he reminds some of them, like Lee Radwell, where they came from and that God, not social status or personal gain, is the One who changes hearts and defines our lives."

"I'm surprised it's so many, though."

"Well, I have to say most of them go there because they aren't ready to accept Sam, not because they won't ever accept him. It's a small town with small-town ways. Sometimes a person has to prove his sincerity to win folks over, and that can take time."

"So only a few are the real problem?"

"None of the lot of the troublemakers wanted to serve on the committee to bring a permanent preacher in, of course, but they sure told those of us who did serve what we did wrong when we selected Sam Moss."

"And so?"

"And so, the men still wanted their date at Dewi's, and some of the gals wanted to deliver a message. That's what they called it, 'deliver a message' to us and Sam by starting up their own Sunday morning Bible study."

"And they are holding services in Dewi's?"

"They're holding coffee cups in Dewi's, but they are not holding back and they are not holding their tongues."

"Poor Sam."

"Sam'll be just fine in this, young lady. The real hurt, the one you need to rest your eyes and prayers upon, is the way this hurts the body of Christ."

Nic nodded, her heart heavy. "I see your point."

"It's wrong. It's dead wrong what they are doing."

She had rarely seen her Aunt Bert's eyes pool with tears, but when she had, it had always been over an injustice done to someone she cared about. In this case, Nic understood without asking that the one Aunt Bert felt so deeply for, the one she saw as the real object of pettiness and outright betrayal was Jesus. No wonder she took this ugly business of divisiveness and pride so hard.

Nic slid her arm around her aunt's round shoulders. She had nothing to add beyond Bert's assertion that those meeting at Dewi's were wrong, so she just sat there, hugging her aunt lightly.

The organ music swelled to conclude some old hymn that Nic no longer remembered the name of, and almost instantly the organist, Shirleetha Shively, launched into another song. They could not wait much longer before even this small, faithful group got restless, Nic thought, glancing around another time. Even looking the other direction, she could still hear Willa thumping her shoe against the back of the empty pew in front of them. She started to turn to tell her child to sit still when the crinkle of cellophane made her whip her head around.

"Tell Aunt Fran and Aunt Nan not to give her the whole bag of those mints," she whispered to Petie.

Her sister looked like she didn't know what Nic wanted and, in fact, like she scarcely recognized Nic's face.

From the back of the church the creak of the door swinging open again registered in Nic's mind, but she stuck to her goal of preventing the disaster she saw coming in the mix of kid and candy. "Stop daydreaming about New Year's, Park, and the Twelve Tunes and tell them not to give Willa a whole bag of candy."

"Huh? What are you talking about?"

From the corner of her eye Nic saw Big Hyde enter the church, stand at the back of the center aisle, and shake his head. Bad as she felt about what that meant, she also understood it cut her time short for taking care of the situation at hand.

"Take the candy away from Willa." She nudged Petie with one elbow to urge her to act, then pointed toward her aunts. "Pass it on."

Mrs. Shively sounded the solid notes that concluded all their hymns in a booming amen. Then the place fell silent except for some shuffling at the front of the sanctuary.

Petie turned slowly as if she needed to study the situation with Willa firsthand before allowing herself to get involved.

"Never mind, just let me—" Nic lurched across her sisters.

"Please rise for the singing of hymn 124," Sam's rich voice carried over the hushed scene.

Nic stumbled forward as the row of Dorsey women stood. She managed to get her footing in time to get her fingers on the bag of mints seconds before Willa would have dumped them onto the floor. Remembering the slant in the floor, Nic sighed in relief to have avoided the spill.

She pulled at the thin material of the candy bag hoping to snatch it away. Under the cover of the singing of the hymn and the thundering organ music, she planned to explain to her daughter that she'd return the precious pink treats after the service.

The congregation all drew in a breath at once.

Willa scowled at Nic.

Nic scowled back.

The organ music surged, swelling to fill the place to the very ceiling.

Nic gave the bag a tug.

Voices rose in harmony in an old favorite Christmas song.

Willa set her jaw, blinked behind her thick glasses, and yanked the candy back with both hands.

At least the candy didn't go arching upward, which might have sent it raining down on Nan and Fran, winging the cottage family, and perhaps plopping down as far away as Aunt Lula's lap in the first pew. Instead, the bag ripped and the candy tumbled downward. One landed in the empty hymnal slot. Two or three landed flat on the floor around Willa's feet. The rest bounced and tumbled and hit just right to send them wheeling down the slanted floor like ball bearings down a sliding board.

The hymn ended just as the last two mints struck the edge of the platform directly in front of Sam.

Nic put her hand to her forehead. She had worn her best dress and been considerate in where she had her family sit in order to make this day run as smoothly as possible for Sam. Now this.

Down the row of women, Willa jounced up and down on the balls of her feet, her arms tucked in to her body but her hands flailing. Her lower lip stuck out and trembled. At any moment she would burst into a wailing cry.

Putting her pride aside and ignoring her chagrin over the incident, she scooted past her sisters, intent on taking Willa in her arms and sweeping her off to comfort her in private.

Head down, she could not see what commotion they had caused. She did hear the murmuring, the scuffing of feet from the front of the church, then something so startling that she had to stop before she got to Willa's side and look in the direction from which it came.

Sam was laughing.

Not a mean, sneering laugh that would ridicule Willa for what she had done, but a gentle, rolling chuckle that filled the room with a sweetness to rival the carol they had just finished.

Nic looked at him, then Collier and Petie, then back at him. Finally she looked at Willa, who had calmed down enough to only be shaking her hands and rocking slightly. Fat tears clung to her long, dark lashes but they did not stream down her cheeks. She sucked on her lower lip and sniffled, her gaze never leaving Sam at the front of the now silent church.

He came from behind the pulpit, stepped off the platform to the place littered with mints, and extended his hand toward Willa.

She looked to Nic, her brown eyes questioning.

Nic bent forward and brushed the tears away. "You can go up there to Sam if you want."

"Can I have the candy?" she whispered.

"No, we'll get you more candy after church. But you can go up there and offer to help pick up the candy you spilled."

"Okay." Willa looked to Sam again.

"Come on down here, Willa, honey. There's something I want to say to you and to all our friends gathered here today."

Willa gulped, made her way to the center aisle, then took the short walk up to Sam with a somber reverence that did Nic proud.

When she reached him, Sam sat on the edge of the platform

and held his arms out. "I wanted to tell you not to worry about dropping the candy and sending it rolling toward the pulpit, honey. Believe me, I know *exactly* how that feels."

Everyone laughed lightly and the tension around them broke.

"You do?"

"Yes." He smiled. "Except I had a bag of marbles, not mints, and the floor was just as sloped then as it is now. But the response, that was, um, a wee bit different."

The laughter came out a bit more stiff this time.

Sam didn't seem to notice, he just looked at Nic's daughter, his arms open.

Willa fit neatly into his embrace and laying her head on his shoulder said, just loudly enough for everyone to hear, "I'm sorry about the candy. I'll help you pick it up, and Mommy can get us more candy when you're done churchin' us."

"It's a date," he said against the side of her head. Then he lifted her to sit on his leg and looked out at the small gathering before him.

"I suspect most of you recall the great marble misadventure of my youth. I expect most of the town remembers it."

The older folks nodded and murmured their agreement.

"I think of it every time I take the pulpit in this church where I was once told I was no longer welcome." He seemed to make eye contact and look into the heart of every person there as he spoke. "I thought of it this morning with anxiety and discouragement weighing heavy on me as I prepared for the morning service. I was tired of the fight and ready to give up. I was considering coming here this morning to tell you all I would not stay on after the new year."

"No."

"You can't give up on us."

"Please don't."

Words of support came from the congregation.

"It's true. I was ready to walk away from the church in the lurch because I felt like it could never be anything more than that, a body of believers without solid grounding. Or if it could be more, then I simply was not the man to help guide it to that point."

Nic swallowed and lifted her chin to keep from giving in to the threatening tears Sam's earnest confession inspired.

"That all changed when I saw those little pink candies come rolling down at me." He gave Willa a squeeze and she grinned at him. "When I had the chance that so many of us wish we had in life but so few of us actually realize—the chance to actually do over something that went wrong and set it right again."

"I see where you're going," Big Hyde spoke out, as was his way in church.

Sam nodded and smiled. "I'm not going, Big Hyde. That's the point. I should never have been turned away from God's house. I certainly won't let the same people who did it to me before drive me to it again."

"Good for you." This time Aunt Bert raised her voice, as was *not* her custom—at least not in church during the service.

"Who'd have thought that God could use a little pink mint to remind me that we all belong here, worshiping Him, following His will, and spreading His message of love and redemption?"

Nic took her sister's hand and sighed. Much as his words comforted her, seeing Willa and Sam together before the church did churn up her protective urges. She had to wonder if this would become fodder for speculation over Sunday lunches all over town.

"Who'd have thought God could use a man with a sullied past

such as mine? Or a little girl with big brown eyes who only wanted a piece of candy?"

"That's me." Willa pointed to herself.

"Who'd have thought it? No one. No one but the very people who could believe that He would use a tiny baby born into a family who had nothing more to offer Him than an animals' manger for a bed?"

"That's Jesus," Willa said with quiet authority.

"Yes, that's Jesus." Sam stroked her hair back from her cheek.

She beamed.

Nic held her breath to keep from blubbering like some great gushing bowl of motherly goo.

"The people who believe that God sent His only Son down to earth to teach us, to show us the way, and to bring salvation and forgiveness to anyone who asks—anyone—those are the people we have here today. We all belong here. We are all welcome here, and it is our job as believers in that baby and the Savior He became to make all people welcome here."

A gentle murmur of approval worked over the gathering.

"We have one Sunday after today before Christmas. One Sunday service and the Christmas Eve candlelight service to go before we celebrate God's love incarnate born to save all mankind. It's not a lot of time but it should be enough. Let's all of us reach out in the time we have left and see what kind of difference we can make."

"How do we do that?"

"Glad you asked. Because I have a plan!"

Fourteen

"Do you think lots of people will come?" Willa looked up from where she sat in front of the family Christmas tree.

"I hope so." Sam shuffled through the selection of Christmas CDs Collier had brought with her. Traditional and religious samplings would suit the mood he wanted to create for the community festivity. His congregation had responded wholeheartedly to his idea, and all afternoon the phone had rung with people saying they thought they had convinced friends and neighbors to attend.

The sisters had not had as much luck canvassing their little corner of town. Though the people living in the cottages all were receptive when Sam stopped in with a personal invite and outreach to people often forgotten in Persuasion, no new families committed to come.

"Do you have enough decorations?" Willa stood with worry etched on her face as she peered into the small box of decorations marked for them to take to the trimming party tonight. "This doesn't look like a whole lot."

"That's the point of us having a tree for the whole town. Everyone is supposed to bring a decoration of their own."

She turned her anxious gaze to him and pushed her small blue glasses up on her adorable nub of a nose. "It's a big tree."

"Yes, it is. But if everyone pitches in, if all the people pick out an ornament they like from home and bring it to the church, we'll fill up the branches real fast."

"They bring their own ornaments? Like from their own tree?" She shook her head.

"Uh-huh. That's what makes it so special. When everyone gives a little of themselves, we can build something bigger and better than it would be if we all kept our blessings to ourselves." He searched her face. "Do you...do you understand that?"

"Is it like when Aunt Collier is cooking and Aunt Petie and my mommy come in and add things and change stuff so it tastes better than if Aunt Collier did it all by herself?"

"That's it." Poor Collier, even the little one didn't let her questionable cooking skills slide. Still he'd noticed no one offered to take the job from her, only to try to improve her work with the little help they chose to offer. Suddenly, Sam felt a great empathy for the youngest Dorsey sister. "You know, though, maybe we had better take a few extra ornaments, just in case someone shows up without any. What do you think about that? About giving a little more than what's expected to help make this the best tree ever?"

"That's a good idea." From the corner of his eyes he saw Nic come into the room.

"It applies to more than just decking the halls, you know. He set the CDs aside and looked at Nic. "When everyone brings their own unique gifts and gives more than they have to, that's when amazing things start to happen."

She fixed her attention on her daughter. "That's nice in theory but it doesn't always work that way. And some things are just too precious to take any chances with."

"Like my snowbird?" Willa cocked her head.

"What, honey?"

"Is my snowbird too precious to take to the big tree?" She reached out and held her small hand under the bird, which swung slowly from its golden cord on a low branch.

"Yes, like your snowbird. Some things you just don't take risks with; you watch over them and take extra precautions to make sure they are with you for a long, long time."

"And yet as humans we are pretty powerless to ensure the things we hold dear will never be hurt, misused, or even lost along the way." He met Nic's eyes.

"We do what we can to keep that from happening. Anything less would be unthinkable."

"If we wrap them in God's love and trust Him to help, if we create a safety net of people willing to give their all and then some in order to help—"

"Are you still talking about Christmas ornaments?" Willa's nose wrinkled.

Sam smiled.

Nic tugged at her sweater. "Willa, honey, why don't you run upstairs to see if Aunt Petie and Aunt Collier will be ready to go over to the church soon."

"Okay, Mommy. Then can I pick out some extra ornaments to take with us for people who don't have any?"

"Sure, but for now get scooting and don't come back down before your aunts are ready to leave, okay?"

Willa hopped up and ran for the back stairway.

"Why'd you do that? Why send her off like that?"

"Because I've always taught her to be respectful of her elders."

"She was a perfect little lady with me."

"Not her. Me. Children learn by example and I don't want to set a bad one for my child."

"Uh-oh. What have I done now?"

"Don't bother trying to pretend you don't know. *If we wrap them in God's love and trust Him to help, if we create a safety net of people willing to give their all and then some?*" She gripped the back of a chair with both hands.

"It's true, isn't it?"

"Don't think I don't know what you're driving at when you say stuff like that. You were so transparent even Willa saw through you."

"Remind me to wear thicker clothing." He put his hand over his stomach.

"I know what you're trying to do, Sam. You and my sisters and my aunts, the lot of you."

"Hey, don't lump me in with that group!" He laughed and raised his hands in mock surrender. "Suppose you just tell me straight out what you're all geared up about?"

She glared at him.

"What?"

She clenched her jaw.

"I didn't say 'calm down.'"

"Sometimes it's what you don't say that says it all."

Sam strained to make that compute.

"You think I don't feel the pressure around this house? Spoken and unspoken?"

"Pressure? About what?"

"Like you don't know."

He shook his head.

"About Willa."

"Nic, I am the one person in this house who does *not* know anything about Willa except that she is a treasure from heaven. As for pressuring you about her? I have no idea what you mean."

Nic hung her head. "I guess it's on my mind so much that I see it everywhere."

"What, Nic? You can tell me. I'll listen. I want to listen. No pressure, I promise."

She chewed her lower lip, shut her eyes, then opened them again. "It's all tied in to selling the house and what I want to do for Willa."

"Okay."

"I'm not happy with her present school. She's not happy there. And more to the point, she's not progressing there."

"I see." He moved around and sat on the edge of the sofa, motioning for her to sit in the chair across the coffee table from him.

"I want to give her every opportunity possible." She looked at the empty seat.

"Of course."

"And I can't afford to lose valuable time again if she's in the wrong place and not getting every bit of help she deserves."

"What do you mean, not lose valuable time *again?*"

Nic tensed.

Sam sighed. "I have no right to ask you to trust me. No reason to think you should. But clearly there is a lot going on concerning Willa and what your family expects you to do. Don't you think talking about it with an impartial third party would do you good?"

She gripped the back of the chair until her knuckles lost all color.

Again, he motioned for her to sit across from him.

Finally her shoulders fell forward slightly. She looked down, rubbed her nose, then moved around practically to crumple into the seat. "I wish you had been around when Willa was born."

He nodded, wishing he had some insightful remark to make to that.

"I mean, I wish I'd had an advisor. Like you said, an impartial ear to hear my side and weigh the information that was being metered out over the next few years by people who did not have my, or her, best interests at heart."

He leaned forward, folding his hands together. He wanted to tell her he wished the same thing but feared it might stop the flow of her outpouring.

"When she was born I can't tell you how much I needed that." She looked away and said nothing for a few seconds.

"What about your family?"

"Can you just picture how impartial they were? Under those circumstances?"

"No." He took a deep breath to steady himself and stepped out in faith that she wouldn't close up or run away when he reminded her, "Because I don't even know what the circumstances were."

"That's right," she murmured. "You don't."

He waited for her to say more. He had promised no pressure, after all.

Finally she sat back and sighed. "Let's just say I needed someone who could look at the big picture without making a big deal of everything. I needed someone to be on my side."

No pressure. Still, he had one question he could not keep from asking. "What about Willa's father? Wasn't he on your side?"

"Nobody but God seemed to be on my side back then." She didn't look at him as she spoke. "Later I could see that my family really was, but so much had happened by then that it shook my faith in people, even people I should have never doubted."

Again she had avoided the subject of Willa's father. It did not sit well with Sam. It raised questions and left in him a sense of vague frustration and dissatisfaction. He regretted the promise of no pressure more than ever. And more than ever he knew if he broke his word to her now, he might never get her to lower her defenses to him again. "Nic, I'm having a hard time following this. What does all this have to do with selling the house and what I said about everyone working together to build something better?"

"Because that's what my aunts and sisters think I should do for Willa. That's their oversimplified view of what's best for her and, I suppose, for me, too. They think I should rely on the support of my family more to care for her."

"That doesn't sound all that far-fetched or unreasonable of a plan to me."

"But it's not the plan I laid out for her. I've put a lot of thought into what's best for my child, Sam."

"Of course you have."

"I did not come to any of my decisions lightly."

"I can't imagine anyone thinks that."

"I've found a school that says it can offer the best education and opportunity for a child with her disabilities. And they even have a scholarship program that they will offer her to discount her tuition."

"Sounds promising."

"But even with the scholarships, it's expensive."

"That's why you want to sell the house so desperately."

"I have to get her out of the school she's in now. The system is overburdened, and the teachers—God bless them—they do their best, but they can't do what the residential program says it can do." She pushed her hair. She rubbed her palms together. She looked toward the low branches of the Christmas tree. "This new place just might be the thing to give her the grounding she needs to make a future for herself."

Sam followed her line of vision to the small, carved snowbird. "Is this school the only way for her to get that grounding?"

"Don't you start with me." She pushed up from her chair.

"I'm only asking. Not judging, Nic."

She went over to the box of ornaments they'd already selected for the community trimming and started picking through them.

"So why is your family against the new school? Is it the money?"

"No. They'd do whatever they had to do to help with that, I'm sure."

"I guess agreeing to sell the house they grew up in and kept in the family for so long proves that."

"Yeah." She looked around the room like she was already saying good-bye bit by bit to her cherished surroundings. Sadness gave her beautiful face a heart-touching quality that only deepened as she touched a glittery red bow on a white package and whispered, "They don't want me to send her away. That's what makes it hardest for them."

"Send her away? To live at the school?"

Nic nodded. The movement sent a single tear streaming down her cheek. "It's the best of all the programs I could find for her."

I could find for her. She hit the pronoun so hard it was like striking a discordant note in a long familiar tune. What *she* could find for her daughter. *Her* experience of distrust for others regarding Willa's birth. The very words that touched this discussion off about people working together to make things better. It all began to fit and make sense to Sam. She still did not dare trust others when it came to Willa. But she wanted to, he could hear it in her voice and see it in the way she wavered in the discussion. She wanted to trust others to help but she just wasn't ready.

Until she was ready, Sam realized, her reluctance would make it virtually impossible for him to do much more than listen, wait, and pray.

"Aunt Petie and Aunt Collier say there is a whole box of ornaments in the back bedroom that would be fine for the outdoor tree." Willa dashed in the room as though her heels had caught fire. "They told me to hurry and get it if I want to ride with them over to pick up Aunt Bert."

"Pick up Aunt Bert?" Nic took a few steps after her child. "Why can't Aunt Bert drive herself? She does pretty well getting around town when we're not here—and when we are here, too."

"I dunno." Willa stopped long enough to shrug. "They said Aunt Lula would be coming with Miss Snooty-Britches and Aunt Bert would feel left out coming alone."

"They did?" Nic didn't like her sisters roping Willa into their ill-fated matchmaking and intended to let them know as much as soon as she got the chance. "Well, you can just tell them for me—"

"Mommy, is that some kind of famous person in our family?" Willa tipped her head and pushed her glasses up. "That Miss Snooty-Britches?"

"Famous? I don't understand."

"You know, like when you were Miss Bode County Butterfly in high school?"

Sam laughed.

Nic scalded him with a look. Well, it did not scald him as much as lit a fire under him.

"You sure you got that right, sweetheart? Butterfly?" Sam asked Willa.

"Butter Queen," Nic corrected, clenching her teeth all the while.

"Is that what you were? Butter Queen? And here I thought you were, yourself, one of the finest Miss Snooty-Britches this town has ever seen."

"Did you get a crown, Mommy? Can I see it?"

"No, I did not get a crown. And it's a good thing, too, because if I had one, I might be tempted to use it to crown a certain some-one who thinks—heaven help him—he's way more clever than he really is."

"Once a snooty-britches, always a snooty-britches," he teased.

She ignored him with a flick of her hair and an upward tilt of her nose, which even she had to concede only played into his jest. "They were making a funny name up for our cousin, Willa, who is acting all high and mighty, that's all."

"Oh. Okay. I'll go get the ornaments now. Aunt Petie said they'd be waiting outside warming the car up."

The back door slammed shut as if to verify the plan.

"Fine. Get the ornaments and give me a second to get a jacket so I can go with y'all."

"Aunt Petie says to tell you there's just room for her and Aunt Collier and Aunt Bert and the ornaments and me." Willa spun around and took off for the back bedroom to fulfill her mission.

"Oh, we'll see about that." She started toward the kitchen, but Sam's hand on her arm stopped her in her tracks.

"I was only kidding, you know."

"I know, Sam."

"I never saw you as stuck-up or snobbish when we were growing up. Never."

The low light made his hair shine golden and bathed his handsome features in a comforting glow.

She pressed her lips together. "I know. It was just a joke. No hard feelings."

"Good. Then why don't you go over to the church with me instead of your sisters?"

"Sam, don't you see? It's just a harebrained matchmaking scheme that I don't want to give in to."

"Then don't."

"I don't intend to."

"Come with me because you want to, not because they tried to trick you into it."

"Because I want...to?" Her thoughts swirled, giving her a lightheadedness that made it impossible to maintain her disgust with her sisters' plans.

"Because *I* want you to." He moved closer to her. "Nic, this is a big deal for me. I'd like to go into it knowing I had a friend beside me. You of all people know how important that can be."

She did. Not too many minutes ago she had actually wished Sam would have been there for her in her hour of dire need. Though this was not so desperate a time for him, it was, nonetheless, the kind of time when having someone on your side could make all the difference in the world.

Willa whizzed by with a box that Nic recognized held some cheap plastic ornaments they'd gotten on sale and never used. "If you are going to come with us, Mommy, you better hurry and get your coat."

"That's okay, Willa. You go on and tell your aunts I'll be going with Sam." She met his gaze and sighed. "Tell them I *want* to go with Sam."

Fifteen

Christmas was in the air. Excitement fluttered in Nic's stomach just to think of it. Not the wintry gold and glitter and the crush of holiday shoppers kind of Christmas she'd have had in Chicago. The slow-paced, serve iced-tea alongside the traditional hot chocolate while country singers crooned carols from a portable unit perched on the hood of a pickup truck kind of Christmas. The *real* Christmas, at least for her. Simple, Southern, and focused on the right things—home, family, community, and not as an afterthought, Jesus.

Nic stuck her hands in her pockets and tipped her head back to look at the top of the extravagant tree Willa and Sam had chosen. They'd set it up outdoors in the untended triangle of a flowerbed where the sidewalks merged to lead to the front steps of the church. Only fitting, it would be there as a symbol of hope and welcome, a gift from the church to all of Persuasion.

It was a good tree, she decided now that she could really get a look at it. Full and fragrant, it had lots of room for hanging rope and tinsel and handmade ornaments. Room still, even after they had gathered around to sing a few hymns and carols and every one in attendance had placed their contribution of ornaments on the waiting branches.

Nic glanced over the people still mulling about the refreshment table. If she were in a count-your-blessings frame of mind, she'd have made note that the event had drawn more than twice the number in the morning service, including more than a couple of the regulars from the Sunday fellowship of Dewi's Market. If she were in a miserly mood, however, she could allow that the Dewi's regulars might have come more to scope out the situation than to participate. She might also concede that more than a few among them had simply seen the lights and music and wandered over for the free cookies and drinks. Optimist or pessimist, she had to conclude that this had not been the booming success she had yearned to see for Sam—for the church, she quickly corrected herself. This was, after all, about mending the rift between church and community, not about scoring points for Sam.

"You gonna help me dig out some of these old decorations to see if we can find some more for the tree or not, girl?" Aunt Bert stood at the side door of the church and beckoned her.

Nic made a hasty review of the surroundings and found Willa trailing behind Sam as he walked about the crowd greeting everyone individually. Her daughter's face rivaled the holiday lights as she beamed with pride, carrying a plateful of Christmas cookies to offer to everyone she met. And everyone who took one had a kind word for the child, even the ones who gave Sam a somewhat chilly reception.

Willa responded to each person with a smile. Sometimes she even spoke to answer the friendliest of the questions people asked. Nic did not know when she had seen her child so relaxed, happy, and radiant.

"Do you want to be a party to all this or not, Nicolette?" Aunt Bert bellowed in her this-is-the-last-time-I'm-calling-you tone.

"I think I do, Aunt Bert," she murmured, walking backward a few steps, reluctant to let go of the sight of Willa in this shining moment. "I'm not sure yet, but I think I do."

"We didn't give people enough notice." Collier went up on her tiptoes to hang a bent construction paper bell on a bare limb two-thirds of the way up the community tree.

"You can't expect much of a turnout on a few hours' notice." Nic held up a golden Styrofoam ball with glittered toothpicks sticking out of it and frowned.

"Not this close to the holidays." Petie flicked at a dark bulb with her painted nails.

"Don't talk like this was a total disaster, girls." Aunt Bert collected the stray bits and pieces of the makeshift ornaments she and Nic had rounded up in the church basement. "We saw plenty of folks we haven't seen at the services since—"

She did not finish but then she didn't have to. Sam fingered a delicate brass harp with a red velvet bow placed on the tree by the family from the cottages. "For those that did participate I am truly grateful. And yet—"

"Just because they didn't come when you thought they should doesn't mean they won't never come." Willa had to tilt her head way back to look up at him from where she knelt on the sidewalk.

"The faith of a child, huh?" He tried not to inject any discouragement in his voice or in his forced smile but he knew he failed. "I wish I could believe that someday people in this town will come around. But I don't think it's wise to cling to that hope and to keep trying half-baked schemes like this one to try to make it happen. Sometimes it's the right thing to do to cut bait and move on, to put our efforts to more productive uses and stop wasting everyone's time."

"The things we ask God to give us don't always come when we think they should. They come when God says they should." Willa scrambled to her feet and took his hand. "Not in our time, in *God's time.*"

"That's a pretty big nugget of wisdom from such a little girl."

"Mr. Freeman told it to me."

"Ahh."

"For the snowbirds."

"The snowbirds?"

"Last year when the only snowbird died and there weren't no more, I throwed birdseed out. I watched every day under all the bushes and looked up in the sky for a storm to come and bring in more snowbirds for me."

"I see." He closed his hand around hers.

The sisters and Aunt Bert moved in close.

"I waited and waited but I never saw one. I prayed and prayed to God for them to find me, for them to come so I could take care of them. But they didn't."

"I know that feeling," he whispered.

"I felt so bad that Mr. Freeman carved the snowbird for me. He said the snowbirds didn't come because of…Mommy?"

Nic moved in and put her hand on Willa's back as she said to Sam, "Because of the droughts and the weather patterns of the last few years."

Willa nodded her head. "The snowbirds have to go where they can get fed."

"More wisdom I'd do well to take to heart." Sam touched her hair.

"But that doesn't mean the snowbirds won't ever come back, just like the people will come to church again."

"In God's time."

She grinned.

On the heels of her aunts and great-aunt murmuring their approval of the child, Aunt Bert yawned and not too quietly suggested, "God's time notwithstanding, it's bedtime for this old lady. Petie, Collier, you gonna drive me on home?"

They moved off, leaving Sam with Willa and Nic. The crowd had thinned to a precious few. Among the hanger-on-ers, the Dewi's delegation clustered together, except Claire LaRue. She strolled up wearing earrings shaped like wreathes that matched the sparkling image on her blue sweatshirt. "Well, hi, y'all."

"Hello, Claire." Sam extended his hand to her even as he sensed Nic bristling in the woman's general direction.

He understood Nic's reservation. When he learned his old pal from his wayward youth Reggie LaRue had married a girl Collier's age, Sam had figured ol' Reg had had to search out someone too young to know better. After his first few weeks in town he'd changed his opinion, and not for the better. Reggie had simply found someone who held the same worldview, Sam decided, based on town talk and the fact that Claire and Reggie's car was often among the first to arrive at Dewi's on Sundays.

It had surprised him to see Claire here with her children and to see how much she tried to really throw herself into the festivities. As a man who had suffered from unfair judgment, it dogged him now to see he might have indulged in the same thing himself. Still, aware that Claire had just come from chatting with people who made no bones about disliking his presence in their town and in this pulpit, he remained cautious. "So good to see you and your family out to support the church tonight."

"Well, if you can't count on the support of an old friend, who can you count on? Right, Nicolette?"

"Hmm." Nic smiled, sort of.

"Are you a friend of my mommy and Reverend Sam's?" Willa craned her neck, her head sort of weaving and swaying as she watched Claire.

Sam followed the movement and realized she was following the movements of the woman's enormous earrings.

"Truth to tell, they are more like old friends of my husband's, sweetheart. The three of them go way back."

Nic put her hand on Willa's shoulder. Her eyes shot daggers but she kept her lips sealed.

"In fact, their friendship goes back to way before Reggie and I were married. Longer than even…" She tipped her head, her short red hair falling against her neck as she tapped her cheek. "What is that expression, Nic?"

Nic turned as if suddenly fascinated by the tree beside them. "I'm sure I don't know what you—"

"Oh, I remember!" Claire snapped her fingers. She fixed her gaze directly on Sam, like a cat honed in on a helpless mouse. "Since before you were a gleam in your daddy's eye."

Nic pulled Willa close.

Sam shook his head, not quite sure where the woman was going.

"I don't have a daddy." Willa blinked up at Claire.

That catlike grin went softer then. The faint lines around her eyes framed them in warmth and kindness as she put her hand beneath Willa's chin. "Maybe that's not the saying after all, sugar. We'll just leave it that they've been friends of my husband's for a long, long time."

"Then y'all should come to church." Willa did not shake her finger in admonishment but she might as well have.

"Willa, show a little respect, young lady." That it cost Nic to remind her child to pay deference to Claire showed in her tight jaw and rigid back.

Claire laughed. "No, no. She's right. We *should* come to church."

"We'd love to have you there." Sam wasn't lying. He would like to see Claire and her children in his church if they came with open hearts to worship God. The churning in the pit of his stomach testified that he did not think that would happen. "Bring Reggie, too."

"Not a bad idea. That man could use some religion." She laughed.

Sam tried to join in but could not make it sound natural.

Nic didn't even try.

"Speaking of that man, I better get back and take care of him. Hope you don't mind that my boys each picked out a cookie to take to him."

"Not at all. We need to be getting Willa home, as well."

"We? You mean the three of you going to your one home, together?"

"We all live in the same house," Willa piped up.

"So I've heard, darling."

"I rented that space in the Dorsey house months before the family—the whole family—came down for their holiday stay."

"Did I suggest otherwise?" She practically pouted like a hurt child as she spoke.

Nic shifted her feet and huffed.

"No." Sam put on his best preacher-in-the-pulpit face in order not to fuel any talk that he had implied Claire LaRue was a liar or gossip. All the while he searched her eyes for any sign of what she might be up to. "Of course not."

"No, *I* didn't."

The heavy emphasis on the *I* meant something, but for the life of him Sam had no idea what.

She patted his arm. "It was a fine time. A good idea, really."

He held his breath a moment as if he could somehow discern her sincerity through that fleeting gesture. He sensed nothing. What good would it do trying to read her motives anyway? She had come tonight and brought her children. She had said she would come to church, and if she did that, especially if she brought others with her, he would be grateful. "I look forward to seeing you in services, Claire."

"And I'll look forward to seeing you, Reverend." She smiled, then turned to Nic. "You, too, Nicolette."

"Uh-huh." Nic kept her hold on Willa, all but tucking the child under her protective wing when Claire bent down to touch the girl's nose.

"And so good meeting you, too. Aren't you just a precious little baby-doll baby?" She straightened and as she turned to go called out, "Night, y'all."

"Good night." Sam waved though she already had her back to them. She probably could not have made out the gesture in the darkness anyway, which might have been a good thing given the way those closest to him responded.

"Good night and good riddance." Nic crossed her arms.

Willa, standing directly in front of her mother mirrored the pose to a tee.

Sam chuckled. "Oh, come on now. She wasn't that bad."

"Smarmy."

"What?"

"That's what she was." Nic narrowed her eyes. "Smarmy and slick, like she was up to something and thought we were either too stupid or too trusting to catch her at it…or worse."

"There's a worse?"

"Yes. If she came over here to try to sniff out a little trash on you or even just to rub your nose in the trash she thinks she and that Dewi's set already have, knowing that as a minister you'd be virtually helpless to defend yourself to her."

"As a minister the last thing I feel is helpless or defensive." He laughed.

"I don't care." She raised her chin. Her line of vision followed Claire LaRue, who gathered her young boys, said her good-byes to those cleaning up, and strolled to the nearly empty parking lot. "I don't trust her and I don't like the way she handled herself."

"Me neither!" Willa added an emphatic nod. "She called me a baby!"

Sam started to make a case for Claire, but when he tried and it became clear to him he couldn't do it convincingly, he just sighed and shook his head. He had to admit the woman had left him feeling a little unsettled, too, though he couldn't put his finger on just why.

"I'm not a baby, am I, Mommy?"

"Of course not, honey. You are a big girl. Big enough to scoot along over to the refreshment table and collect the cookie plates we brought so Hyde Junior can fold up the table and take it back inside."

"Okay, Mommy. I can do that." She stepped forward, then paused just long enough to say to Sam, "Because I am *not* a baby. I am eight and a quarter years old!"

"Eight." Sam blinked at the child, then turned his gaze to Nic. "Eight?"

"And a quarter years old!" Willa smiled with pride before she hurried off.

"Since before you were a gleam in your daddy's eye." Claire's coy choice of expressions suddenly struck him like a bolt out of the blue. He faced Nic, not sure what to think, what to do, what to say.

"I'd better go help her. You've got enough broken cookies scattered around the churchyard already without her spilling another half a plateful." And fast as a rabbit running from a loud noise, Nic was gone.

He thought about stopping her, about grabbing her by the arm and holding her in place until she explained everything to him. But he did not stop her. He did not demand an explanation. It was too big. Too new. The idea that Willa was his child was something he simply could not take in all at once.

Sixteen

ommy, why did you rush me up to bed so quick? I'm not sleepy." Willa raised both hands to let Nic drop the flannel nightgown down over the child's head. "I don't go to bed so early. I'm not a baby."

"Oh no, you're not a baby. You're eight and a quarter years old." She tugged the gown in place.

"I am. I asked Aunt Collier how long until my next birthday, and she showed me on the calendar. Then she showed me how to group the months."

"She did?"

"Uh-huh. How to group them and count them. There are twelve months in a year."

"*Only* twelve?" Funny. These last few years had seemed about sixteen months long, each filled with about fifty workdays, no weekends, and hour after hour that never seemed to have enough time in them. Still, Nic could not let her weariness overshadow this moment when she could affirm and reinforce what Willa had learned. "Actually, honey, that's very good."

Willa tipped her chin up. Her cheeks rounded high to frame a wide grin. Without her glasses on, her eyes seemed deeper brown, and the Dorsey family resemblance was more pronounced than ever. Sitting here in the halo of the bedside lamp she looked like the image of Collier transported through time. At least to Nic she did.

Other folks, even those who knew nothing about Nic's past or who speculation said Willa's father might be, had told her, "She must take after her daddy." But Nic had never seen it. To be fair, she had never looked.

She never searched her child for similarities to anyone but the Dorsey family. Self-preservation, she believed. Seeking clues or confirmations of Willa's parentage in the girl were pointless. It would prove nothing.

"I didn't know you and Aunt Collier had worked so hard on your months," she said too brightly as she folded back the covers on Willa's bed.

"Uh-huh. She spent the afternoon showing me the calendar. I liked it."

"First time I think I ever heard you say you liked having someone teach you something." She helped the child slide her legs between the crisp sheets.

"It wasn't like teaching, Mommy."

"It wasn't?" Collier did have a way of making everything a game, especially where Willa was concerned.

"No. It wasn't like teaching at all. It was like…" Willa cocked her head and rubbed the bridge of her nose. "It was like *learning.*"

Nic sat back a bit, startled by the child's subtle grasp of the difference in how she, at least, perceived the two. "That's neat, Willa. That really is."

"I wish I could learn like that all the time." She put her chin in her hand.

"Maybe you can."

"Really?"

"Sure. They have all kinds of teaching methods at your new school. Things that I, or even Aunt Collier, couldn't begin to know how to do."

Willa pulled her arms in close to her body.

Nic reached out to quiet the flailing hand motions she knew would follow.

Willa curled her fingers into fists and bowed her head. She sat perfectly still.

"Willa? Willa, honey, are you okay?"

"Shh."

"Shh? Willa did you just shush me?"

"Shh, please, Mommy. I'm praying."

Praying. Nic longed to ask what for? but in her heart she already knew. Willa did not want to go away to school. It broke Nic's heart to see how much her child did not want to go, almost as much as it broke her heart to have to send her. But what could she do? She had to think of her child's future.

She bowed her head and offered her own short, sincere prayer. *Father, help me know what to do for my child.*

Sam had to talk to Nic. He needed answers.

He stood at the door of his office in the church. Monday was usually his day off, but today when his frustration at not getting any time alone with Nic made him snap at Collier for the lumps in the oatmeal, he knew he had to get out of the Dorsey house.

Willa had asked him to take her along. She had wanted to show him the surprise her aunts had helped her make for her mother. The little girl's mother seemed to have enough surprises already to Sam's way of thinking. And he'd done nothing but think on the surprise he'd been handed since Willa announced her age last night.

He'd wanted to talk to Nic about it right away, but she had gone up to tuck Willa in and never came back downstairs. Though what he would have said to her, he was not sure. How would he ask? Would he demand? How could he curb his anger over her keeping this secret from him? Over keeping him from knowing Willa was his child while living under the same roof with the girl and her mother?

Funny how all this time the one thing they had avoided, avoided like the proverbial elephant in the room which everyone was painfully aware of but pretended to ignore, was their shared past. Even when others had alluded to it, when situations had brought it to the forefront, when it seemed the only reasonable thing to discuss, they had suppressed the subject. Last night, that all changed.

A night of prayer, rest, and reflection was what they'd both needed, he'd told himself. But looking back at all the lost opportunities he wondered. Maybe, just maybe, he had not really wanted to know the truth.

Willa, his child? The thought staggered his imagination, humbled his heart, and angered him to the depths of his being. He braced his arm against the door frame and looked through his office and out the window that faced toward the house on Fifth and Persuasion.

"Nic, I know I did you wrong." He spoke with quiet power as if she might hear him all the way over here in the church. "I told you I'd love you forever and convinced you to give yourself to me against your faith and judgment in order to prove your love for me. Then I ran off and betrayed you."

He bowed his head.

The wind kicked up. The window rattled. The old church creaked.

"But what you've done, Nic… How do I come to terms with that?"

"We ain't got much of a congregation here to speak of." Bert's palm landed dead center on his back, the heat of her touch spreading out slowly through his tired muscles. "But don't tell me things gone and got so bad you've taken to preaching to yourself."

He lifted his head, wondering how long she'd been standing there, how much she had heard. Instead of asking, though, he simply faced her and tried to make light of things. "Not preaching, thinking. Thinking aloud. Just trying to sort through a few things, figure them out."

"Me, I've found I get a far better caliber of answer when I stop thinking out loud and start praying out loud or otherwise. Stop looking for answers in my sad old self and take it to the Lord."

"I've done my share of that, believe me. But for this one? I'm afraid I need some answers directly from an earthly source."

"Nicolette?"

Tell me about Willa's father. The request burned on his closed lips but he held it in. This was not fodder for a third party discussion. "I need to have a long talk with your niece, but the right time never seems to present itself. Something always interferes."

"Conveniently."

"What?"

"You left out *conveniently.* Something always *conveniently* interferes."

"Are you implying I'm secretly thankful for the missed opportunities?"

"You are here in your office. Nicolette is at her home. Can't get much talking done that way—unless it's to yourself."

"I tried to get Nic to come over here more than once, but she has resisted the idea." He scratched his scalp, his eyes shut tight. "And the house is always too full of people. That won't improve any with Petie's kids coming in this afternoon."

"Then you improve things yourself."

"What? How?"

"I don't know, Sam, but I have to say if it really mattered to me—if I was a man suddenly thrown back together with the girl of my past and she had a child of a certain age—I'd want answers. And nothing would stand in my way of getting them."

She was right. He had not pressed Nic to talk about the past or her "husband" because the only thing he had thought was at stake was the opening of old wounds. He'd had Willa pegged for younger than her eight—and a quarter—years, so the issue had not had the same urgency it now took on. He had to know. Postponing this discussion any longer was simply unthinkable.

"Aren't Scott and Jessica a little old for their mom to help them get settled in their rooms?" Collier slid the first fresh gingerbread man onto a plate in front of Willa.

Nic took a deep breath of the warm kitchen air. The scent of baking mixed with the lingering dampness carried in when Petie's children had left the door propped open as they hauled in luggage and presents.

"Well, Petie wanted Scott to help clear away the last of the Christmas decorations from the back room so Jessica can have it. And with Sam in the master bedroom this year and us having to get creative with the sleeping accommodations, she wanted to make sure Scott didn't feel slighted for having to bunk down on the couch."

"Yeah, but—"

"Willa, honey." Nic brushed her child's hair back from her face. "You can take your treat in by the tree and look through the new presents your cousins brought in."

"Oh, boy!" She leaped up from her chair.

"And practice trying to read your name on the gifts tags, why don't you?" Collier called out. Spatula waving, she nailed Nic with a dead-on, no-nonsense look. "Everything can be an opportunity for her to learn and practice what she's learning, don't you think?"

"Your cookies are burning."

"Oh!" She spun around and rescued the dark brown cutouts from the hot oven. The cookie sheet clattered on top of the stove as she practically pitched it there, spun around, and demanded, "Okay, cookies cooling, Willa is occupied, spill it."

"Okay, here's the thing…"

"Oh, goodie." Collier claimed the chair Willa had just left. "This must be juicy if you had to send Willa away before you dished it out."

"Dish it out? That's a pretty way to put it." Nic pressed her back to the chair and drew her foot up to rest on the edge of the seat. "I only sent Willa away because I didn't want her blurting something out she neither understood nor got in the proper context. You know how sensitive I am about contributing to the spread of gossip."

"With good reason." Collier said it the way only a sister could, head high and loyalty unwavering. "You went through heck back then."

Nic laughed. "But that's past me now. You know, reviewing it through the kind perspective of a lot of years and seeing how Sam is struggling to overcome the long ingrained attitudes around here, I can't feel nearly as hurt and angry about it all as I once did."

"Nic, really?"

She nodded. "Well, what did I expect back then, Collier? A good girl from a solid, church-attending family has a baby out of wedlock and doesn't put it up for adoption? People were bound to talk."

"I suppose."

"Of course. Especially when so many people knew about Reggie's party, and me and Sam and what happened that night."

"Nic, are you saying you've forgiven the small-minded, mean-spirited gossips in this town for making life so hard on you, on Daddy—on all of us—back then?"

"If I can't forgive them, then I'd be guilty of the same sin—holding mistakes that Jesus has washed away against people just because it makes me feel better, justified. Forgiveness, even when we don't want to forgive, maybe then most of all—that's at the very root of our faith, Collier."

"Yes, but—"

"No. No buts. I realized that last night when I was trying to get God to let me stay mad at Claire LaRue. No matter which way I bargained with Him, He kept coming back with the same answer: Jesus died for all our sins, even the people who make me feel bad about myself."

"Oh, Nic." Collier stood up and gave her a hug.

"God is good, sugar, even when people are rotten." She hugged her sister back. "So you can see why I really don't want Willa, even innocently, popping off and starting a new wave of gossip about any of the Dorsey sisters."

"Ooh, that's right." Collier pulled away and perched on the edge of her seat. "You were going to tell me what's up with Petie."

"Nothing earthshaking. It's just that Petie has to tell the kids *something* about their father."

"She's not going to make up a story, is she?"

Nic exhaled hard and long and fell back against the chair.

"Oh yeah, we're talking about Petie here." Collier chewed at her lower lip. "Well, she won't tell them an out-and-out lie, will she? She'll at least stick to one of her likely conclusions, right?"

"I honestly don't know what she will do. I do know I don't envy her situation."

"Oh yes, because your situation is sooo much better." Her younger sister stood and began to wedge the spatula under one of the cooled, overbaked gingerbread men.

Nic opened her mouth to make some smart reply, then found she had nothing to say. Maybe she could thank the sights and smells of the holidays, or the sweetness of her baby sister in supporting Willa and her. Or maybe it was finally giving voice to the ideas that had run through her head last night.

Forgiveness. She often talked about how she expected to have it demonstrated toward her, but how often had she examined how she directed it to others? The gentle nudge of seeing Claire, of facing her own feelings about the people who had hurt her, joined with her decision to really seek God's input on Willa's school, had left her with a great peace. "My situation? It really isn't all that bad, Collier. Not if you think about it. I have so much, have been blessed by God with a loving family and an opportunity to choose the best path for my child's future."

"That's true."

"It's not that bad. Not bad at all." Nic laughed with a lightness in her spirit she had not known in a very long time. "In fact, I'd go so far as to say that even though I didn't want to come here and have met certain, um, obstacles to my original plans along the way, this has all the earmarks of being one of my best Christmases ever."

"Gosh, I hope you hang on to that good mood." Collier frowned at a cookie with a shriveled black clump where his arm should be. "So we can all draw on it when we need it."

"I plan on it, honey. In fact, I'm not sure anything could dampen this mood now."

"Nic!" The door swung open so hard the knob banged against the wall.

Nic put her hand to her mouth. She couldn't breathe.

Sam stepped over the threshold but did not shut the door. A chill wind whipped at the tablecloth and made the curtains flutter like frightened birds.

Collier rushed to close the door, her eyes never off the man who suddenly seemed to fill the room.

"I have to know, Nic."

"Sam, not here." Nic shot a glance toward the living room. "Not now."

"Yes, *now*. We've let this hang between us long enough and now I have got to know." He pushed back his leather jacket and put his hand on his hips. "Is she?"

"Sam, no—"

"Answer me, Nic. I have a right to know now. Is Willa my daughter or not?"

Seventeen

"Are you out of your mind? Marching in here and barking out something like that?" Nic's chair legs squawked over the linoleum. The whole chair would have toppled over backward when she leaped up if Sam had not lurched forward in time to catch it.

She didn't care. Floor-bound furniture was nothing compared to the crashing blow Sam's thoughtless question might deal Willa if she overheard it. Nic rushed to the doorway to check on her daughter.

Not even noticing her mother, Willa stood over the coffee table carefully arranging the Mary and Joseph figurines in the nativity scene. Leaning back against the door frame, she shut her eyes and exhaled.

"I think I'd better go see if Scott and Jessica are settled in or if Petie needs my help with anything." Collier brushed past Nic and into the living room. "Hey, Willa, honey, how about you come with me to find what your big cousins are up to in the back room?"

"Thank you," Nic whispered, fairly certain her sister was too far away to hear.

"I'm sorry." He sounded more agitated than remorseful. "That was uncalled for, but I had to know—I have to know."

"Not now. Not here. Not with Willa just a few rooms away."

"Then let's go to the church office."

Nic clenched her fists at her side. She battled back the swell of nausea rising from the pit of her stomach. "Not the church. That's hardly the place for what I have to tell you, Sam."

"That's where you're wrong." His whole demeanor had shifted in the blink of an eye. "I can see you're hurting. This is obviously not as simple as I let myself believe it must be."

"No." She wet her lips. "It's not."

"Then let's go to the church because—at least as long as I'm still the minister there—that's exactly the place for someone to come to pour her heart out, no matter how bad she thinks her story is."

"You…you really believe that, don't you?" At last she dared to open her eyes and meet his gaze.

"The church that I minister to will be a sanctuary for sinners, not a showplace for the self-righteous."

She managed a twinge of a smile. "So, what? Saints aren't welcome in your church?"

"Of course they are. Everyone is welcome in that church. I just understand that no one is made worthy on his or her own judgment or merit. Jesus alone makes us worthy."

She nodded, her eyes searching his.

"So it only makes sense to go to His house at a time like this, doesn't it?" He held out his hand.

"Amazing."

"God's grace is amazing."

"No—that is, yes. But that's not what I was saying. I am totally amazed that both of us could have come from points of desperation and disappointment through such different roads and yet come to this same place."

"Persuasion?"

"Salvation."

"Ah." Only the vaguest hint of a smile played on his lips as he nodded.

"To know that you strive like I do to live your faith every day, to make your life a witness to the power of redemption." She took a deep breath. The quelling in her stomach calmed. "I only hope you can apply those principles to what I have to tell you, Sam."

"I'll try, Nic. I really will try."

"Because regardless of how bad you may feel hearing all this now, I refuse to beat myself up over it or feel like I have to make a show of how a single misdeed has ruined my life. To me that negates the wonder of forgiveness. If I truly believe that Jesus washes my sins away, I won't go around in filthy rags to appease people who cannot accept that."

"He makes our sins as white as snow, but, Nic, that doesn't absolve us of the consequences of our actions."

"I know that better than anyone." She looked to the nativity where Willa had stood seconds earlier.

He moved around the kitchen.

She did not have to see him to picture him taking a few restless strides in one direction, perhaps touching the laced-trimmed edge of a placemat, glancing toward the window over the sink. Sam in her family kitchen asking the one thing she had dreaded hearing from him for so long. And yet the peace that had come over her before had returned.

She put her hand over her stomach. She inhaled the smells of the holidays right down to singed gingerbread and the leather of Sam's jacket. Nothing. No sickness roiling up inside her. Just peace.

"Will you come to the church so we can talk this through?"

She had to do it. She had put it off long enough. Too long. Her priorities had changed. Her long-term plans for herself, this house, and her child now seemed as irrelevant as the temporary solutions she had offered when she found Sam living in her family home.

She tucked her hair back. "Let me tell my sisters where I'll be."

"Nic." She had not known how close he stood to her until he snagged her by the arm. "Can you just tell me this much now? Can't you just say yes or no?"

"No."

His grip loosened.

"That is, no, I can't tell you. I can't tell you if you are Willa's father, not now or even when we go over to the church—because I'm not sure myself."

Not sure herself. Sam jangled his keys in his open palm as they walked along the side street toward the church. The silence of a town wrapped in winter weighed down on them. No cars passed, no people sat on front porches to wave and call out hellos.

The vacant houses with For Sale signs so old the paint had flaked away and the frames had gone to rust added their own shading to the quiet around them. When the wind picked up, the bare branches rattled like old bones. The cross on the church steeple stood watch over it all.

It took every ounce of reserve Sam had not to take Nic by the shoulders and demand she explain herself immediately. Only another minute now before he'd know everything. Then what?

He stole a sidelong glance at Nic. Her thick brown hair fell like a curtain along the side of her face, obscuring her expression. She kicked at stones in the rutted road with her dusty hiking boots. Her upper body hunched forward slightly. Whether that was from the chill or her emotions, he couldn't tell. The way she kept her hands jammed deep inside her sweater pockets, he suspected the chill.

The anger and frustration that had motivated him earlier vanished as he watched her in profile. He knew this woman like he knew his own heart. He knew her as a blessing to her sisters, a credit to her family, and a wonderful mother despite difficult circumstances. Whatever story she had to tell, he would listen to it without anger-clouded judgment.

He opened his mouth to tell her so as they reached the opening of the church driveway, but the crunch of tires on the gravel cut him off.

"Hey! Imagine finding you two out together—and heading for the church, no less." A mammoth SUV pulled alongside them with Claire LaRue's head poking out of the driver's side. "Out for a romantic stroll or here for official purposes? Not that it's any of my business."

Sam stepped up to the stopped vehicle. "That's right, Claire."

"What's right? Y'all out and about in the name of romance or religion?"

"That's right, it's none of your business." Nic closed in behind him, taking what he had offered as an answer without an answer and given it an antagonistic twist.

Sam cleared his throat. "What she meant was…"

"Oh, I think she said what she meant, Reverend. And she's right, to a degree." The bells on Claire's holiday earrings jingled softly as she shook back her red hair. "I see where your daughter gets her directness, Nicolette."

Nic scuffed her boots in the gravel.

"And her wonderful smile, Sam."

"Claire, if you have something specific to say to me, I'd appreciate if you just said it plain out."

"I admit, I did come over to the church today hoping to find you in. I thought I'd call later but now that we've run into one another—can we talk?"

"Do you want to come into the church?" Sam motioned.

"No, honey, Reggie bought me this fool thing as an early Christmas present, and I haven't mastered the knack of backing it up without running up over curbs and sidewalks and more than a few flower beds. I'm afraid I'd take down the whole Christmas tree if I tried it. Can we just chat like this? Won't take a minute."

"Nic?" He glanced over his shoulder. "You want to go on inside and get warm?"

"Actually she might want to stay. This does concern her."

Nic's fingertips dug into his shoulder.

"What concerns her, Claire?" He anchored his feet and folded his arms.

"Now you know, Sam, Reggie's family as well as my own are long-standing, respected members of this community. My mother's people were in on the very founding of this church." She said it in such a bright and friendly manner that only someone who had reason to suspect her motives would have perceived even the hint of threat in her claim.

"To be sure, Claire. And I hope you're showing up for the tree decorating service is just the start of your—and your family's—renewed commitment to the church we're rebuilding here."

Her breezy smile clamped down tighter and her eyes went a bit on the squinty side.

"Can we count on seeing you at the Christmas Sing on Wednesday night?"

"I have never missed a Christmas Sing—and never neglected to bring more than a fair share of donations for the needy—in my life. Why should this year be different?"

"No reason that *I* know of." He grinned. "And of course, we'll see you again on Friday. Should be a beautiful candlelight service."

"Candlelight you say? On Friday? Do I dare hope you're talking about…?"

"Christmas Eve."

"Christmas Eve? Oh, of course, Christmas Eve." She started to tip her head back but the headrest bumped her forward. She scowled. "I asked Reggie for a peignoir set, a pair of sparkly earrings, and a book. I got this contraption. Aren't men who try to come up with surprises for their women just the most precious things, Nic?"

To Claire's credit, that got a giggle out of Nic, even if she did try to suppress it at the last minute and disguise it as a cough.

"Anyway, forgive me, but when you mentioned a candlelight service, and seeing you two out together today, and being more of the direct woman kind of person than the going around the briar patch man kind of person, I'll just say it."

"Then say it." Nic relaxed her grip on Sam's shoulder and stepped to the side.

"I thought you had a wedding in the offing."

"A wedding? Are you out of your mind?" Nic voiced Sam's thoughts precisely.

"Actually I am quite sound of mind. It's you two I was worried about." She fussed with her hair, her jewelry, even adjusted her rearview mirror, before angling her shoulders toward them and aiming that too-too-sunny smile their way. "Do you think there hasn't been talk? Did you think this could go on, in light of your combined and separate pasts and with these present circumstances?"

"The dissension among the membership? The group that meets at Dewi's wanting me out?"

"I'm not talking about the circumstances at the church. I'm talking about the circumstances at home, your home…the home the two of you share."

"I rent a room and bath with kitchen privileges."

"Share? With my entire family, my sisters, and now her kids and my aunts coming in and out all day."

"Which only gives people the impression that you have their blessing. It doesn't stop those who want to assume the worst."

"That's a dangerous rumor you're starting, Claire." He held out his arm to keep Nic back, not sure if it was her or the woman in the SUV he was protecting.

"I didn't start anything. Your actions did and in an already volatile atmosphere. I'd have thought you'd both know better."

"We're not *doing* anything," Nic protested.

"Aren't we supposed to stay away from even the impression of wrongdoing?"

She had them there. Sam hung his head. "I should have thought of it from that angle. You're right, Claire."

"I didn't come here to be right. Believe it or not, I came to be helpful."

"Helpful?" Nic huffed.

"I believe you, Claire."

"I came to warn you that the talk has already begun. No doubt fed by those who want you out, Sam, for reasons that have little to do with your present personal life."

"Claire, I know you've been in with the Dewi's bunch. Why

exactly do they want me out so badly?"

"There are only a few. And you know the reasons. There are people here like Lee who can't abide the idea that someone who thumbed his nose at the entire town could be allowed to return and take a position of honor and respect among us."

"I know that."

"And there are those who feel strongly that a man with your past might serve in the church but should not lead it, should not be an example to young people. People in small towns have long memories."

"No kidding," Nic muttered.

"Some folks fear the message your ministry might give the youngsters of Persuasion is to have all the fun you want while you're young, then get right with God when you grow up. Or worse, that if you go to church on Sunday, it doesn't matter how you are the rest of the time—that's what they'll say if they buy into the story of you and Nic living together."

"I can see that." He put his hand over the lowered window of the black SUV.

"Most of us, Sam, we're looking for a sign, for a reason to go one way or another." She put her hand on top of his but just briefly. "Inviting folks door to door to come decorate the tree was a good first step. But it will be for nothing if you don't stop this rumor dead in its tracks."

"But why suggest marriage is the answer? I can just move out of the house."

She shook her head. "I doubt that would be enough, and I think you both know why."

"No, why?"

"Because of the child."

"You're out of line there, Claire. Be careful what conclusions you jump to."

"I'm not jumping anywhere, Sam." She ran her fingers over the steering wheel. "I'm not starting rumors nor casting stones. I have no right. I was at that party that night. None of us were acting like the good Christian girls our mamas raised. I hope you know I never was one of those who talked behind your back."

Nic wet her lips and yet her voice came out dry as dust. "Thank you."

Claire acknowledged her with the slightest of nods. "Now I didn't come here to deliver an ultimatum. I hope it didn't come off like that. I'm just shouting a heads-up and telling you what it may take to set things right with folks."

"Understood and appreciated." Sam touched her arm.

"Certainly. But I can't help thinking…would it really be so bad?"

"What?"

"The two of you getting married?" Claire laughed. Her earrings jingled. "Why, just look at the pair of you out together today. It looks right, I tell you. And last night, with your little girl between you…with *Nic's* little girl, I mean. Anyone can see it."

Nic tugged at the opening of her cardigan, wrapping it tightly over her. "See what?"

"You were meant to be together. The two of you loved each other a long time ago. Everyone knows that."

Sam eyed Nic, not sure of his feelings at present but unable to deny Claire's view of the past.

Nic shifted her shoulders and did not look at Sam.

"You've both suffered plenty for bad choices and bad judgment, isn't it time you set things right? The way they always should have been?"

Sam never took his eyes from Nic; she only met his gaze for an instant before she bowed her head and kicked at the gravel under her feet.

"Think about it, at least." Claire gunned the motor. The window whirred as she started to shut it, then stopped. "Don't forget everything I told you, okay? And Merry Christmas!"

"Merry Christmas!" Sam shouted back, though he knew she could not hear him as the SUV roared away. "Has she taken leave of her senses or have—"

He turned to face Nic only to find he was talking to himself.

"Get yourself inside this church, Sam!" She motioned to him from beside the Christmas tree. "This has gone on long enough. It's time we got everything out in the open, once and for all."

"Which is why I brought you over here in the first place," he muttered under his breath as he started across the lot toward her.

"Don't drag your feet now. We don't have time to waste. I think it's finally time we do exactly like Claire suggested."

He stopped in the middle of the lot, blinked, then shoved his hands in his pockets. "Get *married?*"

"No." She put her hands on her hips. She looked absolutely immovable except for the wind-whipped ends of her hair. Shoulders straight, she raised her head the way she did when she was putting her family members in their places. "No, I think it's time, finally, that we do like Claire said and set things right once and for all."

Eighteen

"You did not show up that New Year's Eve."

"I'm well aware."

"You promised me that you'd come for me, that we'd get married right away. I based some pretty uncharacteristic decisions on that promise, and those decisions changed the course of my life."

"Believe me, I know that."

"You took advantage of my innocence and trust."

"And have lived to regret it. I hope you know that."

"You didn't show up that night."

"Yes, we established that." He smiled, obviously hoping to lighten the mood, if only a little.

Nic raised her chin. Though her eyes remained dry, her throat closed and she forced out her next words in a strangled sob. "You broke my heart."

Sam sat on the edge of his desk and folded his hands in his lap. "If I could undo that fact I would."

"I don't want you to undo it. You can't no matter how much you wish you could." She held her breath to steady herself, then exhaled slowly. "I want you to acknowledge it."

"All right."

"It's not all right. Saying it's all right doesn't affect the outcome one bit." She pushed her hair back, wincing as her fingers snagged in a tangle.

"I'm well aware we are dealing with things that are in the past. Things that a few sympathetic responses will not mend. Believe me, I understand that."

"I want you to *understand* that on the heels of that heartache and after already making a string of decisions that went against my own beliefs, the way my family raised me and God's expectations for me, I was in a very fragile state of mind."

"Sure. I can see how you would be."

"I'm not laying blame here. I'm not making excuses, either." She paced as she spoke. She used big, slashing gestures with her hands that both emboldened her and underscored her thoughts with power and finality. "I accept my part in all this. I made those choices knowing full well they were wrong for me and would carry consequences for my family and my faith. But I went on ahead with them anyway."

"I wish I could say I had no idea what that's like, but I've made a few monumental eyes-wide-open blunders myself."

"In that way I should bear more of the blame for it all than you should."

"No, Nic, I thought we weren't going to assign blame here and certainly not try to start divvying it up as to who should accept more or less of it. And if we were, I was certainly more—"

"*I* was a Christian when I made those choices. I knew better."

"I knew better, too." He fixed his gaze on her and held it until she raised her eyes to his. "I just put what I wanted ahead of what I knew was right."

"So did I, Sam. But I had to turn my back on God to do it." She laced her fingers together. "No matter how much I justify my actions, that was, in the end, my biggest sin."

He only nodded.

Years ago he would not have understood at all, but now she knew that he did—completely. That strengthened her resolve to go on. "I regret that my choices hurt so many people, of course, but I won't wallow in regret—much to the disappointment of certain people around town."

Sam chuckled. "I hear you there."

"A lot of people want me to walk around under the dark cloud of my past, a tragic figure, an example of what not to do. It galls them that I am happy, that I don't see myself or my life as devastated by my mistakes or defined by my missteps."

"Many people find guilt easier to handle than redemption."

"Not me. I have sinned. I slip up and sin far more often than I'd like to admit, but I don't live by my transgressions, I *live* by my faith. I don't walk in my sin, I walk in His grace."

"Well put."

"I knew you'd get it, Sam. But I had to make sure we were on the same wavelength before I spill out the whole story. And I have to say, so that there is no misinterpretation, I do not consider Willa or her disabilities my cross to bear or my punishment."

"Of course you don't. Anyone who knows her, who has seen you with her knows she's a blessing."

"A blessing, yes, but no less a consequence of my actions. Living a life with my sins washed clean does not take away the consequences of my actions."

"No."

"Funny, isn't it?"

"Funny?"

"You know, how I made those choices hoping…well, hoping

for the exact opposite of what really happened. Hoping that you would marry me and take me away from Persuasion."

"And here we are, neither of us married to anyone and back in town. Though that's not necessarily a permanent deal for either of us, is it?"

"It may be for me."

"Really? You're thinking of staying in Persuasion?"

"If I don't send Willa to that residential school, I'll have to do something different. Her present situation is not working."

"And you could do that, with your business and all?"

"I could sell my business. There are some other cleaning services around town that would love to buy me out."

"Then what?"

She shrugged. "Willa likes it here. It's a safe place to grow up, and we have enough family here to lend support and work with her with the kind of love and patience you can't find anywhere else."

"Speaking of patience, I think I've shown quite a lot of it since my, um, outburst. Afraid I'm running out, though. You ready to talk to me about whether I'm Willa's father or not?"

"I already told you. I don't know." She put her hand to her forehead, but not even the coolness of her palm quieted the throbbing in her temples. "I thought I knew, and then we came back here and I saw you with her and she took to you so immediately. She never does that and…maybe that's just all wishful thinking, though. You know?"

"Uh-uh." He shook his head and rubbed his knuckles over his cheek. "No. No, I have no idea what you're driving at unless it's… Nic, you can't be trying to tell me you have *no idea* who Willa's father is?"

She turned toward the bookshelf and let out a shuddering sigh.

"There was me, of course. Then I assume you met someone else shortly after I left town?"

"Very shortly." She squeezed her eyes shut as tight as she could, but she could still see Sam's face and could imagine the horror and disgust she would find there once she told him the truth.

"Nic?"

"It was at the party—where I was supposed to have met you that night."

"I see."

"I waited and waited. I kept telling myself that you had car trouble or maybe got into a fight with your father, even that you had cold feet. But I never doubted you'd show up, that you'd come for me."

"Well, I did have a fight with my father, but then that was an everyday occurrence so that wasn't what kept me away. And you know how I doted on that old Chevy, restored it to perfect running order, not so much as a ping or a knock from that engine."

"Cold feet." She nodded. "I figured that out—but not until I'd had a few drinks."

"Too many drinks?"

"For a girl who never had anything more than a sip of sherry at Thanksgiving, anything was too much." She opened her eyes but did not look at him. "By the time the fireworks shot off to welcome in the new year, I was lit up like a rocket myself."

"And so you...*met*...someone. Or did you already know him?"

"No, I...I still don't know him." She bunched her hands into her sweater, then turned to the window that faced in the direction of her house. "When I wasn't home by curfew, Daddy came looking for me. Tracked me down at the party about three in the morning."

"I was already across the state line by then."

She didn't know if he'd said it as an apology or simply as a means of accounting for his whereabouts. It didn't matter either way, she supposed, and wondering about it was only going to put off the inevitable for mere moments. She cleared her throat, wound a strand of hair around her finger, and forced her focus back to her story.

"Like I said, Daddy tracked me down and found me, wearing just my T-shirt passed out in a back bedroom with a boy whose name I did not know and never found out."

"I'll bet Collier Jack was just thrilled about that," Sam deadpanned.

Nic mustered a laugh at that, but she could not sustain the lightness of the moment. Heaviness filling her chest, she wet her lips and pressed on. "He told me he and Mama thought I'd been killed in a car wreck. Frankly, given how he found me and what happened afterward, I often wondered if he would have preferred that to the truth."

"Nic, don't say that. Your father loved you dearly."

"Yes, he did. And I repaid his love with pain and deceit."

"Just like I did to you." He stepped toward her, his hand out as if to brush back her hair.

She dodged the gesture, then spun around to face him. "Have you not been listening to a word I said, Sam? I was found in a bedroom with a stranger."

"I heard. That hardly proves he is Willa's father."

"As far as my daddy was concerned, he had to be." Nic inched closer to the window again, pressing her fingertips to the cold glass. "I couldn't let my father think that I'd been with him *and* with you. I couldn't let him know what a mockery I'd made of my beliefs and his."

"According to Claire the town gossip holds that—"

"Don't start with me about town gossip. I endured the worst kind of it back then. Mean gossip, ugly rumors, and coming from people who had known me all my life, from friends who sang alongside me in the church choir and sat beside me in English class in high school. Worse yet, Mama and Daddy and even Collier had to suffer through it, too."

"And then Willa came along."

"And then Willa came along." She laid her forehead against the windowpane and closed her eyes. "And some of those same people whom I longed to look to for help and support turned their vicious tongues on my sweet, helpless child. They said it was my punishment from God that she was not right."

"Then why would you even consider moving back here, Nic?"

"I told you, my aunts and my home are here and…" *You are here.* She almost let it tumble out, but in her moment's hesitancy she held back, thought it over, and then could not do it. "There are a lot of factors at work here. I can't say for sure I will stay, but I have to consider it as a real possibility. I can't afford not to."

"Can't afford?"

"Maybe I should say Willa can't afford for me not to. It's one thing to talk about forgiveness and facing consequences, it's another to live them out."

"If you move back here, it would show a great deal of forgiveness on your part toward—a lot of people."

"And being back here, talking to Bert and my sisters, seeing my home through eyes that thought they had come to say good-bye to it forever, it's changed my outlook."

"I hope that's not the only thing that has changed. I hope that in that multitude of reasons to think about staying in Persuasion that I count, at least a little."

"At least." Whispering the echo of his own words was the only concession she could make at present. "But the main focus, the person I have to keep uppermost in my decision, is Willa."

"Nic, I can't believe you think you're the kind of mother who doesn't put her child first."

"I put her *future* first, Sam. There's a difference."

"Why don't you explain it to me?"

"Ever since I found out that she had this, this, this thing, this…" She hated saying it. She had always pretended it did not bother her, that she had not simply accepted the truth but had embraced it fearlessly. But that was hope and false bravado. She swallowed hard and made herself do it. "This brain damage, and that no matter how many doctors we saw or what we did—short of a miracle—it would not get better. We prayed for miracles, for healing. We still do."

"You didn't even have to tell me that. I knew. Offered a few of those fervent prayers myself since meeting her."

"You have?"

"Uh-huh."

"Sam, that means so much to me."

He gave her a crooked smile. "Hope it doesn't hurt your feelings if I remind you I didn't do it to impress you."

"Doesn't hurt my feelings one bit." She managed a smile back, a weak one.

"I care about Willa, about what happens to her. I don't think you should beat yourself up that you do, too."

"I'm not beating myself up, Sam. I'm looking at myself, my actions, honestly. Far too long ago I stopped concentrating on Willa day to day, moment by moment, and began to fixate on her future. To how she would get along in that great big, scary world out there."

"Sounds like a wise strategy."

"Was it, really?" She shook her head. The weight of it all settled down on her shoulders and she leaned against the window frame for support. "My sisters have been telling me I'm too hard on her. I don't give her the breaks I'd give a normal eight-year-old. My aunts say that I haven't rooted her deeply enough in the family."

"That's easily taken care of."

"Not if I put her in a residential program."

He held his hands out to concede her point.

"I thought it was best for her. It comes so highly recommended and it works wonders for some children. Now I just don't know anymore if Willa is that kind of child, the kind that will thrive and flourish there. She will receive the training there that she needs to survive in life, but at what personal cost?"

"You mean selling your family's home, walking away from a lifetime of loving traditions, sending her to live away from you?"

Hearing it out in the open gripped at her like a hand around her throat. She blinked and through a wash of tears, tried to make out the gables, the huge magnolia, the fence post, something of her house. "Am I putting too high a value on her staying alive and not enough on her having a remarkable life?"

"A remarkable life." Sam said it so quietly it resonated with the ring of an epiphany. "I can see that for her, Nic. I truly can."

She sighed and wiped the dampness from beneath her lashes. "These past few days I've seen how best laid plans and good intentions don't always produce the desired results. I've seen how family connections can become fragile and how friendships can grow strong. I realize that I've been wrong."

"Wrong?"

"In the way I handled Willa. I need to lay a better foundation for her and trust God and that foundation to take care of her future."

Pride and excitement welled up in Sam's chest at the conclusion she had come to, but he didn't let himself get carried away with it just yet. "And you think you can accomplish that by moving back?"

She turned to face him at last. "There are enough good folks around that I believe I can find the kind of support I lacked back then."

"Really?"

"More people here to really care about Willa's development and well-being than in a residency program away from everyone who loves her."

"Point taken." The old, uneven floor creaked as he moved behind her. "And there's one other thing she will have here that she won't find anywhere else in the world."

"What's that?"

"A man who realistically and biologically probably is her father."

Her back went rigid and she turned around, her shoulders straight. "Sam, I—"

He put his finger to her lips. He fixed his gaze on hers and did not waver. He laid his hand on her shoulder, waited for her to react.

She did not withdraw.

He pulled her into his arms, his heart full of celebration. "Maybe Claire's idea isn't so off-the-wall after all."

"Marriage?" She asked with her mouth pressed against his shirt.

She did not relax in his embrace as he had hoped. "Sam, are you talking about us getting married?"

"I never told you this before because, well, you weren't exactly receptive to me, to say the least. But now knowing about Willa…"

"We don't know anything more about Willa than we did before. Not for certain."

"I know how I feel about her. I know I would be a good father to her, even if, by some wild chance, she is not mine."

She searched his face, her lower lip caught between her teeth.

She was weakening, or rather, warming to the idea. He could sense it. "The thing I haven't told you is one of the reasons I came back here. Not the only reason. I have no doubt the Lord called me back here to do a work of faith in this church, but one of the reasons I came back here was for you."

She shook her head.

He didn't blame her for not understanding, what with his less than suave attempt at babbling out the truth to her. "I came back to find you again, Nic."

"Finding me again and marrying me are too entirely different things, Sam."

"Obviously." He laughed. "But that's not an answer."

"Are you…are you seriously proposing?"

"Maybe not proposing, more trying to see where you stand on the matter."

"Where I stand?"

"Yes."

"You want to know where I stand?"

"That's why I asked."

"I'll tell you where I stand."

"Will that be anytime soon?"

She disregarded his teasing remark with narrowed eyes and the staunch set of her jaw. "I don't stand…no, I *won't* stand for this nonsense. And I certainly won't stand still for it, either."

In a flurry of head tossing and pushing away from him, she pivoted and started for the door. He wanted to call out to her but to say what?

There was nothing to say, really. Not to Nic, not now. He watched her go, his heart aching and his thoughts racing. He may have just lost his best opportunity to win Nic, but he had not lost everything. He had his church, his faith, and in his heart, he now had a daughter.

All was not as he'd expected, but that did not diminish the joy he felt in his new role as Willa's father or discourage him in any way.

"In God's time." He repeated Willa's advice via Big Hyde as he watched Nic practically sprint across the road toward her home. "In God's time, not my own."

Nineteen

Nic's boot heels slammed onto the concrete steps outside the church. The jarring beat rivaled the pulse pounding in her temples. She gritted her teeth, lowered her head, and forged on through the parking lot. At the end of the entryway she glanced right, then left, then right again. But she hadn't really checked for traffic before she darted across the street.

Not that there was any traffic. She had not actually put herself at risk, but the fact that she had pushed herself so carelessly onward made her stumble to a stop on the other side of the road. Slipping behind a tree, she leaned back until the rough bark snagged her hair and rasped against her jacket. She drew the crisp winter air deep into her lungs and held it.

Sam wanted to marry her. No, *wanted* might be too strong a word. He felt obligated—by his morals, his congregation's pending mandate, and the embellished memory of the girl she had once been. The girl he had loved.

She bit her lip. Love? Had he actually said that? She exhaled slowly and laid her head back. No. If he had told her he loved her, she would not have run. She would not have leaped with joy into his arms and accepted his proposal, either.

"What *proposal?*" She pushed away from the tree and stole a peek at the church across the way.

"...*not proposing, more trying to see where you stand on the matter.*" Sam's far from ardent angle on the matter rattled her nerves more than ever. She had come so close to trusting him completely. She had gone into his office ready to lay bare her whole story, to try to face the situation concerning Willa with reasoned compassion, hoping for a new understanding between them, and what had happened?

· *Good question,* she thought as she tried to fit the pieces together. *What did happen?*

Sam Moss mentioned marriage. Well, whoop-de-do, not like he hadn't done that before and left her to regret he ever opened his sweet-talking, ever-lying mouth. But that was the old Sam—or rather, the *young* Sam—not the man she knew now. This man cared about Willa and wanted to be a father to her whether she was his biological child or not. He saw possibilities for her little girl that Nic wanted most of all: that Willa would have a full, loving, faith-filled, and remarkable life.

This man, this Sam whom she had loved so long ago, and probably still did if she could ever let her defenses down long enough to admit it, had come back to find her. After all these years, it seemed that in some way he had never forgotten his promise to come for her.

Nic hugged her arms tight around her body and shut her eyes. Tears spilled onto her cheeks. She pressed her lips tightly together. He had come back for her, but it was too late. Too much water under the bridge. Too many heartaches time had not erased.

Pulling her shoulders up, she shook back her hair. She would not waste her time dwelling on this. She had plans to make for whether she and Willa would stay on in Persuasion and plans for Christmas, which loomed larger than life now only a few days away. She would not get bogged down in some impossible emotional quagmire. She would be strong. She would be in control. And most of all she would not let anybody else drag her down or divert her from her new priorities.

"Nic, I'm so glad you're back." Collier had Nic by the elbow and began dragging her toward the living room before the back door could swing shut. "We've had a small disaster here."

"Not Willa!"

"No, Willa is fine." She urged Nic into the padded rocker by the Christmas tree. "Scott and Jessica walked her over to Dewi's to get a treat and a loaf of bread and lunch meat for dinner."

"Bread and lunch meat for dinner?" Nic rocked back and forth. Petie having a small disaster was one thing, but her family resorting to sandwiches for dinner during the holidays was something else altogether. "You're not serious, are you? Why didn't you have them pick up a roasting hen or something to make a nice soup?"

"You can criticize my cooking later; right now we have a real problem on our hands."

"Don't be silly."

"I'm not. This is a real problem, Nic."

"You don't *cook* lunch meat sandwiches." Nic refused to play along in her sister's minidrama. She'd had quite an eventful day of her own already and did not need the added strain. "Best I can do is criticize your menu choices, but not your cooking."

"Forget the menu for one minute, would you? The menu hardly matters because in case you've forgotten, tonight's the night The Duets and the odd assortment of cousins are coming over."

"Oh, dear, even if only the odd assortment shows up, that'll be quite a lot of people. Sure you want to serve them sandwiches and suffer through all the snotty remarks and head shaking over not making a very proper Christmas party meal?"

"Everyone is bringing something to eat and you know it. Since when have you known anyone in this family *ever* to show up at a family gathering without fried chicken, a three-bean salad, and a chocolate sheet cake?" Collier pointed to the end of the room and the extra table, the one that their parents had borrowed from the church for one day—twenty years ago. "I'm already set up for as much food as even our family can carry in. *And* I'm well-prepared for the fact that Aunt Lula's lime Jell-O wreath with maraschino cherry accents cannot occupy the same table as Aunt Nan's wreath of pistachio pudding with red hots and real holly leaves on top."

"Not without causing a catastrophic hissy fit of near biblical proportions." At least her sisters came to their overly dramatic streaks honestly. Nic flipped the collar of her sweater up and sighed. "But with all that food coming, why do sandwiches, too?"

"Because Jessica and Scott hate molded desserts, things with tiny, colored marshmallows on top passing themselves off as salads, and especially fried foods."

"Not Willa. She loves that stuff. She even begged me to get a deep fat fryer." Nic reached out and feigned intense interest in a faded construction paper ornament dangling low on the branch of the tree. "Must be in her genes or something. She hasn't lived in the South, but she instinctively yearns for the foods of her forefathers."

"If you think I don't know that you're trying to steer this conversation away from Petie's problem, then you've got another think coming."

"Another think coming," Nic scoffed. "Ooooh, that has me quaking in my boots."

"Stop it, now. This is serious." Collier knelt in front of the rocking chair and stilled its movements with both her hands on the arms. "Listen to me, Nic. Petie is in a world of hurt, and for once it's not a world whipped up in her own imagination."

"You shouldn't let her upset you like this, hon." She patted Collier's hand, then brushed the straight brown bangs from her baby sister's forehead. "You know full well she could march down here any minute completely over whatever had her worked up—or have moved onto the next dilemma that threatens to rend the very fabric of her being."

Nic played the last part up big, hoping for a laugh. Collier's eyes stayed somber. "I think it's just ugly of you to make light when Park and Petie's marriage and happiness hang in the balance."

Marriage and happiness. Like one guaranteed the other. She thought of Sam's most reluctant not-exactly-a-proposal. She pulled her legs up under her body, tucking herself into the comfy old chair as if she were cuddling up in her mama's lap. Marriage was no promise of happiness, not without two people willing to work and sacrifice, two people who went into the union for all the right reasons. That was seemingly not the case for her and Sam—well, for Sam anyway—but even she had to admit it had always been true of her sister and her devoted husband.

"Yes, Petie and Park are going through a rough patch right now, but do you honestly think he would abandon her and the kids? At Christmastime?" Parker Sipes was as predictable as Sam Moss was impulsive. Nic would stake her life on that. "Mark my words, sometime between now and Christmas Eve morning, Park will stroll in that back door, presents in his arms and apologies on his lips."

"I told you once, Parker doesn't buy presents." Petie stood in the doorway.

Somehow, perhaps it was a trick of the light or something she learned from the other women of their family, she managed to loom larger than life and yet appear almost ghostlike standing there, as if she might suddenly rise up to fill the whole room with her unleashed anger or fade completely away to nothing more than a memory in the wink of an eye. She gave off a sense of frail strength that made even Nic sit up and take notice.

"You all right, Petie?"

"I couldn't stand it," she murmured.

"Couldn't stand what, sugar?" Nic extended her hand to her sister.

"The not knowing." Petie took a few steps. "It was the not knowing that had me on the edge this whole time. Bad news a person can handle given time, faith, and a few people to count on to get her through. But no news…"

Her voice trailed off and she seemed to stare unseeing at the Christmas tree.

Collier took Nic's hand and gave it a squeeze. It was all she had to do to convey her anxiety. Worries over Sam and his simplistic solution to their situation fell away. Her sisters needed her and she would not let them down.

"What have you done?" Nic asked her older sister.

"When the kids didn't have any real answers about what was going on with their father, not even a very solid take on his mood or frame of mind, I had to do something."

"She went back into his e-mail," Collier whispered.

"And?" Nic gripped Collier's hand tightly but spoke directly to Petie.

"I only intended to see if it had been active, to see if he was checking it. He wasn't. The same old information remained from last time along with a new string of memos on meetings from his administrative assistant." She cocked her head, her gaze still aimed past the sisters but not appearing to focus on anything. "And then it hit me."

A sour sensation rose in the back of Nic's throat. "What hit you?"

"If Park had taken time off and everyone in his office knew that, why would his administrative assistant keep sending him e-mails reminding him of current meetings?"

"Oh, Petie, no." Nic was halfway out of the chair when her older sister finally looked her in the eye.

She held out her hand to stop Nic from getting up and coming to her. "Yes."

The rocker sighed as she settled back down. "How bad is this, sugar?"

"You mean how far has it gone?"

Nic nodded.

"Near as I can tell, from reading her notes to him—"

Nic tugged at the collar of her sweater, then clutched the lapels together. "You opened his e-mail?"

"Wouldn't you have?" Collier sprang to her big sister's defense like a sheepdog protecting a wounded lamb.

"I'm not proud of it," Petie conceded. "But like I said, it was the not knowing that drove me over the edge."

"So, now you know." Nic did not prod for details. She understood how much more difficult facing a personal crisis could be when well-intentioned onlookers pried for more information.

"I know that it hasn't gone very far. Flirting, innuendo. She's apparently invited him to her home and suggested they have lunch at a hotel a few times."

"Good thing this gal is a thousand miles away or I'm afraid the Dorsey girls might have to take her up on that invitation." Nic rocked forward slowly. "Meet her for a light repast of watercress and regret."

"She is persistent. To Park's credit, he clearly has not taken her up on it—a fact she decries in notes filled with those little on-line symbols for how you feel about things."

"Emoticons," Collier said. "That's what they're called."

"To Park's credit?" Nic spoke over her young sister's explanation. "You saying you feel better after reading these things?"

"He hasn't given in to temptation—as of the last note she sent a few hours ago. She's as baffled by his up and taking off as I am. Except, well, now I'm not so much."

"Not so much what?"

"Baffled. Having this little piece of the puzzle brings it all together for me. It makes perfect sense now that Park has run off."

"Because he needs to think things over?" Collier sat back, cross-legged, and ran her hand through her short hair.

"Thinking? He's not thinking, honey; he's hiding." Petie laughed. "Parker Sipes never had to make a real decision in his life. His family circumstances put him on a path that he has followed from the first time he stepped onto a peewee league football field."

"You don't sound nearly as mad and upset as you did a minute ago." Nic relaxed enough to let her chair rock gently.

"Well, you *have* to laugh, don't you? The man is so on time for his midlife crisis, it's clichéd and apparently *that* isn't even his idea. Poor sweet boy."

"He's hardly a boy." Collier rolled her eyes.

"He is to me," Petie murmured.

Nic didn't know whether to groan or grin. Seeing her sister's burden lightened had lightened her own. She just felt better.

"Right now just thinking back, I can still see his fresh, young face." Petie laid her hand to her cheek. "The first boy who ever kissed me, my date to the high school prom, the nervous groom standing at the end of the church aisle—all of them my Parker."

"Have you lost your mind?" Collier croaked.

"I haven't lost anything. In fact, I may have just found something very precious."

Collier threw her hands up. "Like what?"

"Like perspective."

"Oh, well, now that is the very last thing I'd say you have, Petie." Collier sprang to her feet like a fighter hearing the bell announce the second round. "Only a minute ago you were devastated by what you'd discovered about your husband. And have you forgotten he told your children that he might not come for Christmas?"

"I haven't forgotten." She laid her hand over her heart, her eyes bright with tears. "You think I could forget something like that? Think I can put it out of my mind for more than a few seconds at a time? But there is more going on here than just that."

"Such as?"

"My marriage has taken a slow, downward spiral over the last year. I don't think either of you can deny you've noticed that."

Collier and Nic exchanged glances but held their opinions.

"Sam noticed it when we first got here. He recognized it right off even when my own family didn't seem to take my state seriously."

Nic clenched her teeth and flicked at a strand of tinsel swaying in the draft from the old heating vent.

"That Sam, he spotted it right off as empty-nest syndrome." Petie walked across the room, stopping in front of the tree. She reached out to finger a soft-needled branch tip. "Park and I, our lives have changed drastically now. No kids in the house, no comfortable roles that we both enjoyed and embraced so fervently—that safety net is gone. Sam pegged it just right."

"That hardly excuses Park's actions." Nic wriggled out of her cardigan sweater, not sure whether to blame the emotional intensity in the room or the old furnace for her sudden discomfort. She totally discounted that mentioning Sam and how right he had been could be the cause.

"I'm not making excuses for anyone. I don't think either one of us has handled this past year very well, truth to tell."

Collier cocked her head to the left to study Petie, looking and sounding as innocent as a child when she asked, "So what are you going to do now?"

"Do?" Petie shook her head. "Pray. It's all I can do, and it's still my best plan of action."

Her sister's hair did not move. Even in a time of total crisis, Nic noted, the woman had fortified herself with faith—and a goodly portion of ultrahold hair spray.

"Well, let us in on it, too, then." Nic pushed herself up from the rocker, then held out her hand to Collier. "What shall we specifically pray for, just so we don't cancel one another out?"

"Pray that Parker finds his way." Petie drew her shoulders up.

Nic eased her arm around Petie's back.

Collier's arms fit around both her sisters' waists.

The three of them leaned in just enough to rest their heads together.

"Pray that Parker finds his way home to me," Petie whispered. "And that I find my way back to being his wife, not just the mother of his children. Pray that God restores my marriage, renews all our spirits, and refreshes our love for one another. Can we agree to pray for that?"

"We just did." Nic gave her a squeeze.

"Amen," Collier added.

"Amen." Petie shut her eyes and sighed.

Twenty

"Amen." Sam lifted his head and his gaze rose immediately to the polished wooden cross behind the pulpit in the silent sanctuary. He studied it, letting the beauty of the object and the awe of what it represented sink so deeply into his soul that it actually seemed to converge at the center of his being, then intensify and radiate outward again. It was a poor way of explaining the magnificence of the Lord affecting a man grasping for guidance, but that's how it felt to him and he praised God for the experience.

It was God's will that Sam had to seek, God's plan he had to answer to, not his own or the town's or anyone else's. No matter what went on in this town, in the floundering church in the lurch, even between him and Nic, grace would carry him through.

He shifted on the hard seat of the pew and sighed. Grace would see him through, but that did not guarantee a smooth ride or an easy road. The frustration left brewing since his talk with Nic in his office two days ago flashed hot in his chest.

He had hoped, in the time since their initial confrontation of the situation, they would have both thought things over. That they would be able to discuss it calmly and openly. If by openly he had meant in an open forum of all her family members, then yes, that could have been accomplished. Calm was another matter.

Nothing about Christmas in the Dorsey household bespoke calm. First there had been the rafts of relatives descending for too much food, too many joke presents, and too many mouths moving at once. That had gone on long past the time Sam had retreated to his room, purely a matter of self-defense so he didn't get caught praising one of The Duets' potluck contributions more highly than another and starting a war.

After a truly dismal budget meeting, for which they had to pull Big Hyde in off the porch of Dewi's to attain a quorum, Sam had returned to the Dorsey house to find the sisters had gone, lock, stock, and family portfolio off to the bank. He suspected Nic was examining her options regarding staying versus selling the house but knew better than to ask anyone when they returned in the mood for hot cocoa and a Christmas video. By late afternoon another round of friends and family crowded into the living room to send Lula off to her daughter's for the holidays.

For a woman traveling an hour or so away for all of a ten-day visit, the other Duets made out like she was boarding the *Titanic* for the new world, never to be seen again.

And much as he had kidded them about it, something in Sam envied it. No one had ever cared much whether he came or went anywhere. His mother walked away without so much as a real good-bye. His father never asked where Sam was going or cared when he'd be back. Even at his old church, where he'd had lots of friends and felt he'd made a real impact for Christ, no one had made much ado over his leaving. They had the party, made the expected jokes, wished him the best, then turned their attention to the new minister coming to take his place.

Sam had hoped that Persuasion would be different. He had

hoped this church would be a home to him in ways he had never known before. He had hoped…

Foxes have holes and birds of the air have nests, but the Son of Man has no place to lay his head. The verse from Luke echoed in his mind again. Surely the Lord was telling him something with this. Was it that Sam, too, would not find a home? Might never find a home? He could not believe that was what God wanted for him, and in mulling the verse over again, that message didn't bring him resolve or serenity. No, that was not what the Lord wanted him to understand.

He folded his hands and fixed his eyes on the cross again. "I will seek peace in Your will, O Lord. I will find strength in Your grace. Everything I had hoped and planned for has fallen away it seems, but I know You have a better plan than my own. Help me to embrace with gratitude the gifts You have given me. Guard me against bitterness and despair and guide my ways. Amen."

Sam stood, drew a deep breath, then smiled and walked down the aisle and out of the sanctuary. He paused beside the outside door long enough to grab his leather jacket off the peg in the foyer and zip it up. Sometime in the last twenty-four hours a storm front had blown in and left things as cold and dreary as his mood of late. The weather would lift, he told himself, and so would this cloud over him. Nic could not avoid him for long, and after all, it was Christmas.

He peeked out the window of one of the large doors. The community Christmas tree, though not thick with ornaments or contributions, did look beautiful. Petie's son and daughter had decided upon their arrival that what the tree needed was popcorn garlands. It had taken all three children, all four of The Duets, Collier, and a handful of volunteers from among the scads of folks in and out of the house the better part of a day to create enough strings for the big tree.

Sam had helped Willa with her part of the project. She had been especially clingy to him the last two days, but he didn't mind, not one bit. He loved the child. Loved her enough to want to protect her from anything the world, or his own desires, would do to hurt her.

He could tell she had wanted to ask him something. She kept working around to it, working her courage up. But before she could get to it, Sam had always changed the subject or distracted her. He wasn't 100 percent sure what she was going to ask him, but he sensed it was not the kind of thing he should field. He cared about Willa with his whole heart, but even if he were her biological father, he was really a virtual stranger to her and did not fully understand her. There were some questions he had no right answering.

He wasn't even sure he had the right answers. That was Nic's territory. He would not intrude, not now while it was all so fragile and new.

His gaze rose to the top of the tree then down again, smiling at their recent handiwork. By nightfall yesterday they'd marched over and ringed the big evergreen with the ropes of popcorn. Sam had to admit it did it a world of good and hoped it would offer the birds some nourishment just as the weather had turned wicked.

A flutter in the shadows of the lowest branches drew his attention and he grinned. Spirit lifted, he pressed his hand flat to the door, gave it a big push, and stepped outside. The flurry of small, dark wings welcomed him as the tiny flock beneath the tree took flight. He squinted skyward to watch them. Sparrows, he thought. No, too dark for sparrows. Maybe chickadees or…

The birds rose above him, exposing their white underbellies. At last he could see the reddish beaks against the slate gray of their feathered heads. Just like the delicate ornament he'd held in his hands when he first met Willa.

It wasn't miraculous, Sam understood that, but it was a marvel. A gift, he believed, from the Lord to remind him to stay faithful and wait for God's timing. He smiled, tucked his hands in his pockets, and looked heavenward as he started out for the house. He couldn't wait to tell Willa. The snowbirds had returned to Persuasion.

"Did you really see them?" Willa skipped along at Sam's side. "Really?"

It did Nic's heart good to see the child's eyes glowing with excitement like this, but selfishly she wished she'd played more a part in putting it there. Everything that seemed to matter to Willa now had to have some connection to Sam. For the last two days, Sam, Sam, Sam.

"Yes, ma'am, I really did see them." He maneuvered his hands to keep his grip on the cardboard box filled with groceries and still manage to point to the tree across the street. "A small flock of snowbirds right under that Christmas tree."

"Sam saw the snowbirds. Sam saw the snowbirds!" Willa singsonged the chorus she'd regaled them with at least a hundred times since getting Sam's news and their getting ready to walk over to the church for the Christmas Sing.

Nic scrunched her collar closed in one gloved hand. She huffed out a sigh that created a puff of moist air.

Sam elbowed her in the side. "Sort of makes you yearn for a

few days back when she got stuck singing the last stanza of 'Grandma Got Run Over by a Reindeer,' doesn't it?"

"Sam saw the snowbirds." The family-sized can of soup Willa had insisted she would carry all by herself jounced up and down with each step, making Nic grateful he had not let her carry the bottle of soda pop she'd originally requested.

"I wish she had seen them, too," Nic said, not realizing how soft and wistful her voice would come out.

"She will." He stopped long enough to command Nic's gaze to meet his. "In God's time."

Sure, *now* he preached the virtue of patience and waiting. How she wished he had taken that advice earlier, before he'd offered her a marriage born of obligation and duty, not love and devotion. They had hardly spoken since then. Nic liked it that way. She had too much on her mind to allow the distraction of Sam wanting to use her and Willa as a solution to his own problems to intrude in her thoughts.

But it did intrude. Thoughts of Sam, of his predicament and her own seemed hopelessly intertwined in her mind and heart. She no longer carried any anger toward him, not even for the thoughtless way he had talked about the possibility of them sharing a future.

"Do you think the birds will still be there?" Willa waited at the side of the road for the approaching cars to turn into the church lot.

"Not very likely, honey." Nic tugged the child's scarf in place. "Not with all the coming and going today. Folks are bringing by donations for the food baskets and gathering for the Christmas Sing."

"But they're around and that's what's nice to remember." Sam gave her daughter's shoulder a squeeze, and Willa beamed up at him.

The next car stopped. The driver motioned for them to go on across, and Sam started off, his hand guiding Willa gently along.

Nic didn't know what all emotions clashed in her at that sight; they came too fast and furious. At once she thought of snatching Sam's hand away or pulling Willa protectively close to her, but that passed almost instantly, and she pushed her misgivings over the growing bond between them aside. Head down, she did a quick half step to catch up to the pair.

Placing her hand on Willa's other shoulder, she smiled up at Sam. "He's right, Willa. You don't have to see them to believe they are back and be happy about it."

"I hope we do see them, though."

"I hope so, too, honey. I sort of saw them as a reminder from God of His faithfulness and presence even when we feel we're all alone." Sam met Nic's gaze. They paused in the parking lot to allow a family in a beat-up truck to maneuver into a tight space. "And you know when God is at work in the world or in people's hearts, anything is possible. Wouldn't you say so, Nicolette?"

She had not meant to smile at him, but she couldn't stop herself. When she couldn't hold his gaze any longer, she leaned down to Willa. "What do you say we toss some food out for the birds tomorrow morning and see if that entices them to show themselves?"

"Not this food." Willa had to use both hands and a push up from her knee to hold the big can aloft. "This is for someone who won't have a nice Christmas unless we help."

"So right, Miss Angelface." Sam tousled her hair. "Besides, those birds have traveled a long way. I'll bet they didn't even think to bring a can opener, and it's too far now for them to go back and get one."

"Birds with a can opener! That's not right." Willa giggled.

"Really? I could have sworn I saw a crow around here with a big, old can-o-matic tucked under his wing."

"A crow? That's not right. You didn't get any of that right. You better ask my mommy to help you get it right next time." Still laughing, Willa hurried to the large box beside the Christmas tree to put her donation inside.

"I would love to ask your mommy to help me get it right this time. If I ate a little crow of my own and didn't try to rush things, I'm hoping she might just give it a shot. What do you think?" He turned to Nic, his expression sincere.

"I think…" She met his eyes, and whatever she intended to say faded from her thoughts.

The gentle teasing, the practiced preacher, the usual defenses she had come to expect to see in him had disappeared. In the quiet of dusk becoming darkness, as they stood to the side of the old church that had been so much a part of their past and present, she truly saw him as he was. Sam. The man she loved.

Beyond the two of them she was aware of streetlights and Christmas lights coming on one by one, then in bright colorful strings, casting a warm glow about the scene. But it was the light inside Sam's eyes that held her transfixed.

"Nic, I never told you this before, but I didn't meet you at that party because I knew I couldn't give you the kind of life you deserved. I'd already…taken too much from you. I didn't want to take any more. I left because…because I loved you."

"Sam…I…"

"That's why I hoped to find you again when I came back to

Persuasion. Why I didn't think Claire's suggestion was all that far-fetched or unreasonable. Because I still love you, Nic."

"Sam!" She pressed her hand to her chest and could feel her heart pounding beneath her fingers.

"I know I shouldn't say it here, with people around and all," he rushed on, leaning over the box of groceries between them, his voice hushed. "But I figured if I had to wait until I got you completely alone, it might never happen."

She raised her hand to cover her mouth. When she blinked, tears pooled on her lashes.

"Or if I waited too long, you might have made your decision about whether or not to stay without having all the information you needed to do the right thing." He took a deep breath, then let it out again. "Believe me, Nic, having done that exact thing in this very relationship, I can tell you I never want either of us to make that kind of mistake again."

"Aren't you two coming inside the church?" Collier whisked past Nic, bumping her shoulder as her suede boots and corduroy skirt swished out her brisk pace.

"In a minute." Nic tore her gaze from Sam's long enough to glance over her shoulder. "Wait, Collier, would you take this box of groceries to the donation bin?"

She had scarcely slid her hands beneath the box in Sam's arms when it lifted out of both their grasps.

"I've got it, Aunt Nic," Scott smiled his all-American boy grin at her and winked. "Just in case you need to have your hands free to do a little…"

"Finish that sentence and die." Jessica nudged her brother from behind, propelling him in several awkward lunges in the right direction as she followed behind.

"They are such good kids." Petie patted Sam on the arm.

"Well, you gave them a good foundation," he said, placing his hand on hers.

"That is exactly what I am counting on, Reverend. A good foundation." She slid her hand from under his, then touched his cheek. "A solid foundation. Faith, family, and life built on the things that matter."

"I have a feeling you're not just talking about your kids now."

She smiled and pushed Nic's hair back as she walked by. "Y'all don't stay out here too long now. You know how people talk."

Without so much as looking, Nic nailed her sister with a long backward swing of her purse and landed a swat on Petie's behind. "Too bad she had on that long coat," Nic complained loud enough for her sister to hear.

Petie's laughter answered from somewhere near the church steps.

"She's in a much better frame of mind." Sam folded his arms. His leather jacket bunched up to show his thin black sweater beneath.

"She sent Parker an e-mail. I'm not sure what all she put in it, but when she checked last night, the account said he'd opened it." She watched as the last of the crowd worked their way inside. "She's been almost endurable since then."

"I like her, even when she's being insufferable. I like Park, too. I hope they work it out." He stepped closer. "They aren't the only ones I hope can work out their differences."

"Sam, this is…"

"Yes?" He inched close and put his hands on her shoulders.

She wet her lips and tipped her head up.

The opening chords of "Joy to the World" reverberated through the nearby windows.

She stepped away and shook her head. "This is such incredibly bad timing."

He laughed. "Well, I wasn't planning on starting something up right here on the church grounds, but I did sort of hope you'd acknowledge what I said to you before we go inside."

She nodded. "I understand about that night. We've both come so far since then. I think it's what we've become, not what we were that could—*could*—give us the basis, the foundation, like Petie said, for something solid."

He waited a moment, then seeming to sense she would say no more, he smiled, leaned in, and kissed her forehead. "Okay then. Let's get inside."

"Good idea." She hurried to keep pace with his stride. Just as they reached the top of the stairs she held back a moment, let him step forward, and to his back, with the strains of her favorite Christmas hymn in the air, she whispered, "I love you, too, Sam."

Twenty-one

Nic loved him, his church was nearly full tonight, and they were singing the praise of the birth of the Savior. He had hope of family, hope of healing the congregation he served, and hope of life everlasting. What more could a man of faith want? Heart full, he sang the last verse of "O Come All Ye Faithful."

He glanced at Nic over the top of Willa's head, the three of them sitting in the front row, just like a real family. Someday— soon, he hoped—that dream would become reality. Sam doubted that anything could ruin this one special evening for him.

"Thank you. Thank you everybody for coming tonight." Mrs. Stern, who had spearheaded this year's food drive and thereby won the "honor" of hosting the annual Christmas Sing, stepped down from the platform where she'd been directing the group in song. "And special thanks to Mrs. Shirleetha Shively for her flaw-less performance at the organ tonight."

Shirleetha, looking quite surprised for the acknowledgment but pleased as punch for it all the same, rose halfway from the bench and gave an awkward but endearing curtsy.

Sam led the applause to show his appreciation for one of the few people who had stood beside him in building this church from day one.

Others joined in quickly save a few sour faces here and there who sat, arms crossed and eyes locked forward. Probably old school, Sam thought. The kind that believed applause belonged in places where individuals seek personal glory and require recognition, not in God's house.

"It does my heart good to see so many familiar faces in our dear little church tonight." Mrs. Stern continued to clap softly as she spoke even though Mrs. Shively had taken her seat again and the rest of the group had quieted. "I do hope this turnout is a foretaste of the many joyous—and well-attended—services we will all share in the future."

A spattering of applause broke out in enthusiastic reception to her sentiment.

Mrs. Stern smiled as brightly as her narrow, lean face allowed.

The room grew quiet.

Someone coughed.

Willa wriggled around in the pew and onto her knees to stare at the rows of people behind them, as if to say, "What is the matter with you people?"

Nic scooted in close to her child and, just loud enough for Sam and Willa to hear, whispered, "Turn round and sit right, young lady. Don't make me give you a pew pinch right here in front of God and everybody."

"Well, now, this is not a night for regular services nor do we have anything planned strictly speaking, but it does seem appropriate that Reverend Moss get up and say a word or two and dismiss us with a prayer and benediction." Mrs. Stern held her hand out toward Sam.

He stood.

One or two people started to applaud then stopped short, for which he was grateful. Much as he longed for support and respect here, his true role was to serve not to be revered.

He would offer only a short, sincere prayer tonight. A thanksgiving for all who had come that would lay the foundation to rebuild this church. Tonight, he understood, giving a nod of thanks to Mrs. Stern as she took her place at the front of the sanctuary, would lay the groundwork for whatever he hoped to accomplish in Persuasion, Alabama.

"First I would like to reiterate Mrs. Stern's welcome to everyone who turned out tonight and who brought food to share with those less fortunate. Having been a child whose sole means of Christmas often came from the benevolence baskets provided by this very church, I can tell you all how much it means to those who would otherwise do without. Thank you again."

A murmur went through the crowd.

"It's good to see so many folks here tonight, and I hope each of you will join us this Christmas Eve for our candlelight service. We'd love to have you then and at regular Sunday services. If there is one thing I want to emphasize, it's that each of you has a place here at All Souls Community Church."

"Each of *us* has a place," a male voice muttered from the back of the room.

Let it go and launch into the prayer. That would be the easiest way to deal with this now. But God had not called Sam into the ministry to take the easy way. Sam had come to it fighting his way through almost every bramble and setback a sinner could know. When he answered that call, took up the challenge, and said he would follow Jesus, he did it knowing what it might cost him. He came to the Lord willing to give his all. He would not do less tonight. Lifting his head, he searched the area where he'd heard the scoffing remark. "Did you have something to add?"

The murmuring grew louder.

Nic put her arm around Willa and pressed her lips together, her anxious gaze trained on Sam.

But he could not let her apprehension deter him from his duty. "Speak up. If you have something to say, stand up and say it to my face for everyone to hear."

"Okay, I will." Lee Radwell rose slowly. "Nobody here has a problem feeling we got a place in this church. Most of us was christened here, baptized here, and attended a goodly portion of our friends' and families' weddings and funerals inside these very walls."

"And me right beside you, Lee."

"No. No, that ain't true, *Reverend.* You got kicked out of this church a long time ago."

"If I recall right, I wasn't the only kid who caused a stir in church and was asked not to come back without proper supervision. The difference was I didn't have a parent who cared about supervising me in anything, least of all church services."

Lee puffed up his barrel chest and tugged at the waistband of his dark jeans.

Sam met the antagonistic posture with a gentle smile. "I don't want this church to be like that anymore."

"Why do you get to decide that?"

"Because I'm the minister." He held his hands out, palms open. "It's that simple. The board brought me here to lead and to serve this church."

"I didn't have no say in it. Lots of people didn't have no say in it."

The whispering in the crowd grew louder.

Sam moved his hands to his hips and did not try to make any further response.

"Speaking as a member of the board." Big Hyde rose from his seat, though it took the old fellow a minute to get fully upright; the congregation waited in silence for him to go on. "Speaking as a member of that very same board that voted to bring Reverend Moss to town…"

Sam caught the old man's eye.

Big Hyde must have seen the sheer shock Sam felt to learn this man, who had given him grief on his very first day in town, had participated in bringing him here. He broke into an ornery grin and took his seat again. "I think I speak for the whole board when I say we got no quarrels with his leadership, his preaching, nor any other part of what he's done here since he got back."

"That's right," someone murmured.

"Thank you for saying it," Aunt Bert chimed in.

"No quarrel with anything he's done?" Lee crossed his arms. "Not even his private life?"

"If you are trying to dredge up my past, I'll gladly talk about how the kid you all knew became the man I am today. In fact, it's one of my favorite illustrations of God's grace, but—"

"Have you throw in our faces how we got a minister who came up from a no-good childhood? One who got into who knows what all trouble? One who thinks he's so much better than us that he can get up in a pulpit to tell us everything we do wrong? No thanks."

"I don't think I'm better than anyone, Lee." Sam stole a glance at Nic, but it was Willa's sweet face and worried expression that made his heart still and brought his mind back to the immediate moment. "And I'd be happy to carry on this conversation with you and anyone else interested but not tonight. Tonight we have come to give to the needy and to sing praises to God for His greatest gift—our Lord Jesus. I regret we've gotten sidetracked from that."

"You asked me to speak my mind," Lee reminded him.

"Yes, and I thank you for doing that, now—"

"*Ain't* done it. Not yet. You never let me finish what I had to say. Guess that comes with all that leading and serving you came to do here. You *lead* the way you want the talking to go and cut it short when it don't *serve* your purposes anymore."

Sam clenched his teeth to keep from calling the man a liar in the house of God. Taking a deep breath, he bowed his head and shifted his weight to rein in any anger the evening had churned up in him. When he looked up, he offered only kindness to Lee Radwell and all the people gathered before him. "I can see how my actions might look slanted to my advantage, but then it would be in keeping with the old church in the lurch to have a minister who knows how to handle an incline."

Quiet, approving laughter lightened the tension in the room.

"Knows how to work the angles is more like it."

"Mr. Radwell, Reverend said this ain't the time nor place." Big Hyde did not rise from his pew as he spoke this time, but Hyde Freeman Jr. did scoot forward in his seat enough to lend his support to whatever the old man decreed. "Let's all just join in prayer, then get on with our evening and take this up another day."

"And what? Let him rub our noses in his arrogance as long as he sees fit to do it?"

"What arrogance?" Nic covered her mouth the second the question had slipped out.

Sam gave her a smile and a wink. A few days ago she might have sided with Lee and company about him. That made her unguarded remark so much sweeter.

"Anyone walking in here tonight who got eyes could see that Sam Moss has taken back up with Nicolette Dorsey." Lee seized the moment to press on with his cause.

"If you have issues with me, then bring them to me. Bring them to the board and we will address them in the proper time and place. Now let's join in prayer and—"

"You see? You see how he cuts me when things get too close to the truth? I know you've all heard about what's going on. He stands up there all high and mighty wanting us to think he's changed; all the while he goes on his own jolly way openly living with his girlfriend and their illegitimate daughter. Right under our noses!"

"That's enough, Lee." Sam stepped forward, not to threaten but to place himself in the midst of his church and to make himself a protective shield between Nic and Willa and the ugliness Lee was spewing. "You've gone too far. I do not want to hash this out here and now, but I won't stand by and let you spread untruths about a sister in the Lord and an innocent child."

"You gonna throw me out, Reverend?" Lee looked around the sanctuary nodding now and again to those he must have found sympathetic to his way of thinking. "Ask me to leave this church you just said welcomed everybody?"

"No."

"No?" Nic's voice resonated with soft surprise.

Sam did not look her way. He did not want to face the hurt and disappointment in her eyes. If he did that, he risked wanting to shelter and stand up for the woman he loved; and that would overshadow his first commitment to serve God and every person who came through the doors of his church in need of the love of Jesus.

"I won't throw you out or ask you to leave and not come back, Lee. As long as I am minister here, everyone seeking Jesus will find His love and mercy extended to them here."

"Amen." Big Hyde held up his hand in an attitude of praise to God.

Lee glowered at him a moment, then nudged the woman sitting next to him in the pew. She and the two teenage boys next to her lurched up out of the pew.

"Let's *all* stand and share a minute of silent prayer." Silent because too much had been said already. Silent because anything more he said might so easily be misconstrued or twisted around by those who had come into God's house with angry hearts and closed minds. Silent because Sam did not trust himself at this moment not to speak as a man, to speak on behalf of Willa and Nic and even himself instead of as God's servant. He bowed his head.

Pews creaked. Floorboards groaned. Shoes shuffled then settled into quiet. Above it all the unmistakable scuffing of footsteps, of people leaving the sanctuary, chafed at Sam's battered idealism.

When the door fell shut and did not swing open again for several seconds, he exhaled, drew his own prayer to a close, and said, "In the name of Jesus, whom God sent to die for our sins, amen."

"Amen," the congregation echoed.

When Sam raised his head, more people remained than he had anticipated. That should have lifted his spirits, but he couldn't look out at his church and not see the empty places. He felt their absence in a way he had not anticipated. He recalled the verse that had played through his head these last few days. *Foxes have holes and the birds of the air have nests....*

Jesus had no place to lay His head. Perhaps Sam had asked for too much when he had expected God to give him a home of his own at last. He looked at Nic, who would not return his gaze. He smiled at Willa. She stared back, her eyes so big behind those delicate glasses, her face pale and serious.

He loved them both so much it made his head light and his heart ache at the same time. And yet he knew at that moment he would have to find a way to make this church whole again, even if it meant he would have to leave.

"So that's it then." Nic had not left the front pew.

Everyone else had gone home already. Collier had taken Willa, and Jessica and Scott promised they'd occupy her with stories and songs until she either fell asleep or Nic got home. One by one the other attendees of the Christmas Sing had filed out, most of them pausing to give Sam a hug or some kind of encouragement. Finally, Sam helped the Sterns take the donated food and money to the office where they could put the benevolence baskets together the next morning.

Throughout it all, Nic had stayed just where she had sat when she'd walked in earlier, so filled with hope for her life and love for Sam. Hope wavering, she tried not to give in to the doubt and discouragement pressing in around her.

Sam walked across the front of the dimly lit sanctuary wearing a smile that did not for one minute fool her into thinking it indicated a true lighthearted mood.

"It's started all over again," she said softly as he reached her pew.

"What has?"

She looked straight ahead. "The gossip, the assumptions, the unfounded rumors, the innuendo, take your pick."

"Nic, I am so sorry you got dragged into a power struggle over the running of this church, over my being the minister here."

"I didn't get dragged anywhere, Sam. I was here at the vortex of the problem from the very start."

He chuckled, but clearly not at her. "Nic, honey, my problems with people in this town started long before you and I had our first date. It was a bold choice to ask me to come back here as pastor."

"And brave of you to come back."

"So many people do so much braver things for their faith. Missionaries and those who work in inner cities, who minister to AIDS victims, who put themselves in the middle of all manner of human suffering all for the sake of sharing the pure, powerful message of salvation—that's bravery. Coming back here? That was more foolhardy than brave."

"Exactly what people of small faith say about people who follow God's will, no matter where it takes them. If the Lord led you here, then it *was* brave of you to leave everything you had and knew and to come." She stood. "Living your faith is a scary business. It puts you at risk of being reviled by people on all sides, believers and nonbelievers—anyone who sees your taking a stand for Jesus as a threat to their status quo."

"Hey, no fair, I'm supposed to be the spiritual leader here."

"The *husband* is supposed to be the spiritual head of the household, and you are not my husband."

"I meant as your minister." He grinned and gave her a gentle nudge with his shoulder. "But if you care to discuss—"

"What I want to discuss, honestly?"

"Yes?"

"Is what I am going to do, Sam."

"I don't get you."

"You saw how it started here tonight. And that's just the beginning. You think word isn't spreading around town even as we sit here, people calling Willa your illegitimate daughter, making up who knows what kind of stories about our living arrangements."

"Speaking of that, your Aunt Bert cornered me in the hallway after the service and suggested I move into Lula's room at their house the next few days."

"She did?"

"Yeah. It'll give you all more room in the house over the holidays, and Bert is just itching for someone to start a rumor about her and me staying there unchaperoned."

"I'll bet." Nic laughed at the idea of her aunt at the center of any kind of scandal. "Thing is, I'm not sure if she wants those rumors so she can take on the gossips or because, like all The Duets and most of the Dorsey girls, she just likes everyone talking about her."

"Maybe a little of both." He folded his hands together, cleared his throat, then shifted his feet on the uneven floor. "I am sorry about what happened tonight. I'd never have encouraged Lee to speak if I thought he'd stoop so low as to attack anyone but me."

"Another lesson learned," she whispered. "When someone gets that self-righteous, he stops thinking about others as people with feelings and begins to see everything and everyone as obstacles to his getting his way."

"I suppose so." He shook his head. "Still, everything about my renting a room at your house was so innocent. I'd lived there a month before you even showed up, and then it was with both your sisters and Willa. We never spent any time alone there."

"And most people in town realize that, I'm sure."

"It never occurred to me that anyone would think otherwise.

But we're not to give even the appearance of wrongdoing, so—"

"You'll eat better at Aunt Bert's, that's for sure." She smiled, then bowed her head. "Of course moving for a few days only provides a short-term solution to a long-term problem."

"The gossip about us, the cruel things people might say about and to Willa." He filled in what she had left unsaid.

"Sam, how can I stay here and raise her in a town where someone will always look at her as Sam and Nic's illegitimate daughter? And that's the nicest of it, I'm sure."

"We talked about forgiveness not wiping away consequences, Nic."

"That's easier to face when it's not your child we're talking about."

"What if it is?"

"What?"

"My child we are talking about?"

"Legally she is my child. Your name is not on the birth certificate."

"Since when did a name on a birth certificate make any man a real father? That comes from here, Nic." He put his hand to his chest. "I know it's not the same way you feel about her. Sure, my connection cannot be as deep or as strong as yours yet, but I do love that little girl."

"I know you do."

"And I understand your drive to protect her. But you can't pack her up in shredded newspapers, put her in a ballet slipper shoe box, and tape the lid down tight to keep anything bad from ever happening to her."

It touched her to hear him conjure up the image of the box that housed Willa's precious snowbird ornament, even if he used it to make her confront her futile actions. "I've never tried to isolate Willa from the harsh realities of the world. In fact, my insistence she learn that it's not a safe, forgiving world beyond our family is one thing my sisters criticize me for continually."

"And in answer to that criticism you consider sending her away to the ultimate shoe box of security, where she'd be both sheltered and forced to learn how to cope with reality."

"The residential school." Nic nodded.

"That wasn't the answer for Willa, Nic. For some kids it's the next best thing to a miracle, but kids with special needs share one thing in common with so-called 'normal' kids."

"Go on."

"They have to be treated as individuals. More than ever by the people who love them. There is no more a single solution for every kid with a brain injury than there is for every kid who needs his teeth straightened or his vision corrected."

"Maybe you are a wise man after all, Sam." She swept her hand along the back of the pew.

"If you stop to think it over, you will see that running away from Persuasion is not the answer." He took her hand in his and pulled her around so that she faced him. "You said it yourself. There are enough good people in town to make this the right choice for raising Willa in a safe, nurturing environment."

"But if Willa and I don't leave, things may get very hard on you."

"Don't worry about me. I have my own plan. Something that gets to the very root of the problem and fulfills my obligation to my congregation and to God—serves the church."

"Sam? What have you got in mind?"

"If anyone has to leave, Nic, it should be me."

"No! That's the last thing you should do. This church needs you."

"It needs someone, but *me?*" He shook his head and let out a low, cheerless laugh. "Not if all I bring to this place is controversy and dissonance."

"You bring a lot more than that and you know it."

"That's all I've ever had to offer the people in this town, Nic." He bowed his head and ran his fingers back through his hair. "You included."

"That's not true. You've brought this church new ideas and new people—people who wouldn't have felt welcome here before, like the family from the cottages. More than that you've brought the standard of Christ's love, grace, and forgiveness back to this place."

"I've tried but I don't see it taking hold." He shook his head.

"Don't see it? Sam, more people came tonight than were here at the tree service, more at the tree service than the Sunday before."

"They came hoping to see a confrontation, not wanting to be left out if it happened."

"Maybe, but more of them stayed after you spoke tonight, and all you did was engage Lee then stand in silent prayer. You didn't give a sermon or anything like that."

"You're saying that as long as I keep my mouth shut, I have a shot at growing my flock?" His mouth tipped up in the hint of a grin.

"I'm saying you are not the first controversial shepherd to find his hometown unreceptive."

He met her gaze, then lifted his eyes to the cross behind the pulpit. His desire to love the Lord shone in his face. He shut his eyes and when he opened them again a great peace seemed to radiate from him. He smiled. "Thank you, Nic. The Lord laid a passage on my heart the first time I saw Willa, and each time I thought of it, I thought it meant something different, but now I think I know."

"What?"

He crooked his finger to stroke her cheek. "Let me mull it over, pray, and read the Word before I talk any more about it, okay?"

"Sure. Does this mean you are going to stay and fight for the church in the lurch?"

"I will if you will." He held his hand out to her.

She swallowed hard. She raised her own eyes to the cross and found a bit of that peace that she had seen in Sam. "Okay." She curled her fingers around his. "I'm staying, too. No one is going to drive me off."

"Sorry to interrupt, Nic." Petie stood in the doorway clutching her winter coat tight around her body. "Hi, Sam. Sorry about this, but Nic promised she'd come with me when the time came, and well, it's time."

"Time for what?" He asked Nic, but his eyes stayed trained on Petie.

"You'll see. You can come, too, but we have to hurry. Time's running out."

Twenty-two

"hat are we doing? Where are we going?" Sam put his folded arms on the back of the front seat of Petie's car.

"Over to the old Bode County High football field." Petie made a wide turn toward what was now Bode County Middle School but had once been the high school.

"The *old* one? From when we went there?" He sounded like that was a thousand years ago. Well, in some ways, he supposed, it might as well have been. Still, why would anyone go out to a football field abandoned nearly a decade ago? "What are you up to, Petie?"

"I told you she wrote Parker an e-mail." Nic hung on to her seat belt as the car went sliding into the straight stretch that led to the darkened field. "Slow down, Petie! Parker will either be there to meet you or he won't. Your wrecking the car on the way over won't improve the odds one iota."

"Be there?" Sam squinted to make out the outline of the battered scoreboard coming up on their left. "Why would he be there and not at the house?"

"Because that's what Petie asked in her e-mail." Nic relaxed as the car pulled to a stop by the lone raft of metal bleachers.

"Okay, we're a little early." Petie turned off the engine then the car lights and scanned the area around them as she spoke. Edginess glittered in her eyes. She sat with one hand on the wheel and the other on the back of the seat, like someone ready to move in either direction at a moment's notice. "Let me get you up to speed. I'd like your opinion on this anyway."

He decided to keep to himself any comment on the value of asking for his opinion *after* she'd already gone ahead with her plan.

"I know that Nic or Collier or Aunt Bert or…possibly the mailman has filled you in on my situation with Parker, about his administrative assistant, that is."

"Yes."

"After I had a while to think on that, and on what you had said about my not adapting all that well to this empty nest business, everything just sort of came together. All at once like an image coming in clean and sharp when you finally find the right focus on a camera, you know what I mean?"

"Actually, I do."

"And it dawned on me that I stood to lose my husband, and not to some other woman; she was incidental, not personally significant at all. Right place right time sort of thing."

"More like wrong place wrong time, if you ask me," Nic muttered. "Which seems to have suited her plans quite nicely, too."

"Yes, she was in the wrong to go after my husband, Nic; I'll grant you that. My point is, she is neither the issue nor the problem here. If you don't take care of your house, let support beams rot, the roof fall in, and the very foundation crack and crumble, you can't blame some storm that comes along for knocking the whole thing down. You've got to take responsibility for your part in it all."

Sam put his hand on Nic's shoulder. "Funny thing, your sister and I just had a talk about responsibility for things that go awry in our lives."

"How having your sins washed away doesn't do away with the consequences of your actions," Nic said.

"Sure, of course not. But then, in my case, if I forgive Parker as I'm ready to do right now, then I want to be able to go on as if it never happened. Washed white as snow. I'd like to think that's the kind of thing Christians grasp, appreciate, and practice more than anyone else."

"White as snow," Sam murmured. He nodded. "I'd like to think that, too, Petie. But we've seen tonight how difficult practicing the kind of forgiveness that Jesus taught can be. As humans and flawed from the get-go, a lot of us take comfort in measuring others by the size of their sins and not by the magnitude of God's grace."

Nic laid her hand on top of his.

Through the windshield a thousand tiny stars littered the night sky. The town lay quiet around them with only a few Christmas lights still glowing here and there. Sam checked his watch. It was almost ten o'clock. "What time did you ask Parker to meet you here?"

"He should show up any minute now." Petie chewed her lower lip and pinched the top button of her closed coat between her thumb and forefinger. "In my note I confessed everything, how I'd checked his e-mail and knew about his…about how confused and unhappy he is. Then I did the only thing I had left to do, offered him the only thing I still had to offer."

"Which was?"

"My heart." Her tear-filled eyes met his. "My whole heart, not just the bit left over after I divvied up the pieces between the kids, my family, and the part I held back out of fear over growing older and things changing."

"Oh, Petie, after all the things you've told us about Park lately, what if—"

Sam gripped Nic's arm to keep her from voicing any doubts. If it all fell apart, he knew she would not want even the inkling of an I-told-you-so to stand between her and her sister.

"I told him how much I love him, how much he has always meant to me. I let him know what I should have been saying to him all along over all these years. He has always been my hero. He was in those days on the football field at homecoming. He still is each night when he drags in from work dead tired and sometimes grumpy but *home.*"

"That's really great, Petie. It had to mean a lot to him."

"I guess we'll soon see. I told him if he wanted to rekindle the relationship we knew back when it was just the two of us, to meet me here on the field at ten." She clicked the key in the ignition over a few notches making only the lights on the dash come on.

Sam checked his watch. He hoped against hope that he would find the car clock running fast and could tell Petie it was not really fifteen minutes after the hour already.

"He could be running late." Nic moved her hand to her sister's shoulder.

"Held up by what? Traffic?" Petie stared straight ahead as if she thought the answer lay out there on the dead grass of the empty field. "It was a foolish idea, wasn't it?"

"No." Sam and Nic spoke at the same time, though the joining of their voices did not strengthen their weak replies with greater confidence.

"Don't patronize me. It was dumb. To think one e-mail could

make up for at least a year of letting things slip away. He told the kids he might not even come for Christmas. That's how bad things have gotten. Why did I think my one letter could..."

She sighed. Or had she stifled a sob? Sitting behind her, Sam couldn't tell for sure, and before he could move closer to comfort her, she cranked the key in the ignition. The engine growled to life. She flicked on the car lights.

Nic's hand jolted out toward the steering wheel. "Petie, you can't drive when you're this...oh, my word!"

"Well, I'll be!" Sam sat back in the seat, blinking against the sudden bursts of brightness as one by one the stadium's huge overhead lights hummed then sprang to life.

Petie cut the engine and flung open her car door. She scrambled to stand by her seat, hanging onto the open door with one hand and shading her eyes with the other. She peered over the car's roof toward the bleachers. "Park? Parker Sipes, are you out there?"

"I'd almost given up on you coming, darlin'." All those years up north had not put a dent in Parker's low, lazy drawl.

"I been sitting here in the dark since before ten," she called back.

Laughter answered her. "Guess that's a fine metaphor for us lately, isn't it? Two people right next to each other, both completely in the dark about what the other one needs or wants."

"Oh, Parker, I love you!"

"I love you, too, sweet thing. And I have missed you more than I ever thought possible." He started toward the car, and as he passed from the shadow where he had stood to the brilliant light, it became clear he was wearing his old Pirates football jersey.

"You stay right where you are!" Petie held up her hand. "I'm coming to you."

"How 'bout you meet me halfway?"

Petie hopped to the ground and began working open the buttons on her coat as she bent down to grin at Nic, then Sam. "He came!"

"I'm so glad for you both." Nic scooted over to the driver's seat, then reached up to give her sister a quick kiss on the cheek. "We'll take your car back to the house and see you there…well, we'll see you when we see you."

"Thanks." Petie gave Nic a wink, then pulled her coat off to show her old cheerleader's uniform.

Nic probably had something to say about that, but Petie never gave her the chance. *Wham!* The door slammed shut and Petie was gone in a blur of box pleats and bouncelessly perfect hair.

"You going to sit in the backseat and let me drive you home like a chauffeur?"

"Hey, I don't want to ruin their special moment with the distraction of me getting out and in again." He leaned back like a man of luxury. "Just take me home, driver."

"You mean take you to Aunt Bert's." She backed the car out.

"No, got to go back to get my things. Don't think even Aunt Bert could stand the scandal of the preacher moving into her guest room with nary a piece of luggage nor a stitch of nightclothes."

Nic laughed. "There'd be buzzing at Dewi's for sure."

"Besides, I'd like to tell Willa good night before I go. I kind of got used to our having breakfasts together." Even though his banishment would not last forever, it tugged at Sam's heart to realize he would not see the child's bright face first thing in the morning. "Do you think she'll still be awake?"

"I hope not, but given it's so close to Christmas and so much is going on, she might not have fallen asleep right away." She pulled to a stop at an unlighted corner, then twisted her head around to speak to him. "Awake or asleep. No harm in both of us going in to check on her, if you don't mind my company."

"I'd like that, Nic. I'd like it very much."

"She's sleeping but we could sneak in just to take a peek if you want." Nic left Willa's bedroom door open just a sliver behind her as she spoke to Sam, waiting in the hall.

"We won't disturb her by going in?"

"Oh no. If she's really deep in sleep, nothing bothers her. In fact, when she was younger and had to have so many tests run, I arranged for them to be done during her nap time, and she dreamed her way right through even the worst of it." As soon as the mention of Willa's problems and the allusion to a childhood of tests rattled out of Nic's mouth, she wished she could take it back. Sam had enough on his mind without bringing that into the picture. "Anyway, she sleeps like an angel. I really love going in to watch her; I stand over her bed and say an extra little prayer just for her."

His expression softened. "I like that idea. Willa really is blessed to have a mom like you, Nic."

She turned toward the partially opened door and smoothed her hand down the painted wood. "Is she?"

"Why do you even question it?"

"Because…" She wet her lips and folded her fingers closed on the old glass doorknob. "Because believe it or not, at the end of each day I look back to what I might have done differently, done better. Was I patient enough? Was I strict without acting bullheaded or antagonistic? Did I let her know that no matter what I did, I did it because I love her?"

"I can't imagine otherwise."

She huffed through a half smile. "More days than I care to count, I can't answer yes to most of those questions."

"We all fall short. That's why grace and forgiveness are absolutely amazing gifts. God grants us the chance to start again, completely clean. The old passes away and we are made new."

"But what about the damage already done? How many times have we talked about that lately? I worry about the damage my fumbling as a parent might do to Willa, might have already done."

"Worry is not an act of faith, you know." He reached out and lifted her chin with one finger. "I'm sure all good parents ask themselves the very things you're talking about. If it helps, I think the very fact that you do weigh those kinds of concerns says that you are striving to do the best you can for your sweet little girl."

"But what if my best is only second best?"

"Don't do that, Nic. Don't talk like that. You make it sound like you think you've failed Willa."

"Maybe I have." Finally she forced herself to raise her gaze to meet his. "Failed her—and you all at the same time."

"Failed me?" He brushed her hair back from her cheek, his head shaking. "That's not possible."

"I never even tried to contact you about Willa, to let you know you might have a daughter."

"You had your reasons."

"Yes." Heat rose in her face just to think of those reasons, to know now that Sam knew what she had done that night he left her. "But I should have followed through for Willa's sake and yours. There are tests that can prove paternity, and that would have settled it once and for all. I should have demanded one even if asking that would have caused an even greater rift between Daddy and me."

"I can't stand here and honestly say that in the early years after she was born, I'd have submitted to a paternity test short of a court order for me to comply. I'm not proud to admit that, but it's the truth."

"I suppose."

"Even later as God got my life on track, I doubt I'd have known what more to do than to pay child support and send cards and presents. The idea of family bonds and loving parent/child relationships were foreign to me."

"But all these wasted years—"

"We can't get them back. The waste is in worrying over them. Maybe we needed that time apart for God to do some work so we could lay the foundation for a better kind of family. The Lord had to bring me a long way for that kind of thing to seem remotely possible, you know."

"Translation—it's happening in God's time, not by our dream schedule?"

"I don't doubt that the Lord would have liked us to get marriage and family and children in the right order. But I also don't doubt that He never gave up on us, that He gave us time to mature and grow in faith and life before He brought us back together."

"Are we that? Together?"

"Say the word, Nic. I'll be down on one knee."

She didn't know whether to laugh or cry, or to just take a leap of faith and tell him yes. In her indecision, she bowed her head. "Pretty bold claim for someone who hasn't even kissed me in nine years."

"That can be fixed." He stepped close and tilted her head up. "If you—"

She didn't wait but went up on her toes, wound her arms around his neck, and put her lips to his. His kiss was everything she remembered and so much more. This was Sam. Sam, the only man she had ever truly loved. The man she had always known had the capacity for love and goodness that she saw come to fruition in him now. Sam, who was Willa's—

She pulled away from his kiss and laid her hand on his chest. "But we still don't know for sure if Willa is your child. I can't stand here and pretend there is no chance that that stranger at the party isn't her father."

"I can."

"What?"

"I can stand here and tell you that no man but me is Willa's father. No one, no matter what the biological circumstances, could be to her what I want with all my heart to be—her daddy."

"Sam," she whispered when all other words failed her.

"I've thought it over, Nic. That's what I want if you and Willa agree. I want to be Willa's daddy. No matter what happened between you and me, I want to make that official and irrevocable."

"You don't know what you're asking. You cannot understand the ramifications of taking on a child like Willa. Your obligations to her won't end when she turns eighteen or twenty-one, maybe not even when she is forty-one. We just don't know for sure now."

"I know for sure, Nic." He took both her hands in his. "And I don't need a test to *obligate* me to her. I couldn't walk away from her now any more than I could or would when she is eighteen or twenty-one—or forty-one."

From the gentleness of his touch to the unwavering love in his eyes, she knew he meant it. Shutting her eyes, she laid her head on his chest, savoring the warmth of his arms closing around her.

"Just let me know when you want to proceed, if you want to proceed. You'll probably want to talk to Willa about it."

"And to God. I may need to pray about this for a while, Sam. Even though I do believe everything you said about God bringing us back to each other to be a family…I just…"

"Maybe we should go in and say that prayer over our little girl," he suggested.

"Our little girl." What a sweet, sweet notion. Nic smiled, her hesitant heart buoyed by Sam's generosity of spirit and faith in doing the right thing. "Okay, let's go say that prayer."

They stepped apart.

Sam leaned down to kiss her temple.

She reached up and kissed his cheek.

He smiled.

She bit her lip to keep from grinning like a total idiot, turned, and pushed the door open just wide enough to cast the pale light from the hallway onto Willa's bed. Nic gasped. "How long have you been awake, young lady?"

"You said she was a sound sleeper," Sam whispered in Nic's ear. "You don't think she heard any of our conversation, do you?"

Willa, all flannel pajamas, freshly scrubbed face, and shiny brown hair threw out her arms and cried, "Daddy!"

"Does that answer your question?" Nic folded her arms.

Sam's grin broadened like a searchlight going on high beam.

Whether she felt secure about it or not, it seemed they had just become their own imperfect little family. And as much as she wanted to rejoice in it, two little things nagged at the back of Nic's brain: What if Sam was not Willa's biological father, and how would Sam's acceptance of Willa affect the goings-on at his church?

Imagining the answers to both of those questions left Nic

unsteady and anxious. Knowing they would probably have the answer about Sam and his church in the next few days did not ease her angst one iota.

Twenty-three

It had taken them a while to get Willa settled down again. Even after Sam had kissed his newly claimed daughter good night—not to mention the truly inspiring kiss he gave Nic on the back porch before he left—an air of excitement lingered in the house. Finally, Nic let Willa climb into bed with her, and they laughed and snuggled and talked about Christmas and snowbirds, but mostly about Sam.

Nic had not gone into too much detail. Things like biological fatherhood and the events on the night of the party had no place in this first discussion, not that Willa would have understood. What she did understand was that Sam loved her and wanted to be a part of her life.

Only once as they spoke of it did Willa go into one of her behaviors but had responded quickly to Nic's silent reminder to control her hands. Progress already. Day by day the awkward gestures, the leaping about, the strange little coping mechanisms Willa used to get through a life that was often overwhelmed by the smallest complications had faded. It was nothing phenomenal but just one small step forward and something neither she nor the special education teachers at Willa's school had been able to accomplish in a year and a half of trying. The counselors had said she would likely outgrow it, and she always got better when she felt safe and relaxed. But still, Nic saw it as a measure of how Willa might thrive in the environment of this home, this family, even a new daddy.

Those thoughts stayed with her into the next day and lingered even as she watched her child playing with the salt and pepper pigs in the early evening light at the kitchen table, warming Nic to the center of her being.

"When do you figure the men will be back?" Collier slid a steaming bowl of white beans with a slab of cornbread on the side in front of Willa.

"I guess anytime now. Let's see, Sam came by around noon looking for a break from writing his Christmas Eve sermon—"

"More like playing hooky from writing it."

Nic didn't know whether to laugh or fret over Collier's keen observation about Sam looking for anything to avoid working on the crucial sermon's text. "Playing hooky or taking a well-deserved break, either way Scott, Parker, and Sam can't stay gone much longer."

"I don't know. It's an hour's drive over to the mall in Gilbertville; then they've got all that supposed shopping to get done."

"Shh." Nic held her finger to her lips like a prissy school librarian demanding order in her domain. "Petie will be down here any minute. We do not want her to know I asked Sam to take Parker s-h-o-p-p-i-n-g."

"What are you spelling for? It's not—"

Nic jerked her head toward Willa, who seemed enthralled in arranging the ceramic pigs just so at a little cornbread table.

"Oh." Collier nodded.

"Anyway, the fact that it was my idea, not Parker's, and that Sam and Scott came in mighty handy in influencing him to go buy his wife a gift is something we don't want Petie to ever know."

"What don't you want Petie to know?" She waltzed into the room on a cloud of satisfaction that pretty much verified she had picked up nothing more of the conversation.

"That I used bacon in the beans instead of ham hocks. I know how you hate that."

"You know where you go for lying, little sister." Petie peeked over Collier's shoulder as if she might spy the truth in the bubbling pot of white beans simmering on the stove.

"I'm not lying; I did use bacon instead of ham hocks." She poked the ladle into the pot and drew it out again with a limp, almost colorless strip of bacon dangling from the heaping portion of beans. "I didn't want you to know because I know how both of you like to go on about the quality of my cooking."

"We'd never do such a thing, sugar." Nic popped her napkin in the air, then settled it on her lap.

"No?" Collier brightened.

"Of course not. We'd never use the word *quality* in the same sentence referring to your cooking."

"Very funny." Collier slopped the beans into a bowl and thrust them toward Petie.

"Why won't you tell me what you don't want me to know?"

"Listen to yourself, Petie. You've started talking in likely titles of old country western songs." Nic winked at Collier as the youngest sister sat down at the kitchen table. "Did Aunt Bert, Nan, and Fran say whether they planned to stay out past dinnertime delivering benevolence baskets?"

"Jessica told me she wanted to talk The Duets into going all the way into Gilbertville to the mall after they did their charity work. And Parker let her take his car to do it." Petie sprinkled vinegar over her beans, totally unaware of her sisters trading uneasy looks across the table. "Don't know where that man got off to. Probably down at Dewi's telling everyone for the umpteenth time about the season when he saved the day and won the game."

An endearing kind of pride shone in Petie's face that had not been there before when she spoke of her husband.

"Everything's all right with you two then, isn't it?"

"We still plan to go for some counseling with our pastor when we get home, but, yes, everything is very much improved between us now." She all but blushed like a dreamy teenager. "We talked half the night away in the stadium about so many things we let fall by the wayside and about what we want from each other in this new stage of our marriage."

"Sounds wonderful, sugar." Collier tucked her hair back behind her ear. "But what about that administrative assistant?"

"Collier!" Nic made a violent slashing motion across her own throat.

Petie let out a low and not particularly convincing chuckle. "Don't get on to her, Nicolette. You can't protect me from the reality of that girl."

"True." Nic propped her elbows on the table and watched for any signs of pretense in her older sister. When she saw none, she managed a teasing smile. "Now tell me, who will protect that girl from the reality of *you?*"

"Park is going to ask for a transfer. That's all he can do, really. It may mean a move for us down the line, but in the long run that could prove good for his career and is imperative for our marriage."

"Good for his career?"

"You know Parker. He loves things same old, same old. Everything exactly as it should be. This little fiasco forces him to take

some action, put himself on the line, and try something new."
Petie wiggled in her seat. "Shake things up a little."

"You talking at work or in your marriage?" Nic muttered to
keep Willa from hearing.

"I'm ignoring that remark, little sister." Petie broke her piece of
cornbread straight in two. "I do wonder if I should hightail it
down to Dewi's after a bit to look for Parker. Not that I don't trust
him, you understand, but I do wonder where he's gotten to."

"Someplace bad." Willa raised her chin and batted her eye-
lashes like a person with all the answers. "So bad Mommy had to
spell it out. H...o...p...g...g..."

"Willa, your Uncle Park has not gone anyplace bad. Isn't that
cute?" Collier stood abruptly and lifted her bowl up. "More beans
anyone?"

"I'll take a dab more," Nic said a bit too quickly.

"I'm done." Willa patted her stomach.

"Then why don't you go play in the living room?" Nic pulled
her child's chair out. "You can even see if there is a Christmas special on TV if you want."

"Can I take the piggies?" She held up the salt and pepper shakers.

"Yes, just run along now." She urged Willa to hurry with a light
pat on the behind.

Willa scowled, her eyes stormy behind her little glasses. Then
she tipped her nose up, gathered the pigs in both hands, and
marched off.

"Have I ever told you that you're doing a fine job with her,
Nic?"

"Why are you telling me that?" Nic had expected a good grilling
about Parker's whereabouts, not a compliment on her parenting.

"Because it's the truth, and I don't think I say it to you enough."

"I don't think you've ever said it to me." Nic sat back. "At least not as a compliment in and of itself. If you do say it, it's usually a prelude to some helpful hint or piece of sage wisdom you think I need to hear."

"You're doing a good job, *but...*" Collier murmured. "There's always that long pause, long enough to make you think that might be all there is to it, just a simple offering of encouragement and praise. Then comes the big *but*. No one in this family seems capable of making a sincere remark without that big ol' *but* lurking around the corner like a bear ready to grab you and strangle all the joy out of the moment."

"Is she saying our family is a bunch of bear buts?" Petie put on an act of taking it all quite seriously. "Because that's what I heard."

"Me, too. Bare behinds!" Nic played right along. "Collier, are you accusing us of running around without our pants on?"

"All right, all right." Collier lifted her hands in surrender. "No serious discussion allowed. I get it."

"Actually only one serious discussion at a time." Petie held up one finger, which she then aimed at Nic. "And right now we're telling Nic what a fine job she's done with our Willa, no buts or bears about it."

"It's true, Nic. And your deciding to stay here in Persuasion and let Sam adopt her legally is just sheer perfection." Collier sat down again and smiled at Nic.

Nic smiled back.

Petie stretched her lips so wide it looked painful.

It got quiet. Too quiet.

"Oh, for heaven's sake!" Nic slammed her open palms down on

the tabletop. "Someone just get it over with and say it, will you?"

"Say what?" Somehow Petie got the question out between her eerily taut smile.

"*But.* The big but that lurks behind every piece of praise anyone in this family doles out. I know it's there; I can feel it breathing down my neck." She put her hand under the thick waves of hair tumbling down her back, surprised to find a thin film of sweat at the nape of her neck. "I've done a good job, blah, blah, blah, allowing Sam to adopt Willa, blah, blah, staying in Persuasion...*but...* but what?"

"But..." Collier glanced at Petie who gave a very big sisterly you-got-yourself-into-this-so-don't-expect-me-to-save-your-hide-now shake of her head. "Well...but..."

"What?"

Collier drew her shoulders up. "You never said anything about marrying him."

"Marriage? Marriage is a huge commitment." Nic made big sweeping gestures with her hands as if that would help to explain it better.

"And parenthood isn't?"

"The parenthood thing is already there. Already a done deal. Sort of." She twisted a strand of hair around her finger. "But marriage? I cannot get Sam involved in that final all-encompassing step with so much still...unresolved."

"His church." Petie nodded.

Since she had said it and not asked it, Nic declined to give any reply. Yes, Sam's position with the church was a factor, but not the only factor in her reluctance to make a decision. Her stomach tightened, and she pushed away the bowl in front of her. "If you don't have anything else to add, I think I'll go watch TV with Willa."

Neither Collier nor Petie spoke.

Nic got up. "Call me when you're done and I'll wash the dishes."

Silence answered her again. She tossed her napkin down on the table and walked to the doorway.

"Don't let them ruin your life again, Nic."

She paused and raised her head. "I'm not, Petie."

"They want you to be so stuck in your sins that you can't move on and get past them." Petie's voice rang with compassion and clarity.

"I remember what it was like before, Nic." Collier hardly spoke above a whisper. "That's the only thing that will satisfy people like that. The only way they seem to think anyone who has as public a fall as you did can show remorse is by dwelling on that fall for the rest of her life."

"Don't give in to the temptation to do that. Don't let a sin that Jesus already died for become the focal point of your life," Petie pleaded. "If you do that, you make yourself and your sin bigger than the price Christ paid."

Nic looked over her shoulder. Tears stung her eyes and tightness clawed at her throat. "Thank you. I love you two so much."

Kitchen chairs screeched back over the dingy floor, and in a flash the three of them fell into an embrace from which Nic could draw boundless hope and strength. With her sisters helping her, she would get through this. With her faith and her family they would face whatever lay ahead. Comforting as she found that, she could not stop thinking beyond this small circle to Willa, to Sam, even to the church members and the town and their expectations. Shutting her eyes for only a moment, she prayed for God's guidance through the coming days, when she knew the very way she loved that her faith as well as her love for Sam would be truly tested.

Twenty-four

hy don't the snowbirds come to eat the crumbs at our house?" Willa leaned on both elbows and gazed out the front window of the Dorsey house.

Sam had come by first thing this Christmas Eve morning to sneak in the presents Parker had bought for his wife and children. Feeling so proud of his choices and the way they had kept Petie from finding where they'd been, Parker had not wanted to spoil it by walking in with the packages they had wrapped at the mall. So Sam volunteered to smuggle Parker's gifts in with the presents Sam had brought for the family. He had slipped all of them under the tree, all but one special token for Nic he wanted to keep on him, when Willa ran into the room making a beeline for the window.

"Why don't they come? Why?" She turned to him as he crouched beside her, concern in her sincere eyes. "You said you saw them."

"Yes, I did." At least he thought he did. He had not seen the tiny flock again since that day. He had seen other birds around the community tree and all around town, where his eye seemed drawn to anything that fluttered or flew lately. Once again he wondered, though, if his timely sighting of those snowbirds had been nothing more than wishful thinking. Perhaps he had simply seen sparrows and wanted so badly for them to be snowbirds that he—

He searched the low branches of the Christmas tree until he found the ornament carved by Big Hyde twirled on its golden cord. Plucking it gently off the limb, he held it up to Willa. "They looked just like this. Dark-eyed juncos. I looked it up in a book."

"You did?"

"After you told me about them. I got curious." He held the bird up between them. "I wondered how often they came to Alabama and what kinds of food they ate."

"Could you show me that book?"

"It doesn't have a lot of pictures."

"I can read some words," she said solemnly.

At eight, he knew she should be able to read many of the words in the field guide he had found in the church library. But Nic had explained to him that often work on the outward mannerisms and behaviors, Willa's grasp of cause and effect, and her frustration at not being able to do what seemed simple to others got in the way of academics. She had hoped that in this new environment with so many people to support her that would change soon. "Would you like me to help you learn to read, honey?"

"Could you teach me from the book about snowbirds?"

"It's not about snowbirds, it's..." Sam curled his fingers around the delicate ornament in his hand. "I'd love to teach you from the book with the snowbirds in it."

She smiled. Such a small smile, and yet it held all the world and half the heavens by Sam's estimation. How could he have not known this kind of love existed? How could he have thought he understood something about the way God loved his children when he had so vastly underestimated the depths of emotion a father feels for his child? Without even trying, Willa had opened his eyes to so many things. Most of all it had given him an infinitesimal taste of the fathomless love God had for mankind. He now understood, as well as a person could who saw through the glass darkly, how difficult it was for God to give His Son and how much He must care to make that sacrifice.

Suddenly wanting both hands free, he tucked the snowbird inside his jacket pocket for safekeeping, then took Willa in his arms in a tentative hug. "We'll start the reading lessons right after Christmas. We won't even wait to make it one of our New Year's resolutions, okay?"

"Okay!" She gave him a peck on the cheek.

His heart soared and he pulled her in to give her another gentle squeeze before letting go.

She stepped away from him and immediately began to look around the room with short, jerky movements of her head.

"You want to look and see what packages have your name on them?" He knew he'd promised to start the reading lesson after Christmas, but how could he pass up this opportunity to help her distinguish her name from others?

"Not right now," she said as if it were the silliest proposition on earth.

"No? But I saw you looking around—"

"I want to know where Jesus is." Her eyebrows slanted down over her near scolding gaze. She put her hands on her hips.

"Where Jesus is?" Dozens of ideas and explanations clicked through his head in answer to that broad and curious question, but which one applied? "You mean where is Jesus, like where are the snowbirds? Are you expecting Him to come to the house?"

"No, you big silly."

"Ah."

"He's already in the house."

Sam couldn't argue with that, but still he tried to clarify, "Of course He's in the house. He's in you and in me and in your mother and her—"

"Kitchen drawer."

"What?"

"Maybe He's in the kitchen drawer."

"Jesus? Is in your mother's kitchen drawer?"

"I gave the baby Jesus to her in the kitchen. Do you think she put Him in the drawer?"

"Oh, the baby Jesus!" He took her hand and walked with her over to the nativity set atop the coffee table. Scanning the figures assembled to worship the baby born in the manger, he saw that it now included two fat, happy ceramic pigs, a plastic dinosaur, a small stuffed smiling tomato, a snowman made from marshmallows and toothpicks with a gumdrop hat, and assorted animal cookies propped up here and there. But no baby Jesus lay in the tiny manger where Mary knelt and Joseph kept watch.

He bent at the knees to put himself at eye level with Willa. "Looks like a fine turnout for the big birthday tomorrow."

"But no birthday boy," she said, solemn as a judge.

"No birthday boy." He shook his head. "Now tell me again what the tradition is? Your mother hides the baby Jesus on Christmas Eve and everyone—"

"Everybody has to look for the baby Jesus, and we can't open any presents until we find Him. It's *His* day, you know."

"I know. That's one terrific way of reminding everyone, too. Find Jesus first in everything we do." He brushed his thumb down her cheek light enough to tickle her into a smile. When voices from the kitchen caught his attention, he leaned toward Willa as though striking up a conspiracy. "That's your mother now. Bet if we ask her she'll remember exactly where she put the baby Jesus, okay?"

"Okay."

"Nic? Could you come in here a minute?"

She appeared at the door smiling and drying her hands on a dish towel. For a split second it was like something out of an old TV show, the perfect family at the holidays. Mom in the kitchen preparing a heavenly smelling delight. Father and daughter whispering in excited anticipation by the tree. Of course, in this case, Mom was actually giving Aunt Bert a permanent, which stank so badly no one else would go near. Father was not married to mother—yet—and the daughter...the daughter was the only perfect thing about the scene, he decided, looking at Willa.

"Nic, we just wondered, do you know where baby Jesus is?"

"Baby Jesus?" She cocked her head not thrown for an instant by the question. "Let's see. Willa brought Him to me the first day we got here."

"In the kitchen."

"That's right. In the kitchen." Nic tapped her cheek with the aqua curler in her hand. "But I didn't leave Him in there because I recall distinctly not wanting to risk getting food dripped on him."

"Don't get distracted and leave this stuff on my hair too long and burn it to a frizz, young lady," Aunt Bert called out unseen from the next room.

"I won't." Nic put the tip of the curler to her lower lip and squinted in what Sam could only surmise was concentration. "So much has gone on since then, but it occurs to me that I probably put Jesus in a box and set Him safely aside until we'd need Him. Then everything got so hectic and haywire that I forgot all about Him."

"We're all guilty of that very thing from time to time."

"Why do I think this will turn up in a sermon some day?" Nic put her hand to her hip.

"Sermon!" Sam stood straight up. "Talk about getting distracted. I have to go over my notes and rehearse my sermon for tonight."

"Want to practice it on us? We're a pretty receptive audience."

"Unlike the one I'll be facing in my church this evening?" Sam's chuckle came out harder than he intended and did nothing to lighten the reality of his supposition. "Thanks, Nic, but—"

Bing, bong. The doorbell cut him off.

"Don't you go running off, Nicolette, and leave me here to try to take these curlers out by myself."

"Would you get that?" Nic stole a quick peek over her shoulder in Aunt Bert's direction.

"You know these old arms can lift up only so high," the older woman went on. "Why, left to my own, the sides of my hair would be waves while the top part would be a fried mess of fuzz like some fancy clipped poodle dog."

Bing, bong. Bing, bong.

"I've got my hands full." Nic raised both her empty hands and shook her head before pivoting on her heel and heading back into the kitchen. "I'm not going anywhere. Probably someone dropping by with Christmas cookies anyway. Sam can get it."

"If they got food, bring 'em straight in here, Sam, honey," Bert bellowed out.

"Will do." His laughter had not died when he pulled open the door.

"Hadn't counted on you being here, Reverend Moss." Big Hyde swept his black hat from his head. Holding it by the crown in one gnarled hand, he jabbed the air with it as he went on, "Thought you'd taken up residence with Miss Roberta for the time being."

"I have. I just stopped over to drop off some gifts. I was just on my way back to the church, as a matter of fact."

"Oh, I see. I see."

"Won't you come on in?"

"That someone with baked goods, Sam?"

"Aunt Bert, sit still. I'll yank out half your hair in the process if you don't settle down."

"A little home beauty parlor treatment." Sam motioned for the older man to come inside the house, then took his hat and coat, draping them over one arm.

"Hi, Mr. Freeman." Willa all but danced up to the wiry old fellow, her hands held up. "My daddy's gonna teach me to read about snowbirds!"

"Is that so?" He took the child's pale hands in his weathered black ones and stuck out his wing tips.

Willa stepped on them light as an angel landing on a cloud, then tipped her head back. "Uh-huh. He found a book about them because he saw some by the big Christmas tree, and now he's gonna teach me to read about them, too."

"So you saw the snowbirds?" He did not skip a beat as he led the small girl in an impeccable box step.

What a picture in contrasts they made, old and young, black and white. Big Hyde in his customary dark pants and white shirt, today set off by a maroon-and-blue bow tie, dancing with Willa in her red overalls and green striped turtleneck. Though his glasses were black with silver trim and hers a little girl's pastel, both their eyes shone with a joy of the moment that made all the differences fade to insignificance.

"Thank you very much for this dance, my lady." Big Hyde deftly lifted the child off his feet, then released her hands and gave a grand bow.

"Thank *you.*" Willa bowed in kind. Then she raised her hands over her head, leaped in the air, and spun around. "I'll go tell my mommy you're here."

"She's really special, isn't she?" Sam watched the child fly.

"That she is...*Daddy.*" He flavored the title with that same disapproving tone he'd used on Sam's first day back in Persuasion.

Looking back now knowing that Big Hyde had helped bring him to town, he heard challenge in the old man's voice, not condemnation. "I plan to adopt her and make it all legal. I want to take care of that child and love her for the rest of my life."

"I'll add that to my prayer list then."

"Thank you."

"If I were the nosey sort, I'd find a sly way of asking what you intend to do about the child's mother." Big Hyde gave him that slow, merciless once-over. "Of course, I'm not that sort."

"Of course not." Sam folded his arms and hardened his expression. This man had helped bring him here and stood up for him in the church, but there came a point where even a preacher did not owe every detail of his private life to his supporters.

"Mr. Freeman, it's so good to see you." Nic stuck her head through the arched doorway. "Come on back and have a cup of coffee, won't you?"

"Didn't come to pay a social call, Ms. Dorsey."

"Oh?" She stepped fully into the room. "Is there something wrong?"

He gave Sam a low, sidelong look, heaved out a sigh, and then clasped his hands together. "Went by Miss Roberta's house first and saw the note tacked to her door saying to try for her here."

Nic shook her head. "Why didn't you just add a *P.S.*—robbers come on in and take whatever you please, Aunt Bert?"

"We ain't got robbers in Persuasion. And even if we did, what have I got that they'd want to take? If you came two blocks out of your way looking for me, Big Hyde, then come a few steps farther into this kitchen. I can't get myself in there without dripping on the carpet."

"Well, now, Miss Roberta, I can't stay and I hadn't counted on the Reverend being here."

"You want me to leave?" Without even thinking, Sam started to put on Big Hyde's hat, ready to hightail it out of there.

"No, no, son. This concerns you." Big Hyde took his hat back and ran his thumb along one crease in the crown. "It's church business. I just thought the news might have come easier out of the mouth of a family member. That's why I came looking for Miss Roberta."

He thought about reminding the old man that Bert was not really related to him but decided against it. He understood the motive and knew it did not bode well for the message Big Hyde had come to deliver. Forcing his biggest smile, Sam put his hand on his guest's back. "You sure you won't sit down and have some coffee while you tell me what's going on?"

"No, no. I can't stay." He took his coat from Sam's arm. "I just wanted to stop in and let Miss Roberta—well, now to let *you* know—they've gone and put a petition up at Dewi's."

"A petition?" Nic placed her hands on her hips. "What for?"

"That's what I say." Bert hollered out. "That place is cut up enough with the way he's got all them racks and shelves in there. Why on earth would he need a partition, too?"

"Not *part*ition, Aunt Bert. Petition." Nic's eyes narrowed in her aunt's direction, then she checked her watch.

"I reckon I can guess what it's about." Sam thrust his hands in his pockets and studied the faded pattern on the carpet.

"They want church members to bypass the board and call for him to step down as minister of All Souls, right?" Nic folded her arms.

"What was that?" Bert's chair legs scraped on the floor, and Sam could picture her scooting it along trying to hear the conversation.

"Not just step down from All Soul's." Big Hyde's face was grim. "They want him banned from the ministry altogether."

The news hit Sam like a punch to the gut.

"They can't do that, can they?" Nic looked from Sam to Big Hyde and back again.

Sam shook his head.

"No." Big Hyde waved the notion off. "I doubt they can even muster up enough bona fide church members to go along with this fool petition to make it worth the trouble of writing it up."

"That doesn't mean it won't get ugly. And it could destroy everything I'd hoped to build here. Divide the church for a long time to come."

"You know that's exactly the opposite reason of why we brought you here in the first place."

"I know." Sam nodded, thinking of that first day back in town. Big Hyde had told him about the people who delighted in picking clean the bones of what had once been a thriving small town. Sam now saw that he was the one the old man saw at risk of being ravaged by vultures.

"Willa, honey." Nic faced the arched doorway and spoke in a

soft tone to her unseen child. "Be a darling and run upstairs and get Aunt Petie or Aunt Collier so they can rinse out Aunt Bert's hair."

"Girl, I'm not so feeble I can't rinse my own hair if it's that time already. Don't send the child off on—"

"No, Aunt Bert. I think you really need someone to help you, and Willa *really* needs to go get her." Nic's jaw hardly moved as she tried to drive the point home. "Run along, Willa, and take your time."

"Okay, Mommy." Willa's footsteps thundered up the back stairs.

Nic hurried into the front room. Not wasting a precious moment to preface her thoughts, she grabbed Sam by the arm. "You have to tell them."

"Yes, I do. I have to tell them, but not what you think."

He stood on the steps of Dewi's as he had that first day in town. Like that first day, Big Hyde was there. He meandered over to the rocking chair and lowered himself slowly into the sagging seat. "You sure you know what you're doing?"

Sam looked at the single page in his hand. It probably wouldn't last the day posted at Dewi's as close to the petition as he could get them to put it. He didn't care. He had to do this.

"You told me that first day that Persuasion wasn't even a town anymore. I've looked around and seen that in some ways that is so. But it's still alive. There are still plenty of good folks here."

"Indeed."

"I won't be a party to tearing it apart any more than it already is." The floorboards groaned as he strode up to the door. "But I was brought here to bring folks together. I promised that everyone would be welcome in my church."

"Yes, you did."

"After all my talk about living my faith, I forgot something else just as important. Living up to my promises." He looked down again at the open invitation for everyone in town to attend the Christmas Eve services. "I said everyone was welcome, but I didn't personally invite them in. I hope this corrects that."

"Corrects it or stirs up such a hornet's nest that whatever happens will come swift and hard."

"I'm ready for it either way." He nodded, then opened the door to Dewi's and went inside.

Twenty-five

ell them? Nic's admonishment still rang in his ears. Tell them what? That there was a slim chance Willa was not his child? Those who had issues with him were not interested in technicalities. They had fixed their attention on his actions. First his actions as a boy, then as a young man, and now as the minister they counted on to comfort and lead them. He had not led a blameless life, but since receiving Jesus into that life, he had always stood firm and accepted the responsibility for his choices. He would not buy his way out of this conflict by standing in the pulpit before the entire town and denying his daughter.

The entire town? Sam peeked out through the door behind the organ and jangled his car keys against his open palm. From this vantage point it looked that way. He didn't know if they had come because of his poster or because they wanted to gawk at him, hoping he would confess to being a fallen pastor.

"Filling up awful early for a Christmas Eve service, Reverend." Shirleetha pressed her back to the wall to get past him sideways in the narrow hall. When she got on the other side of him, she pushed her music books in his direction. Without even looking to see that he took them, she began wriggling out of her coat. "If you'll hang my coat up when you hang up your own, Reverend,

I'll scoot on in there and start playing some hymns until it's time to start the service."

"Thank you, Shirleetha. I appreciate that." He traded her music for the coat. "I won't be too long getting ready."

"Well, my advice is don't start early on account of this group—you know, the ones who came early to get the best seats are not the regular churchgoers, or even the ones leaning toward supporting you should it get to taking up sides." She patted his arm with her gloved hand. "Start when you said you would in the bulletin and on your poster."

"I will, Shirleetha. Thank you." He put his hand on top of hers, and just as quickly she slipped it away, turned, and hurried out into the sanctuary.

Sam shut his eyes. "Lord, please, keep me focused and calm tonight. I have the faith to carry me through the fire if that's Your will, but that doesn't exactly soothe my nerves much standing on this side of potential barbecue of my life, my convictions, and maybe even my new family. Help me, Lord, and guide me."

He took a deep breath, walked back to his office, and hung Shirleetha's thick red coat on the rack. Outside his office window the crunch of tires on the gravel lot, the buzz of voices, and the blinking of Christmas lights only wound the knot in his stomach tighter and tighter.

This was it. The test. He had come back here knowing he would face it. But how could he have known then that it would demand so much of him. That when he took that pulpit tonight he would be fighting for his church, the woman he wanted to marry, the child he would love and shelter all his life, and his place in the town he hoped to make his home?

"Home." He shook his head, pulled off his jacket, and hung it by Shirleetha's. He started to toss his truck keys onto his desk as he normally did, then at the last second decided he'd better tuck them in his coat pocket, muttering, "Never know when a fellow might get run out of town on the spot. Would hate to get tossed out into the night without these."

He laughed at taking the situation to an outrageous conclusion but still took the keys and stuffed them inside the jacket pocket. "What's this?"

He pulled free the snowbird Big Hyde had carved and Willa loved so much. Turning it this way and that, he smiled at how it had brought him closer to the child and, in many ways, to God and to His Son born to die for our sins. "The birds have their homes but Jesus…is in the shoe box!"

He was there all the time. They'd just forgotten. Sam stroked his thumb along the intricately painted white feathers of the bird's underside and looked up. "Thank you, Father."

He knew what he had to do now, but he didn't have much time.

The last chord of "O Come All Ye Faithful" still hummed in the sanctuary as the congregation sat and Sam stepped up to the pulpit. Nic lifted her chin to better see him from the back row where he'd asked her to sit with Willa. She had no idea what he had planned, but she trusted his decisions, whatever they might be.

She trusted him. She folded her coat more tightly around her and tried not to smile too big at that sudden and amazing revelation. Looking up at the man, who nodded his thanks to the organist, then addressed the gathering with his eyes clear and genuine goodwill on his face, Nic's heart soared. She loved Sam Moss.

She always had, she supposed. But now the love that had been too shallow to hold them together before had matured—in God's time—and it was whole and wonderful and too strong to deny ever again. She put her arm around Willa and made a quick, silent prayer on Sam's behalf and for the church and all gathered here.

"Good evening." Sam put both hands on the edge of the pulpit and turned his head to acknowledge every row in the crowded sanctuary.

"Good evening," many churchgoers murmured back; The Duets, the Stern family, and Big Hyde more enthusiastically than the rest.

"What a joy to see so many new and familiar faces come together tonight, especially when I know many of you have meals and parties and gifts waiting at home for you that you are anxious to get to. I imagine the most uttered phrase while walking up the stairs this evening wasn't Merry Christmas but more like 'If that preacher gets long-winded, we're sneaking out the back.'"

A flutter of laughter answered him. Here and there people exchanged sheepish looks for being called out.

"Don't worry, y'all. I promise to try to get you out before the kids get rowdy and the ham gets cold. And as for my long-windedness…" He bent his head for a moment.

The candlelight glinted off his golden hair.

Nic held her breath.

He flexed his hands against the edge of the pulpit and raised his head. "As for the chance of long-windedness—you are looking at a man who has most recently had the wind knocked clean out of him."

Nic could feel the crowd collectively tense up.

"And all I can think to ask you now is one simple question." Sam stood straight.

The congregation leaned forward or scooted to the edges of their seats. More than one person braced their hands on the pew ahead of them.

Slowly, Sam moved his gaze around the room, then, pushing back his black suit jacket, put his hand in his pants pocket and gave an absolutely disarming half smile. "Anybody seen the snowbirds?"

"The...?" People cocked theirs head like they hadn't heard right.

"What did he ask?" Wives whispered to husbands.

"You see, Persuasion used to have snowbirds. You've seen them, I think. Little birds." He held his thumb and forefinger up to show the size. "Come in along about the first storm of winter and they flock under trees and bushes?"

Heads shook. Hushed voices rustled like wrapping paper throughout the room.

"I only ask because..." He leaned forward now as if imparting a wondrous secret. "Because *I've* seen them."

Nic stole a peek at Willa, then under the pew, trying to make the connection between what Sam requested of them and the odd direction of his homily.

"I have it on good authority that they haven't been around Persuasion the last year or so. But I saw them, friends, right here, right in front of All Souls Church, and I was hoping that I wasn't the only one."

"Forget about asking him to leave on grounds of moral turpitude," the man in front of her said to the woman at his side. "They should kick him out for plain ordinary nuttiness."

"Shh." Aunt Bert put a finger to her lips and scowled at the man.

"Two warnings and they get a pew pinch," Willa whispered, nodding her head in confidence.

Nic tried not to picture Aunt Bert climbing over the back of the pews to squash everyone who had a comment about tonight's service.

"They are deceptively plain-looking birds at first glance." He withdrew his hand from his pocket.

"My ornament," Willa said, but not loud enough to attract attention.

Sam held the carved bird with its back to the congregation. "Just a little bit of gray on the ground. Maybe at your house." He dipped his head toward someone on the left of the room, then shifted to the right and did the same, subtly seeming to single out Lee Radwell. "Or yours."

Lee shifted his broad shoulders.

"They could go virtually unnoticed. Whole flocks of them. They can seem that much a part of the landscape of our lives. Until someone draws your attention to them." He caressed the bird with his thumb, studying it before he looked again at his own flock. "Our sins are like that, don't you think?"

Pews creaked. Shoes scuffed against the wooden floor.

"For most of us they are a quiet part of our everyday. We often take them for granted in ourselves and sometimes even in others." He put the ornament down on the pulpit. "Until someone points them out. That happened to me lately, I think you all know. That it was unjustified is not the point, and I won't argue about that here, not on this holy night."

More than one person watched for Lee's reaction.

He folded his arms over his chest.

Sam did not so much as glance in his detractor's direction. "That I have sinned and fallen short—many times—I readily confess. 'Confession is good for the soul.' 'Get it off your chest, you'll feel better.' Even nonbelievers will tell you that. But confession is only part of the story."

He scanned the group, his face somber.

Nic wound her hair around one finger, bit her bottom lip, and met his gaze as it swept the room.

He smiled. "The real miracle is what happens after the confession. What happens between the sinner and God and what happens among our fellow Christians. It is that which sets us apart from the world. Which transforms us."

Willa swung her feet back and forth, holding her hands so tightly together in her lap that her knuckles were white.

"Not much longer," Nic whispered, sensing rather than knowing that was so.

"It's like..." Sam's brow furrowed, then he dipped his chin and his expression mellowed. "It's like this little snowbird here."

Willa beamed at her mom.

"Dark as we are by the sins that clutter our lives, so common we scarcely see them all anymore." He rotated the object in his hand slightly. "Until touched by the blood of Jesus." He put his fingertip to the tiny red beak of the carved bird. "And all our sins are made white as snow."

He took his hand away to show the white underside of the snowbird.

The room grew still.

"White as snow, my friends. When the snowbird lifts its wings, just as we lift our hands to God to seek His grace and praise His name, the darkness is gone."

"Amen to that," Big Hyde lifted his own hand.

Nic sighed her own amen.

"Oh, one more thing about the snowbirds." Sam opened his palm as if he held a real bird in it. "They go where they are welcomed. They don't usually come to this part of Alabama, but year after year they did because people left the right kinds of seed for them. In essence we asked them to come."

All around, Nic could see heads nod.

"The first day I saw this ornament God impressed on my heart verse 58 from Luke, chapter 9. 'Foxes have holes and birds of the air have nests, but the Son of Man has no place to lay his head.'"

Her heart stirred at the memory of him quoting that very verse on that confusing, amazing day.

"I thought at first God must be trying to tell me that Persuasion was not meant to be my home. And events that followed might seem to have substantiated that idea."

Lee snorted out a hard chuckle.

No one else joined in.

"But how could that be? It clearly wasn't talking about *me*." He ran his thumb over his forehead as if trying to fit together the pieces of a puzzle in his mind. "Today my daughter—I think most of you have known her longer than I have, actually."

Willa wriggled in her seat, her shoulders thrown back and her head high.

In row after row ahead of them, heads turned. The smiles on those faces warmed Nic to her toes.

"Today my daughter asked me, 'Where is Jesus?' You see, in the Dorsey family they have a tradition of hiding the baby Jesus from the nativity set, and then they have to find Him before they can open any gifts on Christmas morning."

Now the entire row of Dorsey descendents became the object

of curious eyes. Not a single one of them shied from the attention, Nic noted.

"But today we realized we had lost Jesus. We put Him away for safekeeping and had completely forgotten about Him."

"We did," Willa confirmed softly to her family.

"Now, listen closely, everyone. Here comes the part where I dazzle you by bringing it all together." Sam moved from behind the pulpit. "The Son of Man has no place to lay his head. The snowbirds have left Persuasion. Unto you is born *this* night in the city of David a Savior which is Christ the Lord."

The restless shuffling in the church stilled.

"*Tonight,* my friends, tonight on this sacred night, as we contemplate the greatest gift ever given, you must decide." He pointed outward at no one in particular and yet clearly everyone felt he spoke to them. "Where is Jesus?"

Sam walked the length of the platform, then halfway back, giving everyone time to contemplate the question.

"He had no room in the inn. Does He have one in your hearts? Are grace and salvation and forgiveness *lived* in Persuasion?"

He waited as if he expected an answer. Waited until the congregation grew introspective, began bowing their heads, or lifting their eyes to the cross.

"Only you can answer for yourself. But for our family…" He held out his hand to beckon to Willa.

In a flash she jumped from her seat. She bent to retrieve the ballet slipper box from under the pew, then ran to her father's waiting arms.

A wave of laughter rolled through those watching.

Sam helped the little girl open the box, then lifted her up, her arms around his neck.

"Where is Jesus, Willa?" Sam asked.

She clutched the tiny figure of the Christ child to her chest. "In me, Daddy. In me."

He looked out over the sanctuary. "May you all be able to say the same. Jesus has a home in me and in my church. Merry Christmas!"

Twenty-six

T hat was the best Christmas *ever!*"

"Oh, Bert, you say that every year." Fran walked behind the upholstered chair and surreptitiously perched a big, gold-and-red bow on top of her older sister's poofed-up new hairdo.

Nan took her twin's arm and shared a silent giggle.

"Well, it was. Now you can't argue with me that this wasn't one of our most special Christmases of all." Bert crossed her arms.

"I wish Mama would have been here," Collier curled up on the couch next to Jessica. "That would have made it perfect."

"Oh, I like it this way." Jessica adjusted the shining gold bracelet on her raised wrist. "When we get back home, we still get to open more presents."

"How could you possibly need more presents? I got you way too much to begin with, and then your father—" Petie snuggled close to Parker, sitting on the floor by the fireplace. She smiled at him like a kid in the throes of first love. "Did I thank you for my new ring, sugar?"

"Not properly, but you can do that later," he teased, kissing her cheek.

"Parker." She giggled.

The whole scene would have made Nic sick to her stomach if

she didn't feel positively stupid with sappiness herself today. She hugged Willa close, who sat in her lap playing with a new doll.

"Don't forget to thank Sam, too." Parker nodded at the man standing behind Nic. "He's the one who dragged me off to the mall and headed straightaway to the jewelry store."

"Jewelry store?" Every female in the room but Willa echoed the words and/or turned her head to focus on Sam, but none with more interest than Nic.

Sam winced, then sighed, and his shoulders slumped forward slightly. "Might as well accept it, I guess."

"Accept what?" Aunt Bert jerked her head up and her bow crown bobbed.

"That my days of being able to keep secrets are over."

"Can't keep a secret in a small town, can he, girls?" Bert looked to the two of her sisters present this late Christmas morning.

"Nope." Fran wrinkled her nose in mischief at Bert's wobbling bow. "In a town this size if one person knows what you're up to…"

"Everybody knows," Nan finished for her identical twin.

Nic folded Willa deeper into her arms as thoughts of jewelry stores and Sam's secret fell away to one last deeper concern. "Ain't that the truth?"

His hand caressed her shoulder.

She shut her eyes to savor the warmth of his touch, but it did not ease her anxiety.

"I don't suppose y'all would excuse Nic and me for a little while?"

She looked up at him.

"I thought we might go for a walk through town."

"Hey, you two." Claire drove alongside them, slowed her SUV to a crawl, and rolled the window all the way down. "I'm on my way over to pick up Reggie's mama and take her back to the house for supper. What are you up to?"

"Nothing!" Nic stepped out from under his arm.

"Wasn't tossing out an accusation. I like seeing you two out together. You make a nice couple." Claire laughed, then waved one hand toward Sam. "Didn't get a chance to tell you last night. I loved your sermon."

"Thank you, Claire. Hope this means we'll see you and the boys at services?"

"Count on it." She tipped her head then raised an eyebrow. "But you can also count that it isn't over with Lee and his following. Some people will never accept the likes of Sam Moss as the minister of our church."

"There are problems with me and my upbringing that run deep in this town. I respect that and am willing to address it, but I won't compromise my beliefs to make a few people find my presence here more palatable."

"Good for you. You have more than a fair share of supporters now." Claire nodded. "By the way, don't let me get away without telling you how dear I found it, you bringing Willa up last night. Just precious."

Sam grinned.

"You did the right thing acknowledging her in front of everyone last night."

Nic set her jaw. "Bet it set quite a few tongues wagging around punch bowls and Christmas trees last night, though."

"Oh, let 'em talk." Claire feigned a sour expression. "In the end what can they say really but that soon as he found out about her, Sam started doing right by his child?"

"They can say a lot more than that, and you of all people know it, Claire." Anger and hurt clashed in Nic's brown eyes.

"Me?"

"You were at that New Year's Eve party when my daddy walked in and found me with that boy Reggie invited home from college." Nic shut her eyes and grimaced as if the words burned in her throat. "I don't even know his name and he never knew mine, but everyone in town knows there is that small chance that he is the biological father of my child."

"What?"

"I've told her how unlikely that is and how it doesn't matter if it were true. I am Willa's daddy and nothing will change that."

"Sam, you are a wonderful man. So wonderful I have half a mind not to set the record straight on this because I hate to take away from your truly selfless attitude about that sweet child."

"What do you mean set the record straight?"

"I'd a done it a long time ago if I knew it needed doing." Claire clicked her tongue and shook her head. "Honestly, Nic, you don't really think anything happened between you and that drunken moron at the party?"

"We were in the same bed. Me in just my T-shirt."

"Because you got sick all over your jeans. And no wonder, all that crying and those drinks when you never had so much as a beer before, and you expecting a baby to boot." She rolled her eyes. "We sent you in to lie down and sleep it off in the same room we sent everyone to. If your daddy had come an hour later, he'd have found half a dozen people laying in puppy piles around that room. That was one wicked party."

"But all the talk that went around— Why didn't anyone set the record straight?"

"Because, honey, this is Persuasion. People talk. And when you didn't come out and deny it or name Sam as your baby's father, we all figured you wanted the speculation for some reason."

"I guess I did. It broke my father's heart, but it was easier on everyone to think of Willa's daddy as some kind of phantom, some reckless yahoo I didn't involve in her life. Better that than to look at her each day and see Sam and know he had deserted us." She looked at him and gave a sweet, sad smile.

He pulled her into a tight hug that he hoped would say what words never could.

"But you are together now." Claire's voice literally lilted. "Given any thought to my idea about…you know?"

She began to hum the wedding march.

Sam gazed into Nic's tear-bathed eyes. "As a matter of fact, if we could ever find a few minutes alone—"

"Say no more. I gotta git anyway. Reggie's mama is probably waiting out on the porch for me to drive up this very minute." She started to roll the window up, then stopped and poked her nose above the glass. "Oh, one more thing, Reverend. We saw some snowbirds this morning. Kids practically covered the front lawn with crumbs, and we weren't the only ones."

Sam laughed. "Thank you for telling me, Claire. For everything."

"Merry Christmas, y'all!" She waved, then spun off in a cloud of dust.

"That makes, what? Our fourth report of a sighting this morning?"

"I think some of them might be sparrows."

"Not me." He shook his head. "Besides, how can you say that? You saw a couple yourself?"

"Ours were real snowbirds." She tipped her chin up.

"Real. Yes. Just like we're a real family now and we know it for sure." He wrapped his arms around her waist and pulled her close. "Except for one bothersome little detail."

"Sam?" She cocked her head.

He couldn't tell if he read apprehension or anticipation in her reaction. He decided not to try to figure it out. "I broke your heart nine years ago and made a mess at my first attempt to do this a few days ago. This time I want to do it right."

She bit her lower lip.

He got down on one knee, right there on Persuasion Street somewhere between the church and the Dorsey house.

"Sam, we're sort of out in the open here."

"And that's the way I want it. The way it should be. Nic..." He reached into his pocket and pulled out a small red velvet box. "Would you—"

"Yes!"

"You didn't let me finish."

"If you are going to marry into the Dorsey family, sweetheart, not finishing your sentences is something you'll have to get used to." She threw her arms around his neck and kissed him again and again.

"I guess I can do that." He returned her kisses. "How about a New Year's Eve wedding?"

"A week from now?"

"Why not? Like Claire said, we have a chance to set everything right. Why not start with New Year's Eve?"

"Sam Moss."

"What?"

"I love you."

"I love you, too, Nicolette. I always have and I always will."

They kissed again, then turned to walk toward the house on Fifth and Persuasion.

And from the bushes a few feet away, a flock of snowbirds took flight.

Dear Reader,

You'd think after writing an entire book that the letter introducing you to the story, characters, and myself would be the easiest thing in the world. It's always one of the toughest for me. So please bear with me as I try to explain something of the "heart" behind *The Snowbirds* in a few short sentences.

They say that for writers everything is eventually fodder for a book. My writing about the loss of a mother in *The Prayer Tree*, incorporating memories of my time as a social worker in *Irish Eyes*, and for the handling of elderly characters in *Saving Grace* and *Deep Dixie* certainly proved this true. In this new effort, however, I found a challenge in thinking how deep and how personal I would go to portray a child with special needs and the family who loves her. You see, my daughter is a special needs child. She is not the pattern for young Willa in this book, but I will confess that in some ways I am the model for the mother who struggles with concerns of caring for such a child and fearing that often I have fallen short. But when I began this book, it was with the charge from the Lord: "I will not offer anything that costs me nothing."

And so to tell the story of a special relationship, a dear child, a family who loves one another, and the absolutely amazing gift of salvation and having sins washed clean forever, I drew deep on personal territory. It meant a lot to me to offer this story, and I hope you find it worthy.

Annie Jones

Multnomah Publishers®

The publisher and author would love to hear your comments about this book. *Please contact us at:*
www.multnomah.net/snowbirds

—From—
Annie Jones, bestselling author of *several* inspirational romance novels

Miss Grace needs them. Or is it the other way around?.

Every year on the night of New Bethany's Gala Ball, an eccentric recluse appears on her porch in a tattered ball gown. Four friends decide to reach out to her—and discover they need her as much as she needs them.

ISBN 1-57673-330-0

Sometimes the truth is a well-kept secret.

Family secrets...will they heal or destroy
when the past and future collide?

Deep Dixie

Annie Jones

Dixie Fulton-Leigh is in deep trouble. But when rugged sawmill
owner Riley Walker arrives with a plan to buy controlling interest in
the family company, Dixie can't believe this disaster is the answer to
her prayer.

ISBN 1-57673-411-0

Bound by a promise, four Southern women
struggle against all odds to save a tradition…

ROOTED IN FAITH AND BOUND BY A PROMISE, FOUR OPINIONATED
SOUTHERN WOMEN STRUGGLE AGAINST ALL ODDS TO SAVE A TRADITION. . . .

THE
Prayer Tree

ANNIE JONES

During one life-changing year, four very different women
come together to pray for their community, and end up
helping each other confront—and triumph over—their
disappointments and fears.

ISBN 157673-239-8

More inspirational fiction
^{from} Annie Jones

Irish Eyes
When Julia Reed discovers a boy camped under a billboard, she is drawn into a century-old crime involving a real-life pot of gold—a crime special agent Cameron O'Dea is determined to solve.

ISBN 1-57673-108-1

Irish Rogue
Michael Shaugnessy longs for a new beginning. Fiona O'Dea wants to help him. Yet a legacy of lies and a stolen fortune stand between them and the mending of their Irish hearts.

ISBN 1-57673-189-8

Father by Faith
Alex is praying for a father; his mother, Nina, for a miracle. God gives them both in cowboy Clint Cooper!

ISBN 1-57673-117-0

TEA AT GLENBROOKE

- •Authored by: *Robin Jones Gunn*
- •Artist: *Susan Mink Colclough*

Snuggle into an overstuffed chair, sip your favorite tea, and journey to Glenbrooke…"a quiet place where souls are refreshed." Written from a tender heart, Robin Jones Gunn transports you to an elegant place of respite, comfort, and serenity—a place you'll never want to leave! Lavishly illustrated by Susan Mink Colclough, look forward to a joyful reading experience that captures the essence of a peaceful place.

ISBN 1-58860-023-8

The Guardian

Marcus O'Malley is a U.S. Marshal charged with protecting witnesses in high profile cases. He must protect a family who saw a judge murdered, knowing that the assassin who was hired to kill them before they can testify is one of the best in the world.

ISBN 1-57673-642-3

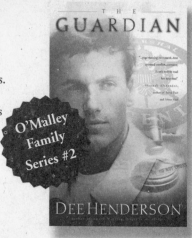

Danger in the Shadows

Sara's terrified. She's falling in love with former pro football player Adam Black—and it could cost her her life. She's hiding from the man who kidnapped her years ago, a man who's still trying to find her and finish her off. Soon Sara and Adam are caught in a web that brings Sara face-to-face with terror—and with the knowledge that only God can save her.

ISBN 1-57673-577-X

The Negotiator

FBI agent Dave Richman never intended to fall in love. But when Kate O'Malley becomes the target of an airline bomber, Dave is about to discover that loving a hostage negotiator is one thing, but keeping her safe is another matter entirely.

ISBN 1-57673-819-1

Faith and purpose collide in the exotic
setting of this powerful love story.
Through mysterious circumstances, Erica
Tanner meets her late sister's only child, Betul.
Within hours, they are kidnapped and taken to
India, where an unexpected friendship with the
handsome Prince Ajari complicates Erica's escape—
especially when she learns he is Betul's uncle.

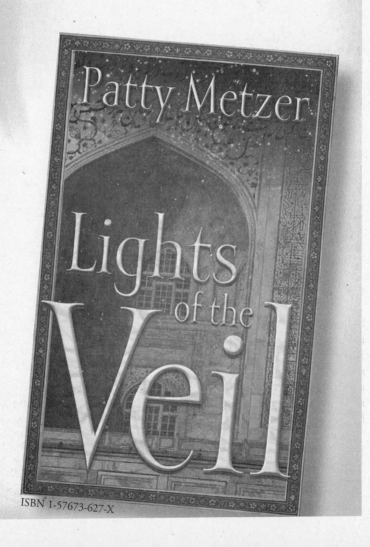

Patty Metzer

Lights
of the
Veil

ISBN 1-57673-627-X

Emotionally Gripping Reads
from Karen Kingsbury

A Moment of Weakness

Jade and Tanner were separated by scandal and one wrong decision. Now only the truth about that long-ago summer can set them free—and rekindle their dreams of forever.

ISBN 1-57673-616-4

Waiting for Morning

Hannah Ryan has lost her husband and oldest daughter in a devastating drunk driving accident. Hannah's faith is tested by this tragedy as she walks the long road of her own modern-day Lamentations. She must learn to forgive and finally discover that God's mercies truly are new every morning.

ISBN 1-57673-415-3

Where Yesterday Lives

Home for her father's funeral and faced at every turn with bittersweet memories of the past, award-winning journalist Ellen Barrett rediscovers what is truly important and eternal in her life.

ISBN 1-57673-285-1

EXCITEMENT, ADVENTURE, BREATHTAKING ROMANCE—LINDA WINDSOR HAS IT ALL!

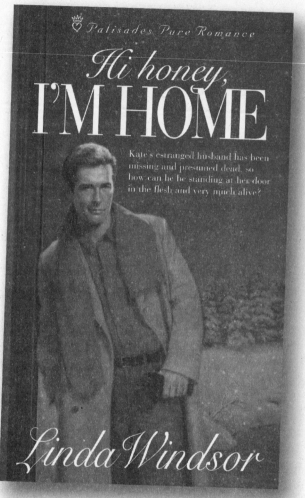

Palisades Pure Romance

Hi honey, I'M HOME

Kate's estranged husband has been missing and presumed dead, so how can he be standing at her door in the flesh and very much alive?

Linda Windsor

Kate finds herself face-to-face with her supposedly deceased husband! An obsessive journalist, Nick was reportedly killed in a terrorist attack five years ago, but there he stands, ready to take up where they left off. Well, she's not interested, but Nick and their precocious boys are determined to prove to her that God has truly changed Nick's heart.

ISBN 1-57673-556-7

Let's Talk fiction

Let's Talk Fiction is a free, four-color mini-magazine, created to give readers a "behind the scenes" look at Multnomah Publishers' favorite fiction authors. **Let's Talk Fiction** allows our authors to share a bit about themselves and gives readers an inside peek into their latest releases. **Let's Talk Fiction** is free and is distributed in the fall, spring, and summer seasons. It features our fiction titles released during these seasons and is filled with interactive contests, author contact information, and fun! Take a moment to review **Let's Talk Fiction** on-line at www.christian-fiction.com and tell us what you think. Contact your local Christian retailer for copies or let us know if you would like a hard copy in the mail. We'd love to hear from you!

www.christian-fiction.com

Multnomah Publishers *Keeping Your Trust...One Book at a Ti*